also by tom leveen

PARTY

TOM LEVEEN

Text copyright © 2012 by Tom Leveen
Jacket photographs (counterclockwise from top right):
© Fancy/Alamy; © Kuzma/iStockphoto; © Ryan McVay/Photodisc/Getty Images;
© Grant Faint/Photographer's Choice RF/Getty Images

Visit us on the Web! www.randomhouse.com/teens

Educators and librarians, for a variety of teaching tools, visit us at
www.randomhouse.com/teachers

Library of Congress Cataloging-in-Publication Data
Leveen, Tom.
Zero / Tom Leveen. — 1st ed.
p. cm.
Summary: After graduating from a Phoenix, Arizona, high school, aspiring artist Amanda "Zero" Walsh unexpectedly begins a relationship with a drummer in a punk rock band, which helps her come to terms with her feelings about herself, her falling out with her best friend, and her parents' personal problems.
ISBN 978-0-375-86921-1 (trade) — ISBN 978-0-375-96921-8 (lib. bdg.) —
ISBN 978-0-375-98932-2 (ebook) — ISBN 978-0-375-87337-9 (trade pbk.)
[1. Self-esteem—Fiction. 2. Dating (Social customs)—Fiction. 3. Family problems—Fiction. 4. Artists—Fiction. 5. Punk rock music—Fiction. 6. Phoenix (Ariz.)—Fiction.]
I. Title.
PZ7.L57235Ze 2012   [Fic]—dc23   2011014893

Printed in the United States of America

10 9 8 7 6 5 4 3 2 1

First Edition

For every Monet and every Patience. Yes, you can.

one

One thing, at least, is certain: everything,
absolutely everything, that I shall say here
is entirely and exclusively my own fault.
—Salvador Dalí

Here's the thing.

You know that whole deal about rainbows being a promise or something?

It's not true.

It's crap. If it was true, I wouldn't be home sitting on the driveway in the rain, a massive sucking black hole of a failure. I'd be packing for Chicago.

The rainbow arching over Camelback Mountain is beautiful, though. It's been raining all day—a rarity in Phoenix—and only now has the downpour stopped. Clouds roll by fast overhead, purple-gray animals growling and flashing teeth. But they haven't moved far enough west to block the setting sun. Its fading rays create the *aforementioned* rainbow.

It's the first time I've even *hinted* at smiling since graduation. A week ago tonight.

Many things suck about living here; the smell of desert rain is not one of them. So I left my room when I saw it wasn't pouring, and still have a soft charcoal pastel stick in hand. I sketch the image on the driveway: a black-and-slate-colored rainbow over the smudged profile of Camelback, which does in fact look like a camel that's lain down.

Or is it . . . *laid*? Ha! For a seventeen-year-old girl, I often feel like a thirteen-year-old boy. So come August, does that mean I'll be *eigh*teen or *four*teen? Discuss.

The driveway is a perfect urban canvas for the rainbow and the mountain. A rogue raindrop splatters right in the middle of the camel's *hump* (ha!), so I smudge it into the charcoal, and suddenly the mountain is in perspective. Not bad.

I wonder if Mr. Hilmer, my junior high art teacher, would approve. "You done good, Amanda," he liked to say, even though ever since about seventh grade, I've been Zero to my friends. Which until last week numbered exactly one. I never talked Mr. Hilmer into using my nickname, but at least he didn't call me Amy like *some other people* I could mention.

Dad's truck rolls down the street and veers toward the driveway as rain starts to fall again, smearing my drawing, bleeding it off the concrete. Good. Sucked anyway.

I don't move. Dad maneuvers around me to park in the carport.

"How's it going, Z?" he calls as he locks up the truck.

I rub my fingers together, creating charcoal mud. "Moist," I call.

"That's kind of a gross word, you know!" Dad shouts, laughing, as I hear him walking into the carport. Our kitchen door opens before he even gets there, as Mom chooses this moment to make an appearance. Oh yeah, this'll end well.

"Amy!" my mother calls, her harpy voice reverberating around the carport. "Come inside! It's raining, for heaven's sake!"

Amy. Like I'm in fifth grade or something. My teachers used to say it, too, before high school. All of them except Mr. Hilmer. He was nice enough to call me Amanda. God, what I'd give to talk to him right now.

Dad, as always, chooses my side. "Oh, hell, Miriam, a little rain won't kill the kid."

"Richard, I don't want her to catch a cold. . . ."

"Colds are caused by viruses, not weather!" I call. Helpfully.

"Amy!"

"Would you get off her back for two seconds?" Dad's voice starts to muffle as it sounds like he muscles past Mom into the kitchen.

"Richard!" my mom yells, and the door slams shut. At the exact same moment, the charcoal stick snaps in my hand.

I fling the broken pieces into the street. My empty fingers immediately tie themselves into sailor knots in my lap. They tend to do this anytime I'm feeling, shall we say, *tense*.

The rainbow over Camelback fades and dies. I blame my mom. Dad hasn't made it any farther than the kitchen; I can hear them screaming even from out here.

"It's not fair," I mutter to Camelback. Instead of starting freshman year at the School of the Art Institute of Chicago like I wanted—like I'd dreamed about since Mr. Hilmer's classes—I'm going to this dumbass community college in September to crank out my dumbass core classes before transferring to a dumbass in-state university.

Maybe by the time I get to a university, I'll be able to at least move out of the house. But the way things have started this summer, I shouldn't get my hopes up. Moving in with my *super-awesome* former best friend is out of the question, so maybe I'll end up living with my parents the rest of my life. Sweet.

"But I got in," I whisper toward Camelback, hoping the mountain will offer some kind of comfort. "I got accepted, and it doesn't even *count*?"

Camelback heaves a sigh and a shrug.

I head into the house, rain plastering my colorless bangs against my (bulbous, fleshy) cheeks. My parents' voices carry from the living room, where Mom is having an epic meltdown.

I head to my room and shut the door. Their acidic voices burn right through the walls, as usual.

That does it; I'm out of here.

Dad'll leave soon enough. It's Friday, which means it's time to pony up to Scotty's Bar & Grill; underline *Bar*. But I'm not going to wait till then. And I'm staying out until it's late enough that Mom's gone to bed and Dad's either still *tossing back a few* at Scotty's or at home passed out on the couch.

I pass my easel—a drafting table cranked to a severe angle—where I've been working on a charcoal trompe l'oeil (*French: fools the eye. Class dismissed!* Thanks, Mr. Hilmer!).

It's a drawing of a candle burning inside an inflated balloon. The candle leaps off the page in pseudo three dimensions, like its gray flame could light a cigarette. Very ironic, very surreal.

Very lame.

The balloon is a flat circle. My shading is all wrong. It isn't very good. Neither are the three dozen heavy impasto oil or acrylic canvases stuffed in my closet. Neither are the faces I've drawn on my ceiling over the past four years or so. Which reminds me, I need to paint over the geometric portrait of Jenn I did last year. I don't need her staring down at me every night. It's not like it's photorealistic, but *I* know it's her, and that's reason enough.

I haven't talked to Jenn since graduation. Up until that whole mess went down, me and Ex-Best-Friend Jenn had planned to bum around all summer; be all, like, young and irresponsible. I'd sketch and she'd cook and life would be peachy until I left for one of the best art schools in the country, and instead—

I scowl up at the portrait, like it's the painting's fault I'm still in Phoenix. I'm terrified I might be what professional artists would call a hack, which is another word for *no-talent lump of shit,* but without the dramatic flair. Maybe I should cut off one ear and develop a solid narcotics habit?

I sign my usual initial Z at the bottom of the drawing, finishing it. My Salvador Dalí clock says it's almost eight; time to get a move on.

I pick up today's copy of the *Phoenix New Times* from my desk and flip through the music section. I catch a break at last: Nightrage has a show tonight at The Graveyard. That'll work.

Nightrage isn't going to be playing in town for much longer, from what I've heard. Allegedly, they're going on a national tour with another *formerly* local band, Black Phantom, who signed with an indie label in L.A. last year and are starting to get some radio play on the West Coast. *Local Boys Make Good.*

New Times says a band called Gothic Rainbow is opening for Nightrage. Haven't heard of them, but the name reminds me of my ill-fated driveway drawing, chalky black and gray. I imagine a large painting . . . maybe from a perspective behind me, where you could see both me drawing on the pavement and the rainbow over Camelback itself—?

Anyway. *Gothic Rainbow.* What are they, gay vampires? I reach for my phone to call Jenn and ask if she's heard of the band. Fortunately, I'm able to jerk my hand back before I even pick it up.

Man, *that* was close.

I root through my dresser for something appropriate to wear. Bad idea, because I can't help but catch my reflection in the glass of one of my four framed Salvador Dalí prints. I refuse to have a mirror in my room, because honestly, I don't much care what I look like. Except when I, you know, *see myself.*

"And we ratchet up the revulsion," I mumble to my reflection in the *Metamorphosis of Narcissus* poster, while poking helplessly at the ring of chub above my waistband. Must cut back on eating, you know, deep-fried butter or whatever. *Stays crunchy in milk!*

I grab my favorite jeans and pull them on quickly to hide the white-hot shame of my reflection. They're a bit baggy—

one of their chief attractions—so I cinch them with this belt I painted on back in eighth grade in Mr. Hilmer's class. What was once empty green leather is now adorned with fading ants, melting watches, and other surrealistic icons associated with the best fucking artist in the galaxy.

Here's the thing.

I wouldn't call it a Dalí phase. It's more of a "Dalí fervent devotion with psychotic tendencies." Salvador Dalí is my hero. I've got the four prints of his on my walls, plus the clock, which depicts *Three Young Surrealist Women Holding in Their Arms the Skins of an Orchestra,* and a handful of T-shirts with his work on them. I painted these Dalí trademark replicas on the belt myself, though. I'm pretty proud of the work, and so was Mr. Hilmer at the time. He called it one of my best expressions. Wearing it reminds me of Mr. Hilmer, who retired after I graduated. He said he waited an extra year just so he could have me in his class one more time in eighth grade. I don't know about that, but it was nice to hear.

Someday, I remind myself as I rummage for a T-shirt, I'm going to St. Petersburg, Florida, to visit (or move into) the Salvador Dalí museum. See his work up close and personal, study the brushstrokes, and probably have a cataclysmic orgasm just standing there. But Florida's a long ways away, and I can't quite muster the guts to borrow/steal money from the account Dad set up to pay for school, which is "hands-off for anything except educational expenses!" A trip to the Dalí museum *would* be educational, in my humble opinion, but I don't think SAIC would hand me credit for it, so no can do.

Then again, SAIC is no longer an option anyway. Goddammit, this is not fair. From May 1, when I got my acceptance letter, to May 28, life was so sweet I didn't even hear Mom and Dad's usual melee. Then last week—hours before graduation, for god's sake—I got the *other* letter from Chicago, the one starting "Dear Ms. Walsh, With regret, your scholarship application has been . . ."

And that was just the start of the worst night/week/ summer of my life.

Whatever. I grab a black shirt from my dresser: D.I., that sweet, old Orange County band that never quite made it mainstream. Nobody ever knows who D.I. is. You can tell the idiots from the cool people by who asks, "What's a D-X-I-X?" The Xs are *periods*, dumbass.

I glance at my hair in the glass pane of one poster. It's still wet from the rain and starting to frizz out, so I yank on my old blue canvas cabbie cap to cover it.

"You pretty much suck," I remind my reflection, and pull the brim of the cap down to shade my eyes. At least my hat looks cool. I shove my wallet into my hip pocket, grab my keys, and go out to begin a night of blessed punk oblivion.

My mother has other ideas.

two

... the secret of my influence has always
been that it remained secret. ...
—Salvador Dalí

She's in the kitchen washing dishes, which means Dad must be
changing his clothes to hit the town. I try to turn invisible as I
hustle behind her to the carport door.

"Where do you think you're going?"

(*They don't understand me/What we need is no moms!*
—Casey Royer, lead singer of D.I. Thanks, Casey.)

"Out. See ya."

"Amy, it's storming out, and it's not safe to drive." Dishes
clatter in the sink.

"Mom, it is not storming," I say.

Thunder rumbles and shakes the windows. Figures.

"Much?" I add.

"Amy, no. It's not safe."

I turn to her. "What the hell isn't *safe*?"

"*Please* do not swear at me. . . ."

"Mom," I say (patiently, of course), "I'm just going to hang out for a while, is all."

"With Jenn?"

Um, *no.* But what I say is, "I kinda sorta rather doubt it, can I go now?"

"Amy, no."

"*Miriam,* yes." Maybe I should've just lied and said I *was* meeting Jenn.

Mom's eyes flash. I try to make mine do the same. We lock gazes and try to stare each other down.

I win. Mom turns back to the sink. I take this as a victory and open the door.

"You step foot outside this house, you will regret it, young lady." She tries—fails—to sound all authoritative.

And, just out of curiosity, when does one cease to be a Young Lady, and what term follows it? Youngish Lady? Young Woman? Gal? Twennysumfin' Lady? I mean, god, I start college in September; "young lady" seems a little stupid.

"I won't be out late," I say, and walk into the carport, slamming the door shut behind me.

I rush to my car, a battered black Peugeot 404 (thanks, Dad), and scamper inside. I can see Mom in the kitchen window mouthing something unhappy as I pull away from the house, leaving our bland tan gravel yard for a more suitable venue to mope in.

Theoretically? I've just sold off a month of freedom for this little escape, but Dad'll overrule any punitive damages my mother tries to hand down. He's handy that way. Especially if I ask him after a few beers. He'll let me off the hook just to piss Mom off. I don't think I've *ever* been grounded.

I roll down my window to let rain splash my arm, and turn on the radio. Sweet; *Flashback,* a local show on every Friday, is just starting. First song turns out to be by Ghost of Banquo, this *way* old funky jazz band. A good sign; I've never been able to find their album—they only released one—so it's cool to hear it. My night improves ever so slightly. It tanks again when the DJ reminds me that the Chili Peppers will be here in September with the Lollapalooza tour, and that I, tragically, will not be in attendance, because while Dad can often bail me out of Mom Prison, his allowance is sporadic at best, and someone named Me wasn't able to get a ticket.

I pull into the parking lot of The Graveyard, which is nearly full. I have to park in the dirt—correction, mud—and run through the rain to get to the door.

The Graveyard is quaking. I expect flakes of monochrome paint to chip off and fall beneath a bass beat I can feel in my fillings. Maybe the sonic boom will rattle my brain enough for me to forget about life for a few hours. The Graveyard is an all-ages punk dive that probably should've been condemned like all the other punk dives that've gone under in the past decade. Not many places left in town for the underage crowd to gather for mayhem.

I pull the door open, go inside, pay the cover, and dive into the chaos. It isn't Nightrage playing onstage, so presumably this is the suck-ass Gothic Rainbow.

Except as I look around the club for a place to hang out—dance floor or indoor patio?—I realize the band isn't suck-ass at all.

More like *kicking* ass.

An enormous pit is going full throttle in front of the stage.

The crowd is awkwardly mixed; toothpick-legged punkers slam beside cloned university jocks in ball caps and flannels. *A recipe for disaster!* Sooner or later, someone with a full hawk is going to have a go at someone wearing a football team baseball hat. (Let the irony sink in.) Blood will flow, the combatants will be ejected, and the night will go on. I am unthrilled the scene is taking a turn in this direction; just last year, punk shows were attended by (gasp!) punks. The fact that these two elemental forces of nature are both enjoying the same band is, shall we say, *remarkable.*

And *damn,* they're good! You know those songs you hear just the first few seconds of but right away you know you're going to be repeating them over and over for the next couple weeks? That's how it feels right now listening to them.

I pick my way through the crowd for a closer look at the band. I secure a spot near one corner of the stage where it looks like I'll be safe from any straggling slam dancers who might get tossed my way.

The singer is a behemoth, two feet taller and two feet broader than me. He sports a mane of long, straight, honey-colored hair and pounds on a black guitar. Screeching baritone vocals punch my (thick, ample) gut. His hair isn't punk—maybe he's being ironic?—but his singing sure is. He salts the lyrics with an occasional *pickitup pickitup!* to keep his fans swarming.

The other guitarist looks more in place in this dive, with short, bleached, spiked hair and a yellow T-shirt that says "Old's Cool." When he spins around, I see "Pathos" scrawled across the back of his shirt. Nice. Pathos is a Chicago-based punk band that has never come to Phoenix, and probably never will. Scene's too small here, which is probably why Nightrage is headed out. Escaping the event horizon that is the boundary of Metro Phoenix: Black Hole for the Arts. Can't say as I blame 'em.

The bassist stands still, a roll of belly hanging over his jeans, barely harnessed by a plain blue T-shirt. He chews his lip like he's afraid he might lose his place.

I shift position to get a look at the drummer, who is relegated to anonymous darkness upstage and camouflaged behind cymbals. I catch a glimpse of hair swinging over his face as he pounds away with a rhythm that sounds more like jazz than punk, but played with the *requisite ferocity* of the genre.

The song ends with a crash, ripping cheers out of the audience. Fists plunge up through the sweaty air. Someone shouts, *"You rock! You rock!"*

"Thanksalot," the singer says into the mic, as the bassist moves to check something on his amplifier and the drummer stands to adjust a cymbal.

Here's the thing.

If you had a couple of priceless sapphires and held them up to the rays of the setting sun in the moments after a Sonoran monsoon, they'd be *lifeless* next to this guy's eyes.

So I'm a girl, sue me, but *oh my god.*

My fingers ache for my paints, something, anything I can use to capture those eyes forever. A blank canvas, the ceiling in my room, one dirty wall of The Graveyard, I don't care, I need my paint *now*. Or my charcoals. It isn't just the *color* of his irises, it's the *intensity* in them I need to preserve.

He's starting to sit down when our gazes meet.

I. Freeze. Solid.

He isn't drop-dead gorgeous, by my or anyone else's standards. He has a narrow sort of face, and short hair except for shiny black skater bangs that reach his chin, old-school style. His body reminds me of a scarecrow, drumstick arms draped by an unpretentious white T-shirt.

But . . . have I mentioned his eyes?

So I stand there like an idiot, my mouth hanging open, thinking, *He looked at me—he looked at me—he looked at me.*

This is No Big.

He must've felt me staring at him and intuitively intercepted my gaze. I'm certain of this as he blinks and resumes his drumming posture without another glance in my direction. Probably I look like a psycho. A step up? Discuss. Wish I had the guts to talk to him after the show—

My rapture breaks as someone smashes into me, almost sending me to the floor.

"Shit, look out!" someone shouts at me.

I regain my footing. Some jackass jock who's been tossed out of the pit stands in front of me, unibrow furrowed, white ball cap askew at a *jaunty* frat angle.

"S-sorry," I say. For what, standing here? Dick.

He assesses me, up and down. "Are you a dude?"

Alas, my wit escapeth me! I have no droll response for yon gent. So I say—I really, truly say this:

"No."

Ten minutes from now, I will come up with the perfect rejoinder, something demure, like *I have some ideas on what you can go do, kind sir, and only half involve your mother.*

The walking penis laughs and shoves past me to the bar.

Welcome to my life.

I push my way to the patio, where I find an unoccupied bar stool. I order a Coke and glance at my reflection in the mirror that runs the length of the wall behind the back bar.

God, *do* I look like a guy? Tonight's nothing out of the ordinary, not a special ensemble I've put together for the evening's festivities. Like tonight, my usual uniform consists of jeans or cargo shorts or maybe overalls, a T-shirt, and one of more hats than I know what to do with. I keep my hair short because I don't care to mess with it.

Oh *yeah*, baby. I'm a peach. (Or Perhaps the Pit, I alliterate. *Snicker.*) But I mean, come on, there are plenty of women in here tonight who aren't dressed any diff—

"Hey."

On the patio, which is separated from the dance floor by thick windows, the noise is considerably lower, so there's no mistaking her voice.

"Oh," I say. "Hey, Jenn."

three

I do not paint a portrait to look like the
subject. Rather does the person grow to
look like his portrait.
–Salvador Dalí

Jenn's dressed to slay, her outfit glamorous, alluring, and casual all at once. Her curly copper hair is wound into a mass of tight, flouncy coils. (Fucking *goddess.*) Jenn's a great cook, and I can smell faint hints of foreign spices as she sits beside me. Whatever she made for dinner, it must've been good.

Jenn tries on a nervous smile. "So . . . how's it going?"

"Fine," I say, lying. I never would've expected her to come here by herself. Usually she's with some guy every weekend. Well, *almost* every weekend.

I haven't made eye contact yet. I make a big show of squinting past her through the picture windows, pretending, sort of, to be preoccupied with trying to catch another look at the drummer. I have a pretty good view now. His toned arms flail mercilessly, his knees popping up and down off unseen pedals.

"These guys are pretty good," Jenn says, filling a pause that looks to embarrass her as much as me.

"Uh-huh."

Jenn leans closer, trying to match my gaze. I counter by leaning backward. I don't think Jenn notices. "What're you staring at?"

"Eh, nothing."

"Got a crush?" Jenn asks with a weak chuckle.

I whirl away from the window. "No."

Jenn keeps studying the band. "Not the singer," she says, like to herself. "Definitely not the bass player. The guitarist?"

"No."

"The *drummer.*"

I take a sip of Coke.

Jenn manages a tense laugh and pokes me in the ribs. "It's him, isn't it?"

For a second, just a *second,* it's like nothing ever happened. I remember *Something Did* when Jenn looks down at her hand and quickly folds it into her lap.

"He's pretty cute," she says with heroic hopefulness. "Maybe you should talk to him."

"Do you not find that comment even remotely ironic?"

Jenn winces. That makes me feel bad. Surprisingly.

"Sorry," I say, coming within an iota of meaning it.

"Nah, it's cool," Jenn goes, all morose. "I get it."

I take another sip and watch the drummer.

Jenn glances out the window again. "Well, if you think he's hot, you should talk to him. I mean, if you think he's cute—"

"I *do,*" I snap. "And I won't."

And it's not that he's cute. Or hot. It's something that's *else*.

Jenn starts to smile. "Oh, come on—"

"Okay, Jenn? I don't think this is a conversation I want to have with you right now, so."

I nod to indicate she's free to leave at any point in the near future. *Now* being one example.

Jenn's smile evaporates. "Oh," she goes. "Yeah, um. Okay." She slips backward off her seat. "Sorry, I didn't mean to bug you. See ya later?"

I almost stop her. Almost. Jenn scowls and goes out into the crowd. She saunters up to a tall slab of meat dressed in jock regalia and rubs against him. Guess she's not alone after all.

And he looks familiar. Oh, *super*! Mr. "Are You a Dude," in the rancid flesh!

The jock strokes Jenn's sides and whispers into her ear. Jenn grins wickedly, as if our little discussion hasn't bothered her at all, and nods to him. But she shoots me this look over her shoulder through the windows.

I shake my head. Jenn gives me the same frowny face she always gives me whenever I bum her out, then they shove their way to the exit and are gone.

Good. Blow the joint with that Cro-Magnon asswipe and leave me here to pine away for some drummer who I will never have the *balls*, if you will, to speak to. And of course she and I need to talk. Just . . . not yet.

But I can't leave, either. There's a good chance Jenn is lingering outside, pressed up against a jockmobile and getting herself nice and felt up before they take off for her house or his dorm/apartment/basement/locker room to get liquored up and bump uglies. Like *hell* I'm going to wander outside and be witness to that. God, I should have stayed home.

Ten minutes. I'll wait ten minutes to make sure they're gone, then go home and pretend to be an artist for a little while before I pass out. Outstanding.

Gothic Rainbow finishes their set with three monster power chords. The audience goes wild, and I'd clap too except that I'd look like—well, a dork clapping all by herself.

"Thanksalot, we're outta here," the singer says into his mic as the other guys start unplugging their instruments. "Nightrage is comin' up next, so stick around. We're Gothic Rainbow, ssssssee ya!"

To keep myself busy, I keep an eye on the drummer as he disassembles his drums, twirling chrome knobs in his fingers and packing cymbals away in black cases. I check the clock over the bar. Seven more minutes.

Nightrage comes onstage as Gothic Rainbow finishes their teardown. There are handshakes and palm slaps all around. I'm sort of surprised; Nightrage is a great band but has a reputation for being assholes. Nightrage sets their gear up and runs through sound check (test one, test two, test test testicles, *huh huh huh!*) as Gothic Rainbow disappears backstage.

Good. I can't handle staring at the drummer anymore. Just thinking about his eyes makes me dizzy.

Three more minutes.

. Nightrage bursts into their first song, one I've heard before at Damage Control, the sole Big Deal club in town. DC caters to none and all, which is probably why it's still in business. Hip-hop, jazz, mellow acoustic, ska—DC hosts anyone who can draw a crowd. Black Phantom used to play there two or three times a month before they left town. Now Nightrage plays there a lot, and I get the feeling Gothic Rainbow hasn't quite made the grade yet. Otherwise, they wouldn't've played first tonight.

I'm counting down the seconds remaining in my last minute of this stupid night when Gothic Rainbow reappears from backstage and worms through the crowd.

Heading for the patio.

All four of them.

I spin back toward the bar and glare at myself in the mirror. Kind of a rarity, really: seeing myself in an actual mirror instead of my posters.

Know what? I whisper-think to the pathetic soul staring back at me. *Screw Mom, screw Jenn, and screw this. Go home. You know you're not gonna talk to him.*

Here's the thing.

I want to.

So, so bad. I want to try, just once. Anything to take my mind off the destructionist paintings that are now emblematic of my *post*friendship with Jenn and my—what was it?—oh yes, utter failure as an artist.

In the mirror, I see the drummer and the band walk onto the patio. They file past me, taking seats at the other end of the bar.

Eleven minutes have passed since I promised myself I'd wait ten minutes. It's safe to get up right now and go home.

But the alternative is facing my mother, who's pr[...]
still awake.

The alternative is letting what happened at Jenn[...]
week continue to bother me instead of moving on. Finding
new friends. Or something.

My hands spring leaks of cold sweat and my heart feels
like one of that guy's bass drums, thrumming and trembling.
Like my body knows before I do that I'm actually going to risk
talking to this drummer guy.

"You've got to be kidding me," I say to my reflection. Like
I have no choice.

Maybe, when all is said and done, I don't. Maybe none of
us do. I dunno.

I slide off my bar stool and chug the rest of my Coke like
it's a shot of Jäger. As if. I love me some soda pop, but liquid
courage it is not. Most liquid courage makes me puke, I've
learned recently. Wish I had Dad's *constitution* on that front,
sometimes.

There's an empty seat next to the drummer. I force one
foot after another toward that stool, which is somehow getting farther and farther away. I pass behind him, reach the
bar stool—

And promptly bang my knee against it as I try to climb up.
"*Ow!* Fuck!"

The entire band looks at me.

". . . Hey," I add.

Three heads tip backward in greeting. The drummer just
stares at me.

He is Caravaggio's *Medusa*. I am a failed Perseus, turned

to stone in his gaze. I want to dive into him through his pupils, swim around, know everything.

"You okay?" he says.

I rub my knee and nod, lying. "Yeah, yeah." I point to the stool. "D'you mind if I . . . ?"

Pop quiz! Which of these is longest?

    (a) An era
    (b) An epoch
    (c) An eon
    (d) The time he takes before answering

"Sure," he says. His voice is low and, like, *suspicious*.

I climb onto the stool and lace my fingers into their usual knots. The other band members turn away and resume their conversation. I decide to dazzle the drummer with my knowledge of all things domestic, foreign, and galactic.

"Um," I say.

He blinks at me.

"My name's Zero," I say, as if this will help.

"Zero."

"Yeah."

"A whole number less than one."

"Yep, that says it all. Heh."

His eyes never leave my face. He says nothing else.

"Well, Amanda, I mean," I say. "I just, you know, like, go by . . . Zero."

And I'm just, you know, like, a jackass. But he's listening. Doesn't that mean something? More likely: he'll let me ramble on for a while before laughing at me and taking off.

I clear my throat. "So, um . . . I liked your music, you're really good."

There. That's Jenn talking. Give the guy a compliment, pump his ego, get him talking about himself. That's her sage advice. Like she has to do anything more than shake her ass to get a guy. I'm afraid if I shook my ass, it would never *stop* shaking. Colossal waves of chub could reverberate for weeks.

The guy raises a shoulder. "Thanks."

"Yeah, uh . . . it was cool. How long have you been around?"

"Couple years."

"Yeah? That's cool. You guys were really good."

Do I have an encyclopedic vocabulary or what? Bloody hell.

Nightrage stops playing suddenly. The singer and bassist are about to swing at each other, while the guitarist tries to break it up. Jerks. They do this at every show. Gothic Rainbow's drummer watches them explode, shakes his head with a grin, and turns back to me. He's shifted position a little, so I can see his face up close and personal. Cute and all, but I don't care. All I can think about are his eyes. Like they know something I don't.

I look at my boots. "So, I just, um . . . thought I'd come over here and have absolutely nothing to say."

"Yeah?" he goes. "How's that working out for you?"

"So far so good?"

I think one corner of his mouth turns up a bit. He sort of squints at me, like he's trying to figure something out. If it's *me*, I wish ya luck, bud.

But he doesn't reply.

I fish for a new topic. "So . . . what, um . . . kind of music do you like?"

He tips his glass and sucks out the last bits of ice, his teeth crunching down, crushing the cubes. "Been known to listen to D.I.," he says.

I twitch, electrocuted. "*This* D.I.?" I say, pointing to my shirt.

He glances at me. "Mm-hm. Underappreciated, in my opinion."

There's this tiny, odd flutter tickling my belly. It, um . . . feels kinda good.

But he doesn't add anything else.

Time to cut my losses. "Cool. So, um . . . maybe I can—I mean, maybe I'll see ya around again . . . sometime?"

"You never know."

"Yeah," I say, my stomach withering. "I guess not."

I suck. In case you didn't notice.

"Well . . ." I spin on my (prodigious, malformed) ass, ready to bolt. "It was nice meeting you."

For no good reason at all, I stick my hand out, amazed that my palm doesn't dump a gallon of sweat onto the bar.

The drummer gazes at me for a moment, looking at me sort of quizzically. "Mike," he says, giving my hand a quick shake. His is dry and calloused but warm.

"Nice to meet you, Mike."

"Likewise. Zero."

We sit there and look at each other. I can't turn away from his eyes; I've got to figure out what the hell is going on behind them. See if charcoal can capture the startling blue with pastel black.

But somehow, I doubt I'll ever get the chance. I'm about ready to make my exit when Mike asks, "So now what?"

Surprised he's initiated more conversation, I say, "Um . . . that's a rather astute question, actually."

"Is it? Hey, thanks!"

And suddenly, unbidden, unanticipated—and kinda neat—I laugh.

Mike does not. But he does sort of give me this little grin.

"We could, um . . ." I search for a solid answer. "I dunno, talk sometime?"

Holy hell, I really just said that.

"We could," Mike says.

Nightrage starts up again—crisis averted—but despite their frenzied thrashing, I'm naked and trapped like I'm in an Edvard Munch landscape; swallowed by dismal curlicues, hearing nothing.

I give myself a shake. "Yeah. Okay, so . . . let me give you my number, then, I guess?"

Why not. I yank out my wallet and pull out a worn business card for Landscapes Art Supply. I have the number memorized. I flip the card facedown on the bar and grab a golf pencil from a mug. Are they kept here for just such an occasion? I write my number down and push the card toward Mike with my fingers, like I'm feeding a tiger.

"Anytime. Okay?"

Mike nods and picks up the card. "Got it."

"Okay," I repeat. "Well, thanks. I mean, cool. I'll, um . . . hope to hear from you, then?"

Mike blinks lazily back at me. But there's this *activity* behind his eyes. Like I'm watching a master artist paint a new piece, but only able to watch his eyes while he works, never seeing the canvas as the painting takes shape. If that makes sense.

"So . . . see ya," I say, and slide off the stool.

"See ya," Mike says. And his eyes sparkle.

I force myself to walk straight to the patio exit. As I pass the other two band members, I hear one of them whisper: "*Nice* ass."

I check behind me in time to see the singer smack the bassist upside the back of his head.

Clearly, I misheard. Must've been *wide* ass.

I walk out of the patio, and I'm compelled to wave to Mike through the window. Mike raises a casual hand in reply. A friendly hand; a no-way-in-hell-will-I-call-you hand.

I should feel, like, *elated* or something as I drive home, but I don't. I feel like a tool. Yeah, so I got my guts up and talked to the guy. No big. I lived to tell the tale, and that's about it. I try to tell myself that's what matters, that I at least gave myself the chance.

Then I tell myself to kindly shut the hell up. I'm tired of thinking about it, sick of the merry-go-round thoughts of it all. Better to just get home, toss in a movie, read a book, paint by numbers, whatever. Forget this whole night ever happened.

When I get home, Mom's still at the sink, like she never left. Awesome. I wonder if Dad pays her to be a housewife or what, because she doesn't have a job.

"Where were you?" she demands before I've even closed the door.

God, for real? "A club."

"Amy, would it be so horrible to let me know where you're going to be?" She rubs her forehead and squeezes her eyes shut.

"Mmm . . . possibly. I'll have to get back to you on that."

"Amy, I—"

"*Dad* home yet?"

Crap. I swear I didn't mean for it to sound like that; all smart-ass. No, I *didn't*. His truck isn't in the driveway; it's not like I could have missed it.

Mom looks at me, slapped. I try to come up with a way to apologize, but Mom walks down the hall to their bedroom and closes the door, massaging her head.

Way to go, Z, you're a champ. I go into my room, shut the door, and start getting ready for bed. This whole night drained me. See! That's why I should stay home. So much for a fun, relaxing weekend.

On the other hand . . . I did talk to Mike. That's, like, momentous. It's *something*. Right? And even avoided talking to Jenn. *Yay*, I guess . . .

I consider trying to capture Mike's eyes on canvas, now that I'm here and have all my weapons at hand. Even before my fingers graze a brush, though, I know it'll be a waste. I'm too tired, too bitchy, and art supplies don't come cheap. Whatever.

I change out of my shirt, and catch myself pausing just before pulling on an old pair of sweat shorts. Biting my lip, I slowly turn around until I can look over my shoulder at my reflection in the glass covering Dalí's *Young Virgin Auto-*

Sodomized by Her Own Chastity. Which is not quite as gross as it sounds.

Nice ass, huh?

"Not . . . *bad,*" I whisper. But not nice. No way.

I climb into bed, wishing I could tell Jenn how I actually talked to a living, breathing male of the species of my own accord.

I wonder what the weather is like in Chicago right now.

I think about charcoal sapphires.

I wonder if my phone will ring.

Ever.

four

Who were my enemies? Everyone, or
almost everyone. . . .
    –Salvador Dalí

"You need new clothes," Mom says on Monday night, ironing a
pair of my jeans.

Jeans. Who the hell irons jeans?

I don't look at her because my video game demands total
concentration.

"'Kay," I say.

"Amy, I mean it. Don't you want something a little brighter
for the summer? Or for school this fall? A nice skirt or two . . .
These clothes are falling apart."

"Well, Mom, most people don't iron their socks."

The iron sizzles behind me. God, why can't she do this in
her bedroom or something instead of the living room, where
I am clearly trying to de-stress from a very long, hard day of
practicing my shading and hatching?

Mom's telepathy tunes to my lazy channel. "Have you

thought about finding a job this summer?" she asks. "Since you chose not to take summer school?"

I didn't *choose* not to take summer school; I didn't think I'd freakin' have to worry about being here long enough for it to matter. But I don't bother telling her this. After graduation, in desperate need of distraction thanks to Jenn and the SAIC debacle, I registered at a community college for fall semester. Still need to choose classes, though.

"Yeah, sure," I say.

It's not a bad idea. Maybe I'll start looking tomorrow. It beats being stuck at home with Mom. Not like I'll be hanging out with Jenn all summer.

"You'll need something nice if you want to look presentable," Mom goes on. "You can't hide in all these baggy things for a job interview. And some color wouldn't kill you."

Maybe it would. *Then* she'd be in trouble! I close my eyes and count to five. When I open them, my game has ended. I'm dead.

"Goddammit."

"Amy, please, swearing is a terrible habit for . . ."

"Ah, hell, let her say what she wants," my dad says, sailing into the living room, his suit coat hanging casually off one finger. "How's it going, Z?" he asks, yanking the brim of my cap down as he ambles past.

"Don't call her that," Mom stage-whispers. "It only encourages her."

"We all need encouragement, Miriam," Dad says, tossing his coat carelessly onto the couch and stepping back out of the room. Mom sweeps the coat into her arms and folds it over the back of her rocking chair, beside the sofa.

"Oh, for chrissake!" Dad's voice blares from the kitchen.

Mom goes back to ironing (my *jeans*!), tight-lipped. I reset my game while Dad crashes around in the kitchen. I'd keep the game system in my room except Dad bought it mostly for himself. Apparently he's training to be (a) a ninja, (b) a mercenary, or (c) a race car driver.

I hear Dad sliding a case of beer into the refrigerator. Glass clanks, and Dad walks back into the living room, a tall brown bottle in one hand. He sits on the couch and sighs.

"Got to hand it to you, Miriam," he says. "You're getting smarter. It could have taken me, I don't know, *minutes* before I found it this time. Well, it's warm and disgusting, if that's any goddam consolation." Dad hates ice in his beer, for some reason. Maybe it spoils the taste.

"Please don't swear at me," Mom says quietly.

"Well, please don't hide my damn beer!"

"I just wish you wouldn't drink before dinner, that's all."

"The hell that's all."

My game ends again. Probably because I didn't use the controller at all. I reset.

"I'm not going to fight with you, Richard."

"Glad to hear it. Hey, kiddo, you done playing? Where's the goddam remote?"

Mom slams the iron down on the board, making me jump.

"Oh," Dad says in mock surprise. "I thought we weren't fighting."

Mom puts a hand to her forehead. "I am not fighting! I . . ." She takes a deep breath. "I just wish we could all use more *civilized* language. . . ."

"Well, I'm an uncultured old bastard, I guess." Dad's lips pop as he takes another drink.

"It's no wonder Amy talks the way she does," Mom says. "It's clear where she gets it from."

My game ends. Probably because I can't make my fingers work. They've tied themselves together in my lap without asking me first.

This time, I reach for the power button.

"Gets what, exactly? My rugged good looks or boyish charm? Maybe both, huh, Z?"

"Or my boyish looks and rugged charm," I offer, searching for a smile to go with the joke. Dad throws his head back, laughs, and takes a drink.

"The sarcasm, Richard," Mom says, pressing a hand to her forehead. "The swearing. Probably drinking, too, for all I know . . ."

"If your daughter wanted a beer, there's not much you could do to stop it. Right, Z?"

I stand up. I've had a swig or two in my time, yes. Mostly girlie stuff like piña coladas. But not anymore, not ever again. Somehow I can't make myself tell them that, though.

"Her *name* is Amanda, Richard. . . ."

"Oh, Christ, would you relax, Miry? Jesus."

Dad only pulls out the old King of Kings to upset Mom's delicate Catholic sensibilities. She hasn't been to Mass in years, but it works every time.

"Richard . . . !" Mom says, and I know the tone. She's ready to throw down now.

I stand up. "Well, I'll be in my room. Enjoy your special time together."

They both look at me like they're not sure what to say. I walk out just as they start blaming each other for my *tone*.

I'm about ready to set clocks by this crap. Dad usually gets home at seven, and the skirmishes with Mom begin not long after. He's out the door by eight or eight-thirty on the weekend to go to Scotty's with work buddies.

I go into my bedroom and slam the door. It's not enough to drown their voices. I can't stay here. I reach for my phone and punch in Jenn's number.

She answers on the first ring. "Hello?"

Oops, forgot; *not ever talking to her again.* I hang up.

I fall back against my door and slide down its length until my knees buckle upward, my arms curled around my stomach. I inhale sharply, trying to stop the salty, bitter taste running down my throat. I feel my sinuses clogging, stomach tightening, face warming. . . .

"Stop it," I whisper. "Just fucking *stop it* for once."

Something crashes in the living room. Wonder what it was this time.

In eighth grade, Mr. Hilmer introduced us to glass etching in his last-hour art class. I fell in love with it, and the next weekend, I bought etching cream, carbon paper, razor blades, and a selection of mirrors and glass. It took me a few weeks to get the technique down, but I got pretty good even by my own standards, and that's saying something. I showed a couple of my pieces to Mr. Hilmer—the class had moved on to watercolors, which I don't like as much—and he said, "You done good, Amanda. These are fantastic." Me. *Fantastic.*

My first truly successful piece was of my dad's face, hidden in white swirls on a circular mirror. I ran into the living room, literally *forgetting* that a fight was in progress. Combat ceased as Dad accepted the gift with a fast smile and faster hug. I took off, ashamed somehow that my presence was distracting them from their *marital strife*.

Then came the sound of broken glass as one of them—I never asked nor wanted to know which—dropped the gift onto the tile floor.

Dropped or threw. Whichev. I haven't etched a single thing since then.

I snuffle up a noseload of snot and glance up at a painting of my own face on the ceiling, expressionistically rendered, split by jagged cracks and splinters. My face in a shattered mirror. Subtle, yes?

"I hate you," I say to the painting.

". . . so damned worried about . . ."

". . . would for once listen to . . ."

My parents' voices filter into my room. Thought I was used to it by now. I will not cry over this. No, I *won't*. But I can feel the whole mess with Jenn stacking on top of my off-the-scale stupidity at The Graveyard on Friday ganging up on me, too, threatening to flood my eyes.

Must make it stop. I get up and turn on my stereo. Minor Threat blares, but I turn it up louder. Ian MacKaye reminds me right off that life's not been good for me. (Thanks, Ian. I appreciate that.)

But it's not loud enough, so I flip on my TV, too. I am pleased to learn that *getting rid of a yeast infection is now easier than ever!* I change the channel to public access. No commercials.

". . . with the drinking every night . . ."

". . . tell me how to live my own . . ."

I grab my palette and squirt black acrylic onto its surface. Dumb idea; I should cut it with gel, make it last, but the hell with it. Pick a brush, any brush, smash it into the goo, and begin slicing across the canvas of a half-finished desert landscape.

Go out and fight, fight, bottled violence, Ian suggests, while two guys on public access introduce me to downhill skateboarding. Camelback Mountain is in the background.

I hold my brush in a fist, making circles now; tight, Möbius-strip curls. Wipe my nose across my forearm, squeeze crimson onto the palette, use the same brush, stab the canvas, refusing to look at my reflection in any of my Dalí posters. I have a pretty good idea what I look like, thanks. It rhymes with *shit.*

That's when I realize my phone is ringing. I'm not sure for how long it's been going. I drop the brush and pick up. Instead of saying hello, I bitch, "*Now* what!"

Nothing. No response. I swear, if this is some kind of sales—

"Uh . . . hi."

"Hello!" I shout again, and jab the TV power button off.

"Um . . ."

"What!" I punch out Ian MacKaye's voice. "Hello!"

"Hi, um . . . is . . . Zero there?"

No. Fucking. Way.

"This is me—her—she," I blurt out, *very* smooth and calm. My nose is still plugged up from crying, so I sound like a sick goat.

"Oh. Hey. It's Mike."

I know!

"We met Friday night at The Graveyard?"

I know!

"Oh yeah, hi," I say. "How's it going?" I look wildly around for a safe place to set my palette down without creating a mess.

"Pretty good, I guess. So, um . . . what're you up to?"

I view my painting, such as it is. *Teaching myself a little Dada. You?*

But what I say is, "Um, nothing much, what are you up to?"

"Well, uh . . . getting ready to head over to Eddie's to jam."

"Yeah? Who's Eddie?"

"Bassist."

"Oh. Cool."

Bang! The kitchen door slams, causing every one of my muscles to cramp. That must've been Dad, out to hit Scotty's, drinking. . . .

"You wanna hang out sometime?" I blurt.

. . . Um . . .

That voice sounded an *awful lot* like mine. Oh, hell, what did I just do? Tires screech off the carport concrete, and I hear Dad's truck peel into the night.

This is my mom's fault. I just made the world's biggest ass of myself, and it's because of her stupid nagging. No way would I have asked Mike out otherwise.

Oh, and speaking of Mike: *insert awkward silence.* My mind is a new canvas, stretched taut, off-white, empty.

Mike rescues me. "Well," he says, "now that you mention it, we're playing this show downtown tomorrow night, at Weidman's Pub, but we'll be done around nine or so . . ."

Oh my god. Is he really going to ask—

". . . and if you want to, you know, hang out or something, we could maybe do that afterward, if you wanted to. Or whatever. I mean, unless you're twenty-one, then I guess we could meet up at the pub. Uh, *are* you twenty-one?"

I say, "Me? No! No, uh-uh. Are *you*?"

"Nah. We can play there, we just can't drink."

"Oh. Cool. But—yeah! Meeting up, I mean. That's cool. Okay."

Smooth Operator Tip Number One: Babble incoherently instead of saying *Yes*.

"Okay," Mike says, with what sounds like a sigh of some kind. "Cool. Where're you coming from?"

"Oh, uh, I can get pretty much anywhere. As long as I can still see Camelback."

"Camelback . . . *Mountain*?"

"Yeah. It's like a, you know, landmark. For, like, navigation."

And I'm, like, you know, *an idiot.*

"Huh," Mike says. "Well . . . okay, yeah. Um . . ."

I (somehow) get a brilliant idea. "Do you do coffee? We could meet at Hole in the Wall Café. That's not far from Weidman's, right?"

"Yeah, I know right where it is. Yeah, sure, that sounds good."

"Really?" The word pops out of my mouth before I can stop it. I wish I could slug myself in the stomach. "Cool. So Hole in the Wall at about nine tomorrow?"

"Yeah, perfect. That'll work. See ya then."

"Bye!"

I hang up and perform eighteen consecutive cartwheels. Only mentally, but whatever!

I'm an idiot, but I'm a *genius* idiot. The Hole is my turf. Home away from home. It's the perfect place to hang out, with its multiple rooms for semiprivacy, but still in public just in case he's an ax murderer, and with plenty of espresso to ensure my tranquility.

Mom's footsteps echo in the hallway. A moment later, I hear their bedroom door close. Guess that's it for the night.

Whatever. I have important things to do. Selecting exactly the right clothes for a first date could take up to several decades, right? I need to get started. I haven't exactly been on a real live date in . . . well, whatever. The point is, I want to look good, and thinking about this beats thinking about them.

However, Mom had a point: my wardrobe isn't exactly varied. Should I wear my D.I. shirt again, since he mentioned them? No, it'll look like I never washed it. Some other obscure punk band to test his taste? No, too risky, and I don't care. What I care about is getting the chance to spend an hour, maybe two if I'm lucky, looking into those emerald-sapphire eyes. Which I could have been trying to paint right now instead of destroying a landscape.

He *called*.

Okay, Z, calm down. Got plenty of time. He liked what I wore Friday, right? Or at least, he didn't *not* like it. I can figure it out tomorrow.

When I go on my date!

I catch a glance at my canvas. One more ruined. Pieces of the original landscape peek through the black and red destruction, like a yearbook photo of That Guy that you blot out with Sharpie. I should pick up kickboxing or something to work out my issues instead of punishing my innocent canvases. Had to pick an expensive dream, didn't I.

My phone rings again. It's going to be Mike, isn't it. Him and all his friends will laugh at me, call me an idiot, and hang up; I know it.

I pick up anyway. "Hello?"

"Um—hey. Did you just call?"

Maybe it would have been better if it was a prank call from Mike and the band. But no, it's Jenn, sure as hell.

"Uh . . . sort of," I mumble. And even though I do not want to talk to her, I have to resist gushing about Mike's call, since it's *not* him calling to say he was joking.

"You okay?" Jenn asks.

"Me? Yeah. Sure."

"Oh."

I should hang up. Yes, I should.

"Well, since I've got you—" Jenn starts.

"Look, I gotta go, okay?"

"Z, come on. Please? I hate this."

Me too. But I don't say it.

"Jenn, look, I . . . I can't, okay?"

I hear her sniff. "It's *not* okay!"

"Yeah, you're right, it's not. But I can't do this right now."

She sniffs again. Is she, like, *crying*? "Okay," she says. "But can you at least promise me we'll talk soon?"

". . . Sure."

Jenn makes a little snorting sound, like she doesn't believe me. Well, that makes two of us. "Fine," she goes. "Can I call you?"

"I guess."

"'Kay. Thanks. See ya."

I hang up without saying goodbye. Dammit, I was feeling pretty good there for a sec.

I pick my brush back up and face the painting. *Hole in the Wall,* I chant as I blend gel into my acrylic. *I've got a date tomorrow, Hole in the Wall, I've got a date.*

It helps.

A lot.

Who needs best friends or parents or art school, right?

five

Something very different was going to
come into my life.
—Salvador Dalí

Hole in the Wall Café is aptly named. It's this low, gray cinder block building with a dirt parking lot and perpetually flickering orange neon sign that attracts only the likes of . . . well, me. Me *and* Jenn, once upon a time. It's owned by this artist, Eli (no last name), who converted it into a coffee shop, redesigned with several rooms with their own unique decor. Local artwork hangs haphazardly on the walls, each piece with a small white price tag affixed. If you like one, you just take it up to the register and buy it.

I debate a lot whether or not to approach Eli about showing my own work. I have the whole scene written out in my head:

I show him my best painting, should such a thing be possible, and his mouth drops open in orgasmic delight at my brilliance, which shines like the light of a thousand suns. He tells me this doesn't belong at the Hole; it should be hanging in the Met, and he knows the Supreme Chief Super High Curator personally, so it'll just take one phone call and I will be rocketed to international glory, fame, and wealth.

Or he'll, like, laugh and tell me to stick with kindergarten handprint turkeys.

That's why I've never tried. I mean, for real—if the Hole won't hang my work, why would anyone else? The vibe here is cool and all, but not every piece is exactly outstanding. The art here is equivalent to garage bands: cool, fun, and full of potential, but only a couple of real standouts. Would I be one of them?

I order an iced mint mocha and head to my favorite room in the Hole. It's painted eggplant purple and has hundreds of glow-in-the-dark star stickers attached to the ceiling. The light level is kept low in here to better show off the stars.

I check the time to see if Mike's late. He's not; not quite yet. Okay. Breathe. Whether or not this is a real live Date, and not just a Hanging Out, I've got to know why he called. I mean, hey, he gets top marks for interrupting a crappy mood last night, but honestly, part of me wonders if he's even going to show.

I shuffle through the random flyers advertising bands, art classes, and garage sales that litter all the tabletops, then pick up a discarded copy of *College Times*, flip through it, mock everyone in the photos, envy everyone in the photos, hate everyone in the photos, get depressed when I realize I'll be *among* them soon. I'm about to toss the paper away, except a headline on the last page catches my eye:

Gothic Rainbow (Almost) Rules
By Joy N. Wickersham

Why, hello there. What are the chances, right? I start reading.

> A good rock band is like a great lover. Their rhythms simultaneously jolt you and calm you. They know when and where to tease you to make it feel the best, how to draw from you the ultimate pleasure. There are some—bands and lovers—who rehearse this rhythm, but they have no soul. Then there are those who were simply born to be so good. They can't help it. Gothic Rainbow is one such band.

Wow. This chick is either having great heaping buckets of sex or hasn't ever.

Not that I would know. Must ask Jenn. Someday.

> Gothic Rainbow appeared on the local scene more than a year ago, picking up gigs at all-ages holes like Phantasm, prior to its demise. Before long, the foursome appeared on bills joining them with local successes Nightrage and Black Phantom.
>
> Jonathan Nelson (vocals/rhythm guitar) must've only narrowly missed the casting call for any given metal band. Hotshot virtuoso Brook Peterson (lead guitar) often adds a Brian Setzer–style rhythm to the band's minor-chord tunes. He'd appear more at home slam dancing with the punkers at Liberty Spike's Bar than playing the bluesy-ska riffs the band is now notorious for. Eddie Smith (bass) and Michael Berry (drums) round out the lineup with provocative rhythms borrowing heavily from jazz, tribal, and commercial punk.

> Nelson's baritone is both ominous and optimistic. His lyrics are
> a maudlin affair punctuated with bursts of oddly mature insights.
> Regardless of subject matter, often standard fare such as angsty
> broken hearts and pure punk diatribes against society, GR whips its
> growing audience into a frenzy. They did just that last weekend at
> The Graveyard.

Hey, I was at that show. Maybe the writer interviewed Mike, and he told her all about this awesome girl he met. Heh.

> Gothic Rainbow is destined for local stardom at least. Let them
> build up the core audience they need to move to the bigger venues
> like Damage Contr—

"Whatcha reading?"

I jump. Mike is standing across from me, holding a mug of something steamy in one hand and a skateboard in the other. A Vision Gator. The underside is scratched and scraped, testifying to its use and abuse.

"Oh, hey, hi," I say, and almost crumple up the paper like it's evidence needing disposal.

"Anything good?" He sits across from me with a little smirk. "Ah, *College Times*. It's the review, isn't it."

I feel absurdly guilty, like I was spying on him. "Yeah."

"What'd you think?"

My mouth goes suddenly, painfully dry as it sets in that we're actually here. Together.

And his *eyes*—

"It's a pretty good review," I say.

"Yeah, I heard," Mike goes.

"You . . . didn't read it?"

"Nah."

"How come?"

"It's just one person's opinion. Selling tickets, on the other hand, harder to argue with."

Touché. Why hadn't I ever thought of that? I mean, how are you supposed to know if you're any good unless the critics say so? But now that he says it, I see that Mike's got a point. I don't always agree with the reviews I read in *ARTnews,* either.

Mike scratches his head and says, "Ah, I'm sorry, that sounded really arrogant. I didn't mean it quite like—"

"No, no, it's cool," I tell him. "I think that's a great way to look at it." Not that I'll ever be able to when it comes to my first showing. I'll probably have an aneurysm waiting for my first reviews. But I respect Mike's point and oh *god* his eyes are beautiful.

"So . . ." Mike snaps his fingers. "I meant to tell you, I liked your belt."

I glance down. "Uh, you can't *see* my belt from there." Perhaps my whale blubber has oozed up over the table of its own accord, taking my belt with it.

"The one you were wearing the other night. Green leather, with the watches and stuff. Where'd you get it? It was cool."

Mike: I will bear you many children. We can start now. Let me just clear off the table.

It's only a stupid belt, I know. But he *noticed.*

"Thanks," I say, knuckles popping in my lap. "It's sort of a Dalí tribute."

"A dolly? Like, for moving stuff?"

"Oh, no, no, no!" I lean across the table to take his hands, to emphasize the error of his ways. I'm halfway there before I realize that I'm doing it, actually about to *make contact,* and it's way too forward a move for little old me, but to pull away now will look brain damaged to the tenth degree. I give one of his hands a quick pat instead of taking them in mine, which would be awesome because I would give anything to feel his hands, his palms, how they must—

Shut. Up.

I withdraw my hands. "Salvador Dalí. The artist. Underline *thee.*"

"Oh," Mike says. "Okay, yeah. Him. That sounds familiar."

Well, it'll do. For now.

"So you're really into art?" he asks, looking around at the walls.

"An epic understatement, but yes."

"You paint?"

"And draw. Yeah."

"You any good?"

Here's the thing.

What the hell did you say? I mean, I clearly know the answer already, but dude, you don't have to remind me.

"Um . . . I don't think I can answer that."

"Why not? It's yours."

"Are you a good *drummer*?" Haha, zing! That'll teach—

"Not bad," Mike says with a shrug. "Not great, but I mean, it's drumming. Not a ton of skill required. At least not what *I* play. Art's totally different. *Are* you any good?"

This isn't the conversation I'd hoped for. My mood shifts from eggplant purple to grayscale.

"I thought I was," I mumble.

"You're not anymore?"

I pull my fingers apart and shake my hands. "Now's not the best time to ask if I think I'm any good or not."

"Oh. Sorry to hear that. What happened?"

"Nothing," I say helplessly. "I mean, literally."

Mike tilts his head. I meet his eyes, and—I dunno, it's not like I want to talk about this, but his curiosity feels genuine, not judgmental. All right, hell with it.

"There's this school I really want to get into," I tell him. "The School of the Art Institute of Chicago? And I got accepted, but my portfolio wasn't good enough for the merit scholarship I needed. They said I had potential but—how'd they put it—I 'lack the level of technical excellence demanded of first-year fine-arts students.' Words to that effect."

Exact words, in fact. I don't even know what they meant, other than that the scholarship went to someone more . . . what's the word . . . *talented*.

"And SAIC is a private university, so tuition is freaking huge, and I needed this damn scholarship to pay for it," I say. "My dad has this school savings account thing for me, but it's only enough to cover a community college. Maybe a year at an in-state university after that if I'm careful."

Mike looks confused. "So aren't there other schools? Other scholarships?"

I choke back a sigh. I can't help it. "Not exactly," I mutter. Bottom line, and I don't want to get into this with Mike at the moment, Dad makes too much money for me to be considered for a lot of scholarships out there. My *expected family contribution* is too high. Neat, huh? Makes you wonder where all his money goes.

Mike's expression switches to something that looks like disappointment, and I straighten up in my seat. I'm being a bummer. Not cool.

"I mean, yes, there are," I amend. "Lots. I just sorta had my heart set on this one."

He nods. "You don't want to settle."

"Yeah. Pretty much."

"But you still enjoy it, right? Painting, drawing?"

"Well, yeah."

Mike shrugs again. "Then you're good. Maybe that's enough. For now."

For one moment, I *forget* that I am scared to death to be sitting here. "Hold on a sec. You're saying as long as a person enjoys doing something, they're automatically good at it?"

"If a person enjoys doing something, they'll probably only get better with time."

"So as long as a serial killer keeps practicing, he'll kill more people, more efficiently."

"If killing people is his goal, yeah."

I bust up. Can't help it. This is ridiculous, and a hell of a lot of fun, and *man,* his eyes are killing me here. And come to think of it, it's not just his eyes anymore, either.

Mike leans back in his chair and grins, just a little. He takes another look around the Hole, and jerks his head toward one wall where several paintings are hung.

"You ever put anything up here?"

"Oh, no."

"Why not?"

"They wouldn't want it."

"Ever ask?"

"Not . . . exactly?"

"Hm. Well, you should. Someday. Like, when you're ready."

He makes it sound so easy. Poor kid.

Mike grabs a neon-pink flyer from a nearby table and holds it up. "What about classes?" he asks. "Taking anything this summer? Maybe you just need a little practice. I know I do."

The flyer is advertising a life drawing class, held in one of the Hole's rooms, starting next week. But the price per class is ridiculous. For what they're asking, I may as well sign up for summer school at my college and get the credit for it. And since I did *not* look for a job today, it might not be a bad idea. It'll help keep Mom off my back, *and* get me out of the house.

I twist my fingers together again. "Yeah," I say. "Maybe."

He takes a quick sip. "What do you like to paint? What're your . . . like, topics."

"Subjects," I correct automatically.

"Subjects," he says with a gleam in his (incredible, mesmerizing) eyes.

"Um . . . I dunno . . . people. Things."

"You're not exactly your biggest fan, are you."

I roll my eyes until they fall out of the sockets, while Mike just smiles.

"Okay," I say, defeated. "No, I guess I'm not."

"How come?"

"Well . . . I had this teacher in junior high. Mr. Hilmer?

He was really cool. He went to SAIC, which is why I wanted to go. And I mean, *he* said I was good, but that was like years ago, and I mean, I was like *twelve*."

"I'm not entirely sure you answered the question there."

Rats. "How come I don't think I'm any good? I dunno. I've never sold anything, for one. I blew that scholarship, for two."

"But you got accepted, right?"

"Well . . . yeah, but. Now I'm stuck just going to get my associate's, then try to transfer to SAIC, hopefully. Someday. But probably not. I mean, that's like two years from now. Minimum. If ever."

Mike chuckles at me. I don't know whether to be mad or what.

"You're a very complicated personality," he says.

And for some reason, that makes me smile. Maybe because he's right.

"Got me all figured out, huh?"

"I think I'm getting the Cliffs Notes, yeah." He smiles, and a feather duster teases my belly.

I try to shift the conversation: "Why do *you* care? I mean, if I try to hang something here or not."

"I just think if you want something, you should go get it."

What I *want* is to feel his hands, look into his eyes. And maybe more, because it beats dwelling on my SAIC failure. But I'm guessing now isn't the time to mention it. I also want international acclaim and truckloads of money, but honestly, that's a distant second—*third*, even *fourth*—to knowing, for sure, that I don't suck. But I don't mention that, either.

"Have you been doing it long? Painting and whatnot?"

"Junior high and high school, mainly. But my high school art teacher was an idiot. He sort of inherited the job; like, he was the only faculty who'd ever taken an art class. Didn't learn much. And he wrote the world's worst recommendation letter for me. But I did get an A all four years. Not that it was hard. Sadly, the grades didn't give me what I needed, which was, oh yes, *technical excellence*. Whatever that means."

Mike exaggerates being secretive as he slides the art class flyer toward me, hinting.

I actually—god help me—*giggle*. "Golly. That was sneaky there."

"Thanks. I'm kind of a ninja."

"Is that like a full-time thing or . . . ?"

"Eh. Part-time right now."

Mike looks into my eyes, and finds a direct line to my nervous system, which seizes up and freezes me in place. I wish I could know what it is he's looking for in here.

Or what it is he's found.

"So, you're going to be around for a while, huh?" Mike asks.

"Looks that way."

And only after I say it in that casual tone do I realize the implication of the question. Am I going to *be around*? Why would he care if I was?

I'm not quite stupid enough to ask for a clarification. "So, way, way, way enough about me," I say, and I get a little grin from him. "What, um . . . what about you, what do you like to do? Besides drumming in an awesome band and carrying out part-time assassinations."

"Skate. Read. Hang out."

"With anyone in particular?"

Translation: Are you dating anyone? I am *such* a girl.

"The band, mostly, you know. Hob."

"Who's Hob?"

"Our singer. Hobbit."

I fold my arms. "Wait. That seven-foot-nine behemoth is named *Hobbit*?"

Mike pulls on a guilty face. "Well, it's not his *given* name." He peers at me through the curtain of his bangs. "Nice use of *behemoth*, though. Kudos."

I tuck my chin into my neck and try to disappear, even as my spine tingles. Okay, I know: I'm not supposed to get all gooey over something like a vocabulary test word. But I mean . . . he gets it. Maybe gets me. Just maybe.

"Thanks," I say. Stupidly. You want fries with that?

Mike continues to gaze at me. Studying. For *what*, I couldn't tell ya.

Then he goes, "So—well, screw it, why'd you talk to me last weekend?"

Hell-oh! Forward much? Slow down!

I mean, I was going to ask him the same question, when it felt like the right time, but I was going to be super-smooth about it. (She said, knowing it was unlikely at best.) I make the dumb decision to tell him the truth, because I am *that* socially retarded. Wait, that's rude—I mean *colossally* retarded.

Mike's still watching me. My mouth goes dry again, and I curl my fingers together into an abandoned church, broken steeple, wrecked doors, no people.

I stall with a sip of my drink. Mint coaxes words at last. "Your eyes," I say at a volume of a quarter decibel.

Mike blinks. "Say again?"

"You have incredible eyes," I say into my lap.

"And hair," I add.

"And I liked your music," I mutter.

Ladies and gentlemen, Amanda "Grace Under Pressure" Walsh! Yaaaaay!

I can feel him staring at me. "Which came first?"

I glance up. "Huh?"

"Was it the band or—you know. Me. I guess."

It should sound like an arrogant question, but Mike's tone isn't that. He looks mildly uncomfortable, in fact. Like he gave the wrong answer in trig class.

My fingers pop, and I pull them apart. They stay curled in my lap.

"Well," I say, "I mean, I'm serious about the band. I really liked your music. But . . . no. It was, you know. You. Does that happen a lot? People coming up to you like that?"

Not people. Girls. Chicks. *Young ladies.*

Mike looks at some art. "Not much."

But I'm not the first one. I know it, like intuition or something. Didn't know I had that.

"I don't usually talk to people like that," I say quickly. "I mean, just walk up and start talking. That was kinda the first time. Ever, actually."

He turns back to me. "Yeah? You don't seem all that shy to me."

"Oh, well, that's because I'm trying to hide how terrified

and vaguely nauseous I feel right now." I am *so* not kidding about this. My heart hasn't stopped ricocheting around my ribs since I got here. It's beating faster than his drums could ever hope to. But honestly, I kinda like it. This is the best night I've had this summer so far.

"Really?" Mike says. "That's good. Me too."

"Oh, whatever."

"I don't make a habit of meeting up with people like this," he says, and there's no trace of a laugh or smile in his voice at all. Which should be a bad thing, but somehow it feels . . . safe.

Feeling brave, I say, "Okay, so then why'd *you* talk to *me*?"

I assume it'll be the D.I. thing. Feels like no one around here knows who they are, so probably he only came tonight to talk about music. Which is *fine* with me. Mostly.

Mike clamps his mouth shut and looks at the tabletop. I can see him choosing his words. Not sure whether that's good or bad.

"I wanted to see if you were for real," he says.

Um . . .

"Could you unpack that a little more for me here?"

"You . . . I dunno. Got something going on."

I *do*? I can't resist a smile.

Mike shakes his head. "And that was a truly lame thing to say."

And I think: *Like hell it was!*

He glances into my eyes. His intensity melts me. "Can we come back to that?"

"Well, I mean, I know I'm not your standard supermodel

groupie," I say, trying to laugh, but it comes out like a sick bark.

Mike sort of winces. "What's that mean?"

I stutter until Christmas trying to come up with an answer. "Well, I just, you know." I stall, rubbing my (enormous, freakishly high) forehead as if trying to stimulate something coherent in my brain. "I'm not . . . like, *hot* or anything. . . ."

Mike squints at me. I squirm under the scrutiny.

"So you're not an anatomically impossible Barbie doll?" he says. "Gotta tell ya, that's not all it's cracked up to be. You got style."

Something unravels in my belly and tickles up my back. Now *that* felt good.

But before I can say anything, Mike's suddenly on his feet, his skateboard popped into one hand, and he's patting his pockets down like to make sure he's got everything.

"Listen, I need to get going," he says, all fast, and I'm like, *Huh?*

Then he pauses and looks at me again.

"Could I call you?"

I lean back. Shields up. "Will you?" Because I don't think I can handle being strung along, and—as much as it will throw me into a deep black well of soulless undeath—I'd still rather know now and get it over with. I mean, I wouldn't have even talked to him if Jenn hadn't surprised me at The Graveyard like she did. I know this is just a meaningless crush. Speaking of which, you ever wonder why it's called a crush? Could it be because that's what it *does to your soul*? Discuss.

Still—gotta say, so far, I'm really liking this.

Mike goes, "If you say yes, I will."

"Then yes."

He gives me the small grin again. "Okay," he says. "Cool. Um . . . probably not tomorrow night because we're jamming, but . . . got plans for Friday?"

"I rather doubt it."

He smiles. A real one, not just the grin. "Nightrage is playing over at Damage Control, we were all going to go see them. You want to meet up there?"

Hm . . . Let. Me. Think.

"Yeah, sure." I somehow manage not to use exclamation points. "Sounds good."

"Cool. Eight o'clock Friday night." Mike smiles and tips his head backward, a reverse nod. "Take care."

"You too. Later, skater."

Mike chuckles; very nice of him. I watch him walk toward the exit, board in hand. Then, as he's about to turn the corner that will take him to the front door, he stops and looks over his shoulder at me.

"Like your shirt," he says, and disappears.

I look down at my (sad, boyish) chest. I went with a classic black Misfits logo tee, but not one where skeleton hands would be cupping my boobs. Clearly the right choice. (*Let's test your threshold of pain, let's see how long you last*, indeed.)

I go for a refill, staring at this circular painting—a.k.a. a "tondo"—I've studied for the past couple years that's hanging near the counter. I'm glad no one's bought it yet, because then I wouldn't be able to savor it. And I *so* don't have the money to buy it myself. The tondo is encircled by a simple ebony frame, but the painting itself always makes my heart race. It's oil on canvas, a shadowy figure in a top hat, cravat, tuxedo, the works, but rendered entirely in a crimson to black spectrum. Elegant and mysterious. When the barista brings my cup back, I almost ask what I need to do to get a piece hung in here.

Instead, I take my refill back to the table, sit down, and call myself a few thousand names, all prefaced with *stupid*. I do this *every time*. I should stop coming here. It just depresses me.

But I've got Friday night to look forward to, so that's something.

I let out a big sigh and take another look at the art class flyer. Maybe Mike's right; maybe I should go ahead and take a class this summer. But at my college, not the Hole; at least there I can get credit for it. What's the worst that could happen?

I spend another hour carefully detailing every possible answer to that question before going home. I decide on the drive to sign up for my first official art class since graduating, hoping I'll get a teacher at least half as cool as Mr. Hilmer. Maybe start over on my portfolio. Just in case. I thought I'd learned a lot since freaking eighth grade. But that's the problem: obviously I had a lot to learn, and no one's taught me anything new since I was twelve, thirteen. Maybe that'll change if I get a good teacher again.

Hey, I can dream.

About a lot of things. One of which, it turns out, is Mike.

I mean, if I'm going to be around for a while *anyway* . . .

six

The first man to compare the cheeks of a
young woman to a rose was obviously a poet.
The first to repeat it was possibly an idiot.
—Salvador Dalí

"Got a date?" Dad asks Friday night as I walk past his bedroom door.

I stop in the hallway. He's pulling on a black sports coat. Must be party time.

"Uh . . . not . . . I mean, sort of." I'm not convinced my *rendezvous* with Mike at Hole in the Wall was a date, so I'm not sure tonight's meeting at Damage Control is, either. Plus, the rest of the band is going to be there. What're they, chaperoning?

"Why?" I ask Dad.

Dad shrugs. "Haven't seen your hair in a while."

I touch my hair. Dad's right; it's been a while since I tried styling it. Probably should've gotten my hair cut before attempting such a feat, but that would make *sense*, you see, and so is clearly beyond my capacity. I've clipped my bangs

58

back with little black barrettes so they're out of my face; a new look, to be sure. Where am I supposed to hide?

"Oh," I say. "Um—do you like it?"

"Hm?" Dad goes, and riffles through his wallet. He doesn't look up. "Yeah, sure."

"Gosh. That's a ringing endorsement."

Now he looks up and smiles guiltily. "Sorry, kid. Got a lot on my mind, I suppose. Work's been a little crazy."

"What's going on?"

"Oh, just"—Dad sighs, turning to the mirror over their bureau—"thought I had a promotion all locked up, but it, ah . . . didn't quite materialize."

"Oh. Sorry."

"Yeah, me too."

"Would it have meant a raise?" Sue me for being selfish, but maybe a nice raise could negate the need for a stupid scholarship.

Dad sees right through me. He winks, and I want to tear the eyelid off with my teeth.

"Hey, Z," he goes. "That was an expensive school you wanted to go to, you know."

And thanks for using the past tense, Daddy-O. He may as well have said, *Since there's no way in god's green hell you'll ever make it there on your own.* I imagine the facade of the main building at SAIC melting in front of me, like it's part of a Salvador Dalí painting.

I shake my head to dismiss the image. "Well, I signed up for a class yesterday," I say. "If that's okay."

"Summer school? Yeah, sure. Get a head start. Took it outta the school account?"

"Mm-hm."

Technically, I could write myself a check out of the education expenses account and run off to Chicago, Santa Fe, L.A., wherever, but that feels messed up. Like, unfair. Gotta say, though, on those nights when he and Mom are clawing it out in the living room, it doesn't seem quite as unfair after all. And after this crap with Jenn, my (ahem) *future* with Mike is about the only thing keeping me here. I guess I just wanna see where it's all gonna go. That, and I'd run out of money after about a semester in Chicago.

"Math? Science?" Dad asks.

Leave it to my accountant father to be all practical and junk. I'm not convinced he wasn't sort of relieved I couldn't go to SAIC.

"Intro to Art." It's a mixed-media class, painting and drawing. Good place to start.

Dad squints at me. "You need that?"

"Prerequisite. Well, elective prerequisite, anyway. For my major." Which, strictly speaking, is undecided, but'll have something to do with—drumroll!—*art*. Duh.

"Well, I'm sure you'll do great." He sits on the bed and pulls on his shoes.

"Going out, huh?" I venture. Obviously he is, but I want to see what he does with it.

"Oh, you know, just for drinks, throw some darts," Dad says.

"What's Mom doing?"

He laughs softly. At what, my naïveté? "That's the million-dollar question, kiddo."

"Well, don't drink and drive," I say.

Dad gives me a mouth click and shoots me with his forefinger and thumb.

With that touching expression, I walk down the hall and through the kitchen. I hear the TV in the living room; Mom's out there alone. God, couldn't they just go on a *date* sometime?

I head out to DC without telling either of them where I'm going or when I'll be back.

Damage Control is this huge box of a building, two stories tall, with this awesome old redbrick exterior. I grab a parking space three rows from the entrance; the lot's pretty full.

I pay the cover and slide into a dark hallway that opens up into one gigantic room. Onstage, this band Black Dot Society—or BDS, as we *in the know* like to say, because we're pretentious punk jerks—is setting up their gear, but Nightrage's trademark red bass drum is at the back of the stage, and their guitarist is fiddling with an amp.

There are no tables or chairs on the ground floor except in back by the bar. A flight of steel stairs climbs along one wall, leading to a balcony surrounding the dance floor in a U-shape.

I don't see Mike anywhere.

The place is almost at capacity, but the houselights are on and it's pretty easy to see everyone. If he was here, I'd see him. Bathroom? Not here yet?

Big F'ing joke on me? Discuss.

I mean, he didn't use the word *date.* Maybe people don't use that word anymore. I keep telling myself that.

I notice someone waving boa constrictor arms at me from

the balcony. It's Gothic Rainbow's singer—Hobbit. (Clever.) He's sitting at a table with the other two band members. Brook and Eddie? I climb the steps and head over to them.

I run through the list of questions for the band that I meticulously planned for tonight. I figure my best bet is to be chill, not act all groupie. Guys like to talk about themselves, Jenn has advised. And she should know. For one second, I really wish she was going to be here to help me not look like an ass.

"Hey!" Hobbit goes as I reach the table. "You're Zero, right?"

"Truer words were never spoken," I say, sitting.

The guys give me a laugh. Well, it's a start. Brook and Eddie introduce themselves to me, but we don't shake hands or anything.

There's a verbal explosion from the stage down below. The guys all grin and lean over the railing to see what's going on, so I do too.

It's Nightrage's drummer and guitarist. The crowd is too noisy to hear exactly what's being said. Something to do with where Fucking Tony needs to Move His Amp, Dipshit.

"I put ten on Tony!" Brook says, laughing, rubbing a hand across his bleached hair.

"Naw way, man, twenty on Rod!" Eddie says gleefully.

"How about fifty on BDS?" I say.

Brook and Eddie laugh; score! Hobbit, though, says nothing, watching Nightrage intently, eyes narrowed. The members of BDS stand aside, looking impatient; they're up first tonight, and Nightrage is probably eating into their set time.

The two guys are getting super heated now. When Rod

slams both hands into Tony's chest, the crowd roars and the two begin wrestling center stage. Some people cheer them on; most shout for them to quit it and let BDS start their show.

"Here's a thought," I say. "If you don't like each other, don't start a band."

Brook and Eddie laugh again, while Hobbit snorts like a bull and nods. The match ends when the other two members of Nightrage show up and pull the combatants apart, dragging them backstage.

Eddie and Brook groan and retake their seats. Hobbit shakes his head.

"That's the dumbest shit I ever seen," he says.

"Maybe it's all part of the show," Brook says. "Get everyone riled up."

"Whatever it is, it's stupid," Hobbit says. "Just play your damn music." He glances over at me. "*You* saw the Graveyard show last weekend," he says. "How was it?"

"Awesome," I say. "It was the first time I'd seen you guys. It was great."

"Yeah? Listen, what'd you think of the chorus on—"

"Hob!" Brook says. "She's not here to pump your ego, man. She's here to see . . ." Brook pinwheels his arms and throws two pointy fingers toward the stairs. *"That guy!"*

I turn just as Mike approaches the table. He's in jeans and a distressed T-shirt with a Ghost of Banquo logo pasted across the chest. The shirt fits him nicely. Just sayin'.

"What's up?" he asks the table, but as he crosses behind me to sit down next to me, his hand touches my shoulder. Just for a second.

I'm a Dalí watch, melting under his hand. Was it by accident? On purpose?

"I don't suppose anyone offered you something to drink?" Mike asks me.

"Not as of yet, no." But I'll need something, stat, because desert dust has mysteriously appeared in my mouth. I need a freaking IV line around this guy.

Mike stands back up. "Gentlemen, I am ashamed of you." Brook playfully smacks Eddie's shoulder, like it's all his fault. To me, Mike asks, "Soda?"

Right then, BDS plays their first chord for their sound check. It underscores the way I feel as Mike looks down at me. Ultra-cinematic. Maybe he timed it somehow.

I can only nod.

"Diet, regular, cola, clear?"

I nod again.

"All four in one," Mike says. "I'll see what I can do."

He grazes my shoulder again as he passes by on his way to the bar. Okay, that *had* to be on purpose, right? I twist my head to watch him until my neck cramps.

When Mike comes back and sits down, he's carrying four sodas. Two dark, two clear.

"Couldn't find one that satisfied all four requirements," he shouts over the music.

"Thanks!" I say, and take one of the colas. Mike takes the other. Eddie and Brook elbow each other to get to the remaining two glasses.

It's too loud to talk easily, so the five of us watch the show. Well, four of us do. One of us watches Mike. That's all I'm sayin'.

After BDS's set wraps up, when we can hear each other again, I ask Mike, "Where'd you get that shirt?" The man's got taste, no doubt about it.

Mike looks surprised. "My dad. Why?"

"It's really cool. I'd love to find one like it." Or, you know, share yours. While you're wearing it. Woo hoo!

Okay, down, girl. Still trying to figure out if this is a date or not, remember?

"They're hard to come by," Mike says. "But if he's got another one lying around, I'll grab it for you."

Eddie looks confused. "I thought you gave your last one to— *Ow!*" He shuts up and reaches under the table to rub his shin.

I'm pretty sure I missed something there.

Hobbit gives Eddie a *look,* then leans over the table toward me. "Mike says you're an artist, huh?"

Note to self: *He talked about me!* That means something, right? I shoot a (mild, ineffectual) glare at Mike. "I never said that!"

Mike smirks back at me. "Didn't you?"

"No, I . . ." I spread my hands out toward the other three. "I do some painting and drawing, is all."

"Yeah?" Hob says. "Like what?"

"Well, um . . . I don't know . . . a lot of different things. Landscapes, lately."

The guys seem to exchange glances; Hobbit, in particular, looks intrigued. I try another glare at Mike for dragging me into this topic, but *damn,* those eyes of his. What is going *on* in there? I forgive him instantly.

I remember my plan to get Mike talking, so before

anyone else can interrogate me, I say, "So, when are you guys playing here?"

"Hard to say," Mike says. "Soon, hopefully."

"When one of the big promoters calls us," Hob fills in. "Four Eyes, maybe Alecia Ruth."

"Wait," I say. "Who what huh?"

Mike tilts back in his chair while Hob looks at me like I must be a complete tool for not understanding him. He's not a jerk about it; it's probably the same look I gave Mike when he asked who Dalí was.

"Those are promotion companies," Mike tells me. "They put lineups together and take them to the venues. Like at The Graveyard, that was an Open Casket show. Open Casket's the promoter."

"A lame-ass promoter," Hob adds. He turns to watch the next band tune up, getting that same narrow look, like he's searching for flaws. It hits me that the expression on his face is probably the same one I have when I look at some of the photos in *ARTnews*.

I'm better than that, his face says. *I think.*

"We'll get Four Eyes, man," Hob says, rubbing his enormous hands together and glaring at the band down below. "One of these days. It's comin'."

"Are they a big deal?" I ask.

Mike wrinkles his nose. "Sort of. They do a lot of shows here."

Brook says to me, "Yeah, Four Eyes is in here every week. Big-ticket shows, lots of national acts. It'd be a step up."

"They gotta ask us first," Eddie says, rather hopelessly.

"They will," Hobbit states, still watching the band down-stairs finish their sound check.

When the houselights dim and the band starts playing, all four guys groan.

"A Black Phantom *cover*?" Eddie whines loud enough to penetrate the steady bass from downstairs. "For *reals*? Why don't they cover 'Teen Spirit' while they're at it?"

"That's what happens when you're famous!" Brook shouts at him. "Everybody covers you!"

"Black Phantom's not famous yet," Mike says.

"Hey!" Eddie barks suddenly. "You guys hear? They're playin' through here on the last leg of that tour with Nightrage!"

This piques everyone's interest. BP hasn't played locally in over a year, since they got that record deal. It'd be cool to see them again. The label, Pharaoh Records, is independent—which is another word for *minuscule*—but does put out some good music.

"When's that?" I shout at Eddie.

"Dunno!" he says. "November, maybe! But they're comin' back before the tour starts, too, for a couple days, so maybe they'll do a show while they're at it!"

The next two bands are unremarkable, and by the time Nightrage finally takes the stage, the crowd's restless. So am I. Not because I'm anxious to see Nightrage implode again, but because every time Mike looks at me, he gets this little smile and, dammit, it's kick-ass! I wish I could tell Jenn about it.

Nightrage tears up their show. They sound even better than they did at The Graveyard. Hob looks like this fact pisses him off, while Mike just kicks back in his chair, hands over his stomach. The fourth song ends prematurely when Fucking Tony smashes into Dipshit John. Whatever. Nightrage can kiss my ass. There's room back there for all four of them.

The guys decide to call it a night after Nightrage's second *fisticuffs* of the evening. I follow them downstairs and out into the warm June air.

"Where're you parked?" Mike asks when we reach the sidewalk.

I point. The guys linger nearby, trading glances.

"Gimme a minute," Mike says to them.

The guys nod and wave us off, heading to the opposite end of the lot, where an enormous orange van is parked. They gather around the back of it, pretending not to watch me and Mike.

Mike walks me to my car. And suddenly I'm about to throw up, wondering if maybe, god, please, he might try to kiss me goodnight.

Here's the thing.

I won't say no.

"Did you think any more about that art class at the Hole?" he asks as we walk.

"I looked into it, but there was a weight limit."

Mike knocks his elbow into mine. My entire arm goes up in flame. "Oh, whatever." The words are dismissive, and they are golden. I feel (a) awesome that he didn't rush to agree, and (b) bummed that I sounded like such a self-pitying tub of ass. Must try to curb that.

I have to shake my head to clear it. "Um, I did sign up for summer school, yeah. At a junior college, though."

"Really? Cool! They got a good art program or something?"

"None that I'm aware of."

We get to my car, and I make a big show of fumbling around for my keys, giving him plenty of time to make A Move. I mean, if he wants.

"Lot can happen in two years," Mike says. "We've only been playing out for that long."

"Well, I really can't afford anything else," I say, clandestinely holding my keys quiet in one pocket while pretending to search for them in another. "Not without that scholarship, and I already tried that once."

"Once."

I stop my fake search. "Yeah?"

Mike gets a thoughtful look on his face. "Do you know how many record companies we've sent our demo to?"

"Mmm, not off the top of my head, no."

"Twelve. Know how many albums we're recording this year? Nada. Zilch. So I guess we should stop bein' in a band." He raises his eyebrows. "Right?"

Ouch, dude.

"Well, but . . . I mean, they already said no. . . ."

"So you can't apply again? Or get a loan?"

"Honestly, I'm not sure. I kind of doubt it, not for that much. My dad makes too much money."

Mike takes a breath, like he wants to ask more, then lets it out and nods slowly. "Lot can happen in two years," he says again.

I have no answer to that. I mean, he's right, I know that. But still. If I wasn't good enough this year to pull it off, what could I do differently next time?

But then again . . . I didn't *have* to sign up for a summer class.

Mike watches my mental gymnastics for a second. "So, *Zero*," he goes, leaning against the rear door. "What's that mean, anyway?"

"Nothing."

And I laugh my ass off. I can't help it. *Zero? Nothing?* Come on! Comic gold! And I get that urge to kiss him again, if for no other reason than he has the smarts to know when to change the subject.

Okay, maybe there are a *couple* other reasons.

Mike gives me a chuckle. "C'mon, what's it mean? That's not a random nickname."

I hope he hasn't noticed I'm stalling, because my keys aren't exactly hard to find. "Well, in junior high, I was—wait for it, now—the loner art chick. And kids were calling me weird stuff. Like negative, nonexistent, that sort of thing. Someone called me zero, and I sorta picked it up."

Mike nods. "But your name's Amanda."

He remembered. Down, girl.

"I try to avoid it. That was another big joke. The jocks would all say, 'Who is that? A *man*, duh!' It bugged me. Just don't call me Amy, we'll get along fine."

"Amy's short for Amanda?"

"So says my mother."

"Huh. Never heard that before. Well, promise never to call me Mikey, and you got a deal."

"Yeah? How come?"

"Someone used to call me that and it didn't . . ." He stops, shrugs. "It's a thing."

A *thing* . . . that has something to do with where his last Banquo shirt went? All hail my intuition! This is definitely about a girl. I glance toward the van where the guys are waiting. Hobbit has Eddie in a headlock and is grinding his knuckles into the bassist's hair while Brook laughs. They don't seem to be paying any attention to us.

"What kind of thing?" I ask Mike.

Mike shrugs again. "Hey, what's your middle name?"

"Is it just me, or was that a really obvious segue?"

Mike's face gets all stony and grim, but only for a sec. Then he smiles. "Pretty obvious. What *is* your middle name?"

So I guess now's not the time and place to ask about this girl. I suppose that's fair. It *is* only our second . . . date-like event. If he kissed me, I'd know for sure. But then, if he doesn't, I'll know for sure anyway.

"Catherine," I sigh.

"It's a girl kind of thing," Mike replies right on top. "Moving on?" His smile still shines.

Moving on is the last thing I want to do, but it's probably also the smartest right now.

"Moving on," I agree, forcing myself to be casual. "So what about Gothic Rainbow? What's that mean?"

"It's, um . . . a study in contrast and irony?"

"Impressive. What else?" I ask this because I can see in his (drop-dead gorgeous) eyes there's more to the story, and if I can hold out just a little longer, he *has* to go for the kiss, right?

"Well, a rainbow is supposed to be this symbol, like a promise?"

"Where troubles melt like lemon drops."

"Right. Whereas, anything Gothic is typically dark, maybe foreboding. The two can't coexist. It's all *very* deep and profound. Also, we were up pretty late that night trying to come up with something before our first gig, so there was a sleepiness factor."

"Well, you guys sound great," I say, just in case I haven't made this abundantly clear. "I can't wait to see you play here."

"Thanks. That makes five of us now."

I glance back at the guys. Brook and Eddie are playing something I can only call Rock-Paper-Scissors . . . Deadleg. Hobbit stands a couple feet away, arms crossed, staring at Damage Control like he's plotting an invasion.

I turn to Mike. "DC is like the next big step, isn't it?"

"Yeah, as far as this town's concerned. It means you can bring a crowd. Means more word of mouth, which means better luck with a tour. We have a better chance of a label taking us seriously if we can prove we have a following. That means we're more likely to make a record. Like, a real one, not just a demo tape. Not exactly a gold record there. Which, personally, is what I'd like to see."

"A gold record, huh?" I have to give him credit for aiming high.

"Yep."

"Well, you'll get there."

Mike leans away from my car. "So will you. When do I get to see your paintings?"

See them? Uh, never.

Except, wait . . . he said *when*. Indicating a future time. So we're not finished here? Tonight? Tomorrow? The rest of my life?

"Um," I say. "I'm not . . . I mean, I'm still learning."

"*Next* week, then." Mike smiles, and something inside me melts. "So, gimme a hug?"

Time me! This is like a precursor; a *prerequisite,* a college student might say. We'll be close, so very close, and it's only a matter of adjusting a little to go for a—

So I wrap him in my arms, around his waist, as his encircle my shoulders. At first he squeezes me, gently, and it forces my eyes closed. Then he relaxes but doesn't let go. He just holds me for an extra few seconds.

A girl could get used to this. One hopes.

When he lets me go, I hesitate long enough to be inviting, not so long as to look like an idiot. When he doesn't tilt his head toward me, I pretend to have found my keys, even though I'm dizzy with lust or desire or some other such foreign thing.

"Tuesday night, you busy?" Mike asks, shoving his hands into his pockets. "Seven-ish?"

"Nope. You?"

"I am now. If that works for you."

"It does!"

"All right," Mike says. "I'll give you a call, then. See ya."

"Later, skater," I say. I don't know if I'm thrilled we made such close contact or sad a kiss didn't happen. Unless I've already been relegated to Such A Good Friend status?

Mike waves and jogs back over to the van, where the band is waiting. They climb in and tear out of the parking lot.

I get into my car and sit for a second, trying to sort my collage of anxieties. Would he really have asked me out again if this wasn't going to turn out romantic? On the other hand, if it is, why a *hug*? Everyone hugs everyone. There are a million different hugs for a million different people, but only a couple kinds of kiss. It would be nice to know for sure where I stood with him, and kissing would be a super-deluxe way to clarify that.

But maybe I shouldn't complain. God knows I could, if I stopped to take stock of the rest of my silly-ass life, which I should *not* do right now—except that's all it takes to envision a cubist rendering of Jenn's house, jagged and sharp, and dammit, why not just call her and tell her everything that happened tonight so she can tell me what to do?

Answer: Because there are only a couple kinds of kiss. That's why not.

seven

I am painting pictures which make me die
for joy, I am creating with an absolute
naturalness, without the slightest
aesthetic concern.

–Salvador Dalí

On Monday, what is now my first real day of higher education, I'm ten seconds from grabbing my keys and heading out
when my phone rings. Like any self-respecting, fallen-for-a-
musician, in-control-of-her-world female, I pick up and
answer with an excited "Hello!" assuming Mike will be on the
other end, because who else would—

"Hey."

—call me. Crap. Ambushed.

". . . Hey, Jenn."

"You said it was okay if I called."

"Yeah, I know, but I'm on my way out the door. I start
school today."

"You're taking summer school?"

"Yeah, so?"

"Nothing, nothing, I just—I thought we were going to blow off summer together."

"We *were*."

Silence. I almost hang up right then. I can't. We've known each other since freshman year. At seventeen, *almost eighteen,* four years is a long time.

Early freshman year, our entire class went to the Phoenix Art Museum to see a Monet exhibit on loan from collections around the world, and I happened to be standing next to Jenn when she pointed to *The Path Through the Irises* and snottily said, "What is that supposed to even *be*?" I spent the next five minutes explaining:

(a) Monet had been losing his eyesight when he painted it, altering his perception of color and light.

(b) He chose to work with a palette of pure light colors.

(c) *She was a stupid witch who wouldn't know great art if it bit her sassy little ass.* Or words to that effect.

Jenn was this cheerleader-looking fourteen-year-old who never was a cheerleader. Honestly, for as popular as I always thought she was, she never really hung out with anyone. Besides guys, I mean. She'd stared at me for a sec, then started laughing. Just when I thought I was going to have to start throwing punches, she slid her arm under my elbow, pointed to a later version of *The Japanese Footbridge,* and asked, "Okay, what about that one?"

I spent the rest of the trip telling her the kind of details only someone like me would care to know. She listened to every word. Almost like she was just happy someone was even talking to her. I never understood that until I met her parents, which took about four months. Mine are psycho in their own special way, to be sure. But they're *there*. Mr. and Mrs. Haight are what you might generously call "absentee."

So of course we became friends. Jenn would have me over and tell me about her latest sexual conquests and create these amazing foods. If she hadn't learned to cook, I imagine she'd have ballooned up, eating fast food every day since her folks were gone so much. I would have her over and show her recent drawings I'd done; sometimes she'd cook at my house, too, much to Mom's surprise and gratitude. We'd go to Hole in the Wall and gossip about school, parents, boys . . . the usual stuff. Everything was fine and fun until the night we graduated.

And the next morning.

"So what're you taking?" Jenn's voice startles me, it's been quiet for so long.

"Uh, Intro to Art. Have you *met* me?"

"Oh, hell, you could teach that class," Jenn says with this short laugh.

"Look, I gotta go," I say.

"Okay, well . . . what about hanging out? Like, tomorrow night? We could get coffee, or I could bake some—"

"I have a date."

"Oh!"

Yeah, and thanks for sounding so surprised, I want to say but don't.

"That guy from The Graveyard?" Jenn asks.

"Yeah. Mike. We have plans." I don't know what they are yet, though.

"Oh," she repeats. "That's— Good for you. Well . . . some . . . other time, maybe?"

"Maybe. I don't know."

"Zero . . ."

"I gotta go," I say again. "See ya." I don't wait for a response, just hang up.

Dammit, I do not need this on my mind before an art class. I *don't*. On the drive, to get Jenn out of my head, I listen to the radio (*How you get so rude and-a reckless? Don't you be so crude and-a feckless.* Thanks, Joe.) and make up compliments my art teacher will give me after our first assignment. It almost works.

After parking my car, I find the art department and pull open this cumbersome glass door to the lobby, where I pause to enjoy blessedly cold air. Phoenix is once again reaching highs in the hundreds. I definitely won't miss the heat, wherever I end up.

I move slowly through the lobby to absorb the student artwork on the walls. The skill and talent on display are mixed. There are some decent pieces but also a lot of . . . I guess *self-congratulatory* work is a good term. It's not like it all sucks; it doesn't. But it feels like the artists are too aware of the fact that they're artists, if that makes sense. Desperate, maybe. *See, see, lookit! I painted this, I drew this, I can draw real good, huh?*

Makes me wonder what mine looks like to someone else. Is my work any different? I've seen what Mr. Hilmer could do, and his work seemed effortless. Probably that's wrong, he probably worked hard on his art, just like I do—but I don't think any of these pieces are SAIC material. Ergo . . . I'm not sure mine is, either.

I tug the brim of my green porkpie hat down to hide my eyes, plunge through the building, find my studio classroom, and slip inside, taking a seat in the middle of the room. My "desk" is a flat stool in front of a skeletal easel. I drop my bag to the floor and try to blend into the surroundings.

At the front of the room, a tall, willowy woman wearing a flowing, multicolored dress, exactly the type Mom would kill to get me in, is pacing back and forth, a clipboard balanced on her forearm. She eyes each of us in turn, neither smiling nor scowling but judging all the same, I am sure.

The instructor demurely clears her throat and recites names off her clipboard. I'm last.

"Walsh, Amanda?" Her voice is high and birdlike.

I gag on a dry throat. "Here."

"Wonderful!" she says. And I'm like, *That I'm here or what?*

She sets the clipboard down. "My name is *Doctor* Deborah Salinger. This is Introduction to Art Application. Welcome to your first day of *art!*"

Doctor Salinger swirls among us as if on tiptoe, using her hands to paint invisible canvases as she speaks. "In addition to teaching you the basic, the ever so *rudimentary* application of various paint media, I will offer lectures on modern art and art history. . . ."

Scattered groans, mine not among them. A couple of granny types twitter excitedly. Junior college appears to be a replica of high school, except with ashtrays and a student body age range of High School Graduate to Older than Sanskrit.

"...which you will not be tested on. Attendance and completing your assignments will affect your grade, naturally. But it is your work on the paper and the canvas that is worth the most percentage points. It is your heart and soul that matter."

Geez. Hippie much? Still—I can't disagree.

A student raises his hand but doesn't wait to be called on. Rebel.

"Is that fair?"

Dr. Salinger raises her eyebrows. "I'm sorry, your name?"

"Frank."

"My dearest, dearest Frank. *Life* isn't fair. I would have expected you to have learned that much by now."

The rest of the class chuckles. Teacher 1, Frank 0. Frank sneers at us.

"I paid a great deal in money, time, and linseed to become the accomplished scholar you see before you," Dr. Salinger goes on, "so I intend to pass all my worldly wisdom and knowledge on to you. *My* pupils."

The older broads coo and titter again. I snicker under my breath.

"Now, I do realize most if not all of you are perhaps *hobbyists*, uninterested in becoming modern masters, and that is all well and good. However, you enrolled in this class to learn how to create and share art, or as I like to think of it, create and share your *soul*."

Uh ... okay. Two *souls* in two minutes? That's a bit much

even for me. A smarmy noise sneaks out of my mouth, and Dr. Salinger stops and gives me a brief glare.

"Sorry," I mutter. Blah. Not a good start. Well, wait till we start drawing; that'll show her.

"We will search for art *together*, experience life at its heights and depths," she goes on. "We will squeeze and knead our experiences without mercy and transcribe the results to canvas and paper." She claps her hands together. "Doesn't that sound simply *wonderful*?"

The older broads cluck again. Oooh, oh, yes, wonderful, indeed, mm-hm!

Like they know. I want to ask them all to name ten American artists of the twentieth century and at least one of their works each, by name.

"We shall plumb, indeed, *eviscerate* our own lives for subject matter and vigorously apply our findings with brush, with pen," Dr. Salinger goes on. "With oil, acrylic, charcoal, watercolor, the pencil. With whatever tools we have at hand. Let's begin at the beginning, shall we?"

She picks up her clipboard and scans the roll. I know even before she says it:

"Miss Amanda Walsh. Tell us, what *is* art?"

I look around the room just to make sure there isn't another Miss Amanda Walsh nearby. "I'm sorry?"

Dr. Salinger stalks toward me. Her eyes sparkle. *Malevolently*, if you want my opinion.

"What. Is. Art?"

A trick question. I swallow nothing and twist my fingers into a knot, trying to recall the vocabulary I learned in high school and from Mr. Hilmer.

"Um . . . art—can—comprise a series of lines? Area, space . . . color?"

Dr. Salinger wrinkles her nose. "I see. By the end of our time together, I hope all of you can answer that question somewhat more effectively. Miss Walsh?"

I cringe.

"We'll try again next week," Dr. Salinger purrs. "Now, what was I talking about? Ah, yes! Art."

There's a short murmuring of laughter. Teacher 1, Zero 0. Ironic? I think not.

There must be some mistake. I wasn't expecting a Mr. Hilmer, because he was a one-of-a-kind, but come *on*! It *is* college. I should have a great teacher, and show off what I can do—what I think I can do—and prove to the world, or maybe just me, that I'm not messing around.

That I'm an artist. That if I took some more time to work, learned new things from a good teacher, maybe I really could apply to SAIC again.

The look in Dr. Salinger's eyes says otherwise.

"Now, let's dive right in, shall we? Paper and pencils, please."

We all dig through our various bags. Okay, this is better; once I have something in my hand, I'll show her.

"Whatever your favorite paper, whatever your favorite pencil. Charcoal, graphite, whatever you prefer."

I pull out my sketchbook and a charcoal pencil. The lady bugs me, but I can't stop my pulse from picking up. I'm back where I'm supposed to be, in a studio, getting ready to create.

"Let's begin with some gestural drawing," Dr. Salinger

says, conjuring an oversized drawing pad and clipping it to an easel. She scans the room, zeroes in on me, and before I can react, snatches my hat off my head and flings it onto her desk.

"Voila!" she proclaims. "Still life!"

No one seems to notice I'm totally naked now; they just look at my hat and watch Dr. Salinger set to work drawing. *My* hat.

"Gesture drawing is about movement," Doc S says as her pencil sketches in long, graceful strokes. "About form and weight. You want the least amount of line with the most amount of information. Start in the middle and work outward. Use a brisk but fluid stroke. . . ."

The class is following along; I am trying like hell to. I've done gesture drawing before, but not the way she's doing it.

"Oh, this *is* one of my favorite techniques," Dr. Salinger says as she draws. "I had my first great success with charcoal. It was such a sheer delight to take my lovers and friends to the Paper Heart, the New York, the Fuller. . . ."

I stop sketching. Those are big-time galleries. She's got, like, background. I go back to my sketch pad but can't make my hands do what she's doing. She's going so *fast*.

"Those were my glory days!" she says as my hat starts taking form on her paper. "Now, you need not make your drawing look like something you'd hang in a gallery, people. But this is one way to prepare for another drawing or painting you'll take a traditional approach to later. For now, your purpose is to be bold. Expressive. Instinctive!"

My pencil snaps.

Dr. Salinger, while still sketching, regales us with a story about a summer tryst with Robert Nanci, this spectacular artist whose work I've seen in a number of books and magazines. What that has to do with how she's drawing, I have no idea. Maybe summer trysts are how you find your muse. And hey, wouldn't I like to have one myself with a certain percussionist? We'll see.

So I sit and stare at my half-assed, half-completed gestural drawing and consider asking for a refund. From *life*.

"And there it is!" Dr. Salinger says, stepping away from her easel. "It's that simple! Now let's see what you've accomplished!"

I bite back a sigh as she swishes around the room, inspecting everyone's work. Her drawing (of *my* hat) is fucking gorgeous. And it's just a *sketch*.

Damn, she's good.

Here's the thing.

As much as her personality gives me cramps, if she's exhibited in those galleries, then she knows what she's doing, and I need to know more if I'm going to have any chance of putting together a solid new portfolio this fall. Or next spring. Or ever . . .

Dr. Salinger appears at my side, looking down at my lap. I'm still clutching the broken pencil. My sketchbook shows only a collection of smeared charcoal lines.

"Oh," she says softly. "Well, that doesn't look like very much, now, does it?"

I shake my head. My hair flies around my face. "Can I have my hat back?"

Dr. Salinger gives me a look I can't quite interpret. "Of course," she says, and retrieves it for me. She hands it back without a word and glides over to Frank.

Oh, well, it's not like anything else exciting is happening this summer. Right?

Except for that one guy.

Who I'll be seeing tomorrow night. Class goes by faster after that, and I'm the first one out the door when Dr. Salinger lets us go. Taking this class was a bad idea, I'm sure of it. Better to resign myself to living in Phoenix the rest of my life.

I spend Tuesday trying (uselessly) to duplicate the gestural drawing Dr. Salinger showed us yesterday. No luck. But I have to draw or paint something, and sort of wander around my room looking for inspiration. When my gaze hits the ceiling, I know exactly what to do. It's destroying, not creating, but then again, maybe this'll help free the muse.

We don't have anything like house paint, so I have to use my white acrylic to cover up the drawing of Jenn's face on my ceiling. It's not her face, exactly; just a combination of circles, triangles, and lines that probably wouldn't make any sense to anyone but me. I never even told her it was her face after I did it.

But even when the bristles are only an inch away from the drawing, I can't quite make myself cover it up.

"Shit," I whisper.

I step carefully off my bed and sit on the edge, holding the brush between my fists. After a moment, it starts to tremble, because my hands start shaking.

Oh, hell, here it comes. I've been successful thus far at

not remembering graduation, not *really*. Even in the parking lot of DC a few days ago, I was able to reroute my mind, get rid of the cubist rendering of Jenn's house. This time, it's gonna be full-color live action, start to finish. I try to roll with the memory, get it over with. . . .

After graduation, I drove us back to Jenn's house. Her parents were gone, as usual; both of them are political lobbyists, her dad for the NRA and her mom for a car manufacturer. Jenn was raised by a series of nannies and au pairs until sophomore year, when her folks pretty much left her to her own devices. They bought her a car, handed her a Visa, told her to keep her grades decent . . . and that was about it. She didn't even decide on a school or anything last year, and they didn't seem to care.

The Haights' house is kept in pristine condition for parties and stuff, which also means they have a liquor collection that puts bars like The Graveyard and DC to shame.

"We should celebrate!" Jenn said when we got inside. "Let's have our own party, huh?"

"Why not?" I said. It sounded fun. High school was at long last over and done with, I was still bent about the SAIC rejection letter, and Jenn hadn't secured herself a guy for the night. But I felt like something was off, like those comics in the paper where you find six differences between the panels, and I was in the wrong one. She'd been invited to a party, while I'd figured I'd spend the rest of the night at home as usual. I had no idea why she hadn't gone, and I never asked.

I was just happy she chose me, I guess.

Jenn cooked up this amazing chicken dinner for us, throwing around French words like she spoke it as her first language. After dinner, we moved on to piña coladas. "What's in it?" I asked. "Pineapple and lada," Jenn said. "Lotta alcohol!" After the first one, I don't know what else we drank.

We sat on the floor of her living room, watching cheesy romantic comedies, which I hate. Bitched about boys. Made fun of our former teachers. Laughed our asses off. The usual.

Sometime later, I was puking her awesome dinner out in a downstairs bathroom. So much for being my father's child, right? I rinsed my mouth with mouthwash, and Jenn got me upstairs to her room and set me down on her bed. I felt like my drawing mannequin, joints and body made of wood, useless and poseable, as Jenn got most of my clothes off and pulled an oversized T-shirt over me; I'd gotten puke on my own shirt downstairs. I collapsed against the mattress, and Jenn crawled in beside me.

"This was dumb," I remember moaning as my eyes swam around uncontrollably in their sockets. It was worse when I closed them.

"Uh-huh," Jenn said. "But at least we were dumb together." Her voice was still thick with alcohol. Somehow, we managed to laugh despite how gross we both must've felt.

Then Jenn said, "You're my best friend. I love you soooo much." She patted me idiotically on my thigh.

My eyes couldn't stay open. "Uh-huh," I said. "You. Too."

That's when it happened.

I was on the precipice of a delightful fall into oblivion when I felt her lips brush against mine. I forced my eyes open again, stared at her; Jenn sort of whisper-slurred my name and kissed me again. No mistake. Mouth open, the whole deal.

She said something else, but that's when I dropped dead

asleep, assuming I'd been mistaken. Drunk still, perhaps. Dreaming. I might've even laughed, because it was a ridiculous situation. Absurd.

Surreal.

The next morning—it was late, almost noon—I woke up slow and painful, except I felt something moving against my stomach.

Jenn's hand. Tracing circles over my belly, under my shirt. I kept my eyes closed, trying to tell myself I was still asleep, dreaming, something. Anything.

A second later, I felt her curl up catlike beside me, very close, and kissing my neck, ear, jaw; all slight, small, but goddammit . . . so *on purpose.*

There are only a couple different kinds of kiss. There was no mistaking this kind.

"Are you awake?" she said.

And I said, out loud: "No."

Jenn laughed a little, and I felt her lips on my cheek. Then her hand, still under the shirt, inching up—

My phone rings, and the brush in my hand snaps in two.

eight

When I was five years old I saw an insect
that had been eaten by ants and of which
nothing remained except the shell. Through
the holes in its anatomy one could see
the sky. Every time I wish to attain purity
I look at the sky through flesh.
—Salvador Dalí

I jerk to attention, hurl my broken paintbrush into a corner, and answer the phone.

"Howdy," Mike says. "I'm all set, you ready to go?"

"Um," I say, and clear my throat. "Yeah, absolutely."

"You all right?"

"Yeah, yes, I was just . . ." I glance up at my ceiling. "Just finishing a painting real quick. I'll leave in about five minutes."

"Perfect," Mike says. "Hey, you like ice cream?"

His voice slowly brings me back to the present tense. I feel my shoulders relax. "On the advice of counsel, I decline to answer. Wait, scratch that. Hell, yes!"

Mike laughs, and I don't resist a grin. Just hearing him talk, even over the phone, has miraculous healing properties.

"Awesome. That's all I needed to know." He gives me directions to his house. "See you in a few."

I hang up and consider taking another minute to go ahead and paint over Jenn's drawing, but honestly, I'd rather get out of here and focus on being with Mike. I can do the cover-up later.

"Going out," I say as I hustle past Mom, who is at her usual post beside the sink.

"With Jenn? I haven't seen her in a while."

For one moment, I really and truly consider telling Mom the whole sordid story, right then and there. She's a big Jenn fan, always has been. What would she do if I told her the truth? Other than possibly not believe me?

"Um . . ."

"I didn't think so," Mom goes, and scrubs a pan as if to wash its sin away. Sinful pan! "Is it . . . a *boy*?"

No, Mom, a fifty-something tranny named Luscious Tits. I consider saying this because there's a decent chance it'll make her head implode. How'd she know about Mike anyway? Maybe Dad said something. But that would mean they're *communicating*.

"As a matter of actual fact, yes," I say.

Scrub, scrub, scrub, be cleansed, heathen pan! "Where exactly did you meet this boy?"

Gotta watch my step here. It's not like she doesn't know I go to clubs, but she's sure they are filled with *iniquity*. She's right, to a degree, but god, it's not like I'm doing drugs or getting hammered or giving clandestine BJs in the parking lot.

"He's a musician," I say, and regret it immediately. Might

as well have him riding a Harley and wearing a German spike helmet.

Clearly that's the vision Mom's got in mind when she whips her head around. "That's not what I asked you, Amy."

I *so* do not have time for this. I'm picking Mike up at seven, and it's quarter till already.

I fold my hands primly, choir girl extraordinaire. "My apologies, Mother, when wouldst thou care to meet him?"

Mom's head sort of drops. She looks so tired. God, I don't have to be such a bitch.

"Sorry," I mutter. "Look, maybe I'll bring him by. Sometime."

Not that I have any intention of letting Mike anywhere near my mother. Or Dad, for that matter. I'd hate to catch him on a drinking night. So that means days ending in Y are out. The problem is, I really want to show Mike my canvases and sketchbooks tonight. No—it's like, I want to *show* them to him, but I don't want him to *see* them. Make sense? I thought I'd bring him over *after* Mom would've gone to bed tonight.

Mom sets the pan aside to dry, absolved of its heinousness. "We're free this evening," she says. "I'm sure your dad would like to meet him as well."

"Mom, we have plans; we're—" Doing. Something. I don't actually know what, all I know is I'm picking him up at his house, somewhere downtown.

"Amy, please, it's a simple request. If you're going to start spending time with someone, we would like to know more about him."

I can't help a prolonged eye roll. "Fine, I'll see," I tell her, and stomp toward the door.

"And where exactly will you be tonight?"

"At a movie," I flat-out lie. Maybe it's not a lie, maybe that's exactly where we're going, but the point is, I couldn't care less. I'll be with him, and that's all that matters. God, wasn't she *ever* seventeen? Just for a couple days at some point?

Actually . . . that's right, she was. I almost forgot.

"I see. And what time is the movie?"

I grind my teeth into pigment. There's only one way out of this. Because if I don't, it'll just be that much harder to see Mike again (and again, and again).

"Fine!" I say. "Tonight. I'll bring him by tonight. I don't know when exactly."

Mom smirks, just a little. "Thank you," she says. "I'll let your father know."

Swell. I boot the door open and go out to my car.

What the hell have I gotten myself into now? Two minutes with my mom and Mike is going to pack a bag for Australia.

Fine. I'll go with him.

Here's the thing.

It's bad enough that Mom wants to meet Mike. But I can at least comprehend it; it's, like, a Mom Thing, right? Perfectly natural, if not unholy and unreasonable, but whatever. What bugs me most is . . . who is it she'll be meeting?

I mean, *is* he just a friend? Or are we something more than that? Because the truth is, if we're not—which makes me want to turn around right now and go home—then I don't care if Mom and Dad ever meet him. But if we're *an item,* or whatever the cool kids are calling it these days, then I kinda want him to see the house. See my room. See *me.*

And if they meet him now, Mom especially, then it'll just save me a headache when I invite him over later.

If we're an item. Or something resembling itemy. Itemness. Itemimity? (Bitch, stop.) I'd better find out for sure. Like, tonight.

It takes me half an hour to find Mike's house. He lives in this section of downtown where these little cottagelike homes were built when Phoenix was an actual cowboy town. They are small but cute. Lots of Spanish architecture, all whitewashed arches and tiling.

I park on the street and climb a short rise of steps covered in rust-colored Mexican tiles. Most of his tiny house is covered by creeping vines. There are no lights on in any of the windows. A disreputable pickup is parked in the cracked driveway, chrome bumper torn, paint flaking.

After I knock, Mike opens the front door. He's wearing these kick-ass narrow black shorts and a sharp white Operation Ivy "Unity" T-shirt that doesn't exactly hug his chest but isn't baggy, either. His bangs hang free and swing in front of half his face. Nice.

"Hey!" he says. He gestures into the house. "You wanna come in real quick, or . . . ?"

Time me! "Sure," I say casually, and cross the threshold. "Is that your truck?" I ask as he passes in front of me after closing the door.

"Dad's. He lets me borrow it sometimes, though."

"So am I going to meet him?" What with turnabout being fair play and all.

"Ah, no. Just missed him. He just walked down to the park."

"What, is he feeding the ducks?"

"Most likely," Mike says, and doesn't smile, so I wipe off my grin real quick. Weird.

On my left is the kitchen. Two cracked vinyl chairs are shoved beneath a cratered Formica table the color of plaque. Mike says, "So, this is the kitchen."

He leads me down a dark hallway. He points toward the living room, names it, and continues down the hall.

"Bathroom," he says, gesturing. "Dad's room. And the Man Cave."

He opens a door and steps aside. I stand in the doorway, letting my eyes wander. It's Spartan in its appointments: scuffed bureau, twin bed covered with rumpled white sheets, gray metallic folding chair, portable stereo on the bureau, and a bookcase filled with paperbacks and tapes. The floor is hardwood, which with some polishing could be gorgeous, but it's buried beneath a ream's worth of scattered paper and the occasional sock.

"So this is the inner sanctum," I say.

"Yep. Abandon hope, all ye who enter."

I step into the room. A polished acoustic guitar is propped on a stand in one corner. It's a thing of beauty. Maybe art. Its body is cedar-dark. An iridescent pearl inlay on the neck depicts a pair of Harlequin masks. Black nickel tuning knobs jut from the headstock. I approach the guitar reverently and reach out to touch its steel strings.

"Wow. This guitar! It's beautiful. You play guitar, too?"

"Not much, actually. This used to be Dad's."

"Oh yeah? He plays?"

"No, not anymore. He gave up a while ago, but he never got rid of this."

"Oh. Why'd he quit?"

Another shrug. "Too famous too fast, I guess."

"Famous?"

Mike points to a wall. There's only one hanging frame, almost lost beside a collage of Gothic Rainbow flyers from old shows, which, I can't help but notice, aren't exactly exquisite works of art. Inside the hanging frame, however, is a gleaming, shimmering album.

"Is that—a *gold record*?" I say. "Like, a for-real gold record?"

"Well, I mean, the whole band gets one, but yeah."

I look more closely at the writing on the small card inset below the record, my jaw slowly dropping. "Wait. Your *dad* was in Ghost of Banquo?" That would explain the T-shirt Mike wore at Damage Control. Which reminds me, who got that last shirt? I hate her.

Mike blinks at me. "Oh . . . yeah. Did I not mention that part?"

"Uh, no! Do you have any recordings? I've looked for the album but can't ever find it. A lot of old ska bands talk about them, like they inspired a lot of other bands? Man, this is awesome!" My eye catches the abandoned guitar. "But what happened?"

"Well, they had one hit—"

"'Wedding Zoo'! They play it on *Flashback* sometimes."

Mike smiles. "'Wedding Zoo,' yeah. They were getting ready for a big tour to support the record and whatever. And then it sorta fell apart."

"How come?"

"Fight with the label. Who owned what. Contract disputes or whatever. The label won. Which they always do. And that was that. I've never seen any copies of the album around."

"So he never played again?"

"Oh no, he played. Six, seven bands, here and there. But nothing that ever really caught like Ghost did." Mike gazes at the album, and looks sort of wistful. "He always wanted that next gold, though."

Ah-proverbial-ha. "So that's why you want one."

"Kinda. He doesn't say much these days, but he supports us. The band. He told me once that if it was what I wanted to do, I shouldn't let anything stop me. So someday, down the road, you know, I'd love to give him one just like that with my name on it." He winks at me. "I'll keep the *platinum* one in my room."

I smile, and my eyes sting for a sec. Must be nice. There's nothing I want to give my dad. Except maybe a wheel kick to the face from time to time, when he pushes Mom's buttons a little too hard. Usually after a drink or five.

"So why's this in your room? Doesn't your dad . . . ?"

"He doesn't like looking at it. Memories and whatever. Bums him out. And he's bummed enough as it is."

"Huh." I take one more look around, fascinated by Mike's . . . everything. "Well. Thanks for the tour. Hey, where're your drums?"

"Eddie's basement. We rehearse there. No distractions."

"Oh. Cool." I take one more lap around the room, memorizing everything. It might be the last time I'm ever here, for all I know, depending on how my *inquiry* as to our status goes.

Passing his bookcase, I spot a photo of a woman, lying faceup on one of the shelves, on top of a paperback of *The Outsiders*. I move for a closer look but don't touch the picture.

"Who's this?"

Mike looks over my shoulder. "Mom. Sasha."

"Sasha . . . that's a pretty name. Where is she?"

Mike's jaw tightens. "San Francisco."

"Oh. Are they . . . ?"

"Divorced. Yeah. It's been a while now. Ten years, say." He shakes his head. "They weren't a great pair."

I sit on his bed. Considering Mom and Dad, this might be helpful info. "Yeah?" I say. "How so?"

"Well, I mean, I guess I love her and all, but she was also kind of a groupie," Mike says. "They met when Ghost was riding high. But back then, my dad was a typical rock star, you know? Drinking, drugs, the whole nine. It's at least half the reason the band never made it past that one album. They were all acting like they were gonna live forever. And according to Dad, she wanted to be part of that, at first. But she had other things she wanted to do, too, and when Ghost didn't really happen, she left."

His jaw is still clenching. I decide to back off. "Wow. I'm sorry."

"'Sokay. Ready to go?"

I nod, and Mike leads me back out of the house. He locks the door behind us, and we walk to my car.

"So where're we off to?" I say as we climb in.

"Find us a 7-Eleven or something, then we'll go north."

I follow Mike's directions to a convenience store, where he buys us each our own pint of ice cream. I pull out my wallet, all Woman Power, but Mike only shakes his head and says, "Got it." Do *Just Friends* buy *Just Friends* ice cream?

Back in the car, he directs me to the north end of town. Mike guides us to the bottom of a hill, the street winding through an upscale neighborhood clinging to the south side of Camelback Mountain.

"See that little turnoff?" Mike says, pointing. "Go there."

We're past the houses now, climbing steadily up the paved road. Below us, interior lights spilling from the neighborhood create a dim orange glow, but the darkness ahead is pierced only by my headlights. I make a slow right turn, taking us off the street and onto a dirt road.

"You gonna tell me where we're going?"

"The road'll dead-end up there a ways. When we get there, you can park."

The road ends abruptly. I pull the car over, park, and stare at a rocky path beyond, bathed in the glare of the headlights.

Mike climbs gracefully out of the car. "Come on."

I shut off the lights, scurry around to join him. He begins hiking up the hill.

I do my best to keep my footing on the slippery gravel, wishing I could hold his hand as we climb and feeling adrenaline shoot into my gut as I remember that one way or another, I'm getting an answer tonight.

After we crest the hill, Mike stops and looks around at his feet. He plops down on top of a large rock.

The entire city is spread out before us, twinkling in the darkness as if reflecting the starry sky above. The air feels fresher and clearer up here, and I can smell creosote bushes, a faint aroma longing to feel moisture again. It's been forever since it rained.

"Wow," I go, a little breathlessly. From up here, at night, Phoenix is sprawled out like a *veduta* (*a representative rendering of a city*; thanks, Mr. Hilmer!), all murk and twinkles but with enough landmarks to assure me I am still, essentially, home. Instantly, I compose a rough sketch of this landscape in my head.

Mike pries open his ice cream. I sit down beside him on the boulder and open my own carton. Mike hands me a plastic spoon, which I completely failed to (a) notice or (b) think about when we were at the store. Genius.

"Thanks," I say. "This is beautiful."

"Yeah? I was hoping you'd like it. You said you were doing a lot of landscapes lately, right?"

Oh, my.

I clear my throat. "Um. Yeah. I am. Thanks."

I dig into my coffee-fudge ice cream and take in a heaping spoonful. As soon as I swallow, I say, "Mm. I don't know if I can finish this. I may go into a coma. Then, death."

"But sweet, creamy death."

I laugh and jam my spoon into the softening ice cream. We fall silent again, looking out over the city. I'm not sure if I can see my house from here or not; it's definitely in our line of sight but too far away to pinpoint. My mom's out there somewhere, checking the clock, waiting for me to bring my boyfr—

No. I can't say it; I can't even think it.

I churn nervously through half of my pint. Fudge chunks course through my digestive tract and seek my thighs. I stick the spoon into the remaining ice cream and set it down beside me. I wipe my hands on my shorts, fold my arms on top of my knees, and sort of watch him out of the corner of my eye, pretending to not do exactly that.

And I decide it's time.

"Can I ask you a question?"

Mike's scraping the bottom of his container. Skinny bastard. Ever notice how much thin guys can eat? *So* not fair.

He licks off the last of the ice cream from his spoon before answering, "Sure."

"Promise you won't get mad?"

"Nope."

Despite my dry mouth and clenching gut, I still have to laugh. Then I take The Deep Breath.

"Um. Is this a date?"

Mike puts his spoon into the empty pint and sets it down. "Do you want it to be?"

"I was kinda hoping for an answer, not a question." Whoa, hello, assertiveness! How lovely to make your acquaintance.

"I'm pretty sure it is."

My stomach gives an anxious twist. "Pretty sure?"

"It's just that . . ." Mike seems to weigh his words before scooting around to face me. "I haven't exactly been dating for a while," he goes. "And I'm not sure that I know exactly . . . how?"

He shakes his head. I can see his long bangs waving, black strands against a violet sky.

"That's not it," he says. "It's just that I'm kind of coming from a bad place. Couple years ago. Girlfriend problems."

Here's the thing.

Should I care? *Do* I? I know without asking that, whoever she was, she called him Mikey. Bitch. This is his Girl Thing that came up at DC.

"She, um—you know, honestly, if we could talk about it some other time . . ."

"Yeah, no, that's okay, that's cool." I pick my ice cream back up but only play with my spoon rather than taking another bite.

Mike sounds relieved. "Thanks. I kind of wanted to be alone for a while, you know?"

"Past tense?"

"Well," Mike says, "if the past week or so is any indication . . . yes."

The tightness in my stomach unwinds. Much, *much* better now. I try to think of something to say to follow this but come up empty. So to move on, I shake my ice cream. "You want to finish this?"

"Nah, I'm good." He peers at me. "Are *we* . . . good?"

"Yeah," I say. "We're gold, Pony Boy."

Mike laughs out loud, and after a sec, I do, too. Adding it up, I have to say, I don't think I've laughed this much in a long time.

"So, since we're being all frank and honest and junk," I say, "I do have some bad news."

"You're allergic to ice cream?"

"Ha! Death first. No, it's not that."

"Good. What's up?"

"It's just that . . . well, I'm sorta hoping-slash-assuming that since this is a date, there might be others?"

"That is the plan, yes." He bumps his knee into mine.

Such small contact, yet such a *thrill*. "Right, good. So, the bad news is, my lovely and charming mother dearest has rather insisted that she meet you. And if not, that could put the aforementioned *future* dates in grave peril."

"Ah. I see. Cool."

"Hold that thought. When I say she wants to meet you, I mean, like, tonight." And I want to show you my work, I think, but can't say it. Haven't really made up my mind there.

"Sure, I don't mind meeting her," Mike says. "Am I dressed for the occasion?"

"We might want to pick up a tux. Or a clerical collar." *That* would be hysterical.

"Done," Mike says. "My limo's in the shop, but what can ya do."

I grin. And my stomach torques again as I dare to tilt my body toward him and rest my head on his shoulder. I feel no tension from his body in response and gratefully let my eyes wander the city lights. A minute later, Mike drapes an arm over my knee. I shiver happily under my skin.

We sit still like this for a while, not saying much, but I am *infinitely* happy. Eventually, I reluctantly pick myself up from Mike's shoulder. Mom's ethereal voice is starting to assassinate my joy. I *so* do not want to make Mike meet her, even if he is cool with it, but I'd rather get it over with.

"Should probably go," I say. "If you still want."

"Yeah," Mike says, scooping up the two ice cream containers. He pours out my melted ice cream and shoves the empty carton into his.

I step gingerly off the rock we've been sitting on, preparing to inch my way back to the car and hoping Mike'll take my hand. *Please.*

"Um," Mike goes, and I stop.

"Yeah?"

"Where do you live? I mean . . . think you could point to it from up here?"

I step back onto the rock. My hands fall to my (wide, childbearing) hips as I study the city lights, looking for a landmark. Then I point.

"I think that's Arcadia," I say. "The football field. If it is, then that over there is the mall, which puts my house, like, a couple miles up that way, so, like, right there. Ish."

I glance at Mike to see if he's following my directions, but Mike isn't watching my hand. He's looking at *me*. I relax my arm, let it fall.

"You really like it up here?" Mike asks. His voice is quiet.

Has he moved nearer while I was talking? Because a second ago, I swear he was fifty yards away, and now he's close enough that I can feel his ice-cream-cooled breath on my neck.

Now?

It's now, oh god, it's now, please.

"Yeah," I whisper.

"You're sure?" Mike goes.

"I'm sure."

Mike nods, still looking into my eyes.

Then he leans in and kisses me gently on the lips.

My eyes stay open, but I see nothing except stars. Even as Mike pulls away and studies my reaction, I can see only the twinkling desert sky, and catch a faint whiff of creosote.

"Um. You okay?"

"Yes," I say, and lift both hands to cradle his chin.

I pull him to me again, and Mike doesn't resist. He surrounds my waist and holds me close as we kiss. My arms tremble, the back of my neck burns; the base of my skull is *tingling*, sending breathless synaptic electricity down my spine and to my fingertips.

Whatever I paint next, the oils will be mixed with *this*.

nine

Love, I said, strangely resembled certain
gastric sensations . . . producing
an uneasiness and shudders so delicate
that one is not sure whether one is in love
or feels like vomiting.
—Salvador Dalí

"Look, I take no responsibility for what's about to happen in there," I say as I park the car in our driveway.

"And what's about to happen?" Mike asks.

"That's just it. I don't know. She's liable to say anything." I turn off the engine and climb out. Mike follows me as I trudge to the kitchen door. "She's probably going to kick my ass," I mutter.

"For what?"

"For anything she can think of. She's psycho that way. But what the hell, my ass is a big target."

I hear him stop, so I do, too, and turn around.

Mike is, like, *glaring* at me. "What?" he says.

"W-well," I say.

"Well, what?"

"Nothing," I say. "Just, you know, my ass is enormous."

He pushes my shoulder with one finger to turn me around. I don't fight it. I *present*.

"It's awesome," he states.

While I don't have a mirror handy—anywhere, actually—I'm pretty sure my face floods crimson. "You're just saying that."

"*Why* would I just be saying it?"

"Because you just . . . wanna . . ."

He raises his eyebrows at me. "What, make out with you? Yeah, 'cause *that* sure proves your theory." He shakes his head and continues walking to my kitchen door, unescorted.

"Wait a sec!" I shout after him, and jog to catch up.

"No," Mike says as his hand touches the doorknob. "Listen, Zero, you have a great body. It's for real. Don't freak about it."

And the next thing I know, I've grabbed his wrists and pulled him close to me, kissing him, every nerve lit up like an F'ing Christmas tree. I devour his lips with my teeth, trying to swallow him whole.

Which is perhaps not the brightest move I've ever made, considering the top half of our kitchen door is glass-paned and the carport light illuminates us entirely.

So anyone who might, I dunno, *happen* to be hanging out in the kitchen—near the sink, let's say—would see everything *quite* distinctly.

The door opens.

"Hello," Mom says.

Well, shit.

We split apart, and fast.

"Hi," Mike says, like this sort of thing happens every day. God, it doesn't, does it?

"Mom! Hi. This is—um—Mike."

I wait for the Fire of Eternal God to consume us both. Instead—brace yourself—Mom *smiles*. "Hello, Mike. It's so nice to meet you. Come in."

I give Mom a suspicious glance, but she doesn't see it. She's checking Mike out. She closes the door behind us and steps toward the living room, where I can hear the TV blaring.

"Your father's out here finishing dinner," Mom says as we follow her. "He'll be so glad to meet you, Mike."

What. The. Hell. Is going on? Who is this woman? What has she done with my mother?

"How was the movie?" Mom goes as we cross into the living room.

Mike wisely neither says anything nor shoots me a worried look. Brilliant man.

"We didn't go," I say. "We went up to Camelback Mountain and ate ice cream."

"Oh," Mom says, and lobs a smile at us. "That sounds like fun." She gives her forehead a quick rub.

Mom passes behind the couch to her rocking chair. Dad's sunk into the sofa, a TV tray in front of him. Three empty bottles are lined up at his feet; a fourth balances on the tray. The news is reporting something about stocks or bonds or something.

"Richard?" Mom goes, taking her seat. "This is Mike."

Dad finishes chewing whatever Mom made him for

dinner and looks over at us with a surprised expression on his face. "Oh!" he goes. "Your mom mentioned you might be bringing someone over, kiddo. Nice to meet ya, Mike. You want something to drink?"

"No thanks, I'm fine."

"No? Beer, something?"

I mentally eviscerate my father.

"Um, no, no thanks. Not really, you know, old enough."

"Hey, neither was I! Ha!"

Mom presses her lips together tight enough to turn them white. She finds a smile and uses a palette knife to paste it on her face. "We're happy you're here, Mike," she says. "If you change your mind about having a *soft* drink, I'm sure Amy will be happy to find one for you."

Dad turns toward Mom, and I imagine an epic brawl about to begin.

"Yep, sure will!" I say quickly to derail any threat. Dad rolls his eyes and turns back to the TV.

"So, do you have other plans this evening?" Mom *inquires* of me.

"Um, no, not really . . ."

"I thought you were going to show me your paintings," Mike says, his eyes lit up with mischief. I don't know whether to beat him senseless or make out with him. Is there a way to do both? How'd he know that was part of my nefarious plan?

"Hey, that's a great idea," Dad says, still watching the TV and not looking at us. "Z's kind of a little artist, there, huh, kid?"

"I hope so," I say. "So I guess we'll just be in my room."

"Oh, I don't think we've repaired the hinges quite yet,

you'll want to keep your door open," Mom says with a casualness that stuns me.

There is, of course, absolutely nothing wrong with my door. No way would I let it be *uncloseable.* But I have to hand it to Mom for making an attempt at not being a jerk. Still— what, we're going to start having sex in there?

"Right, okay," I say. Mike gives my parents a little wave, and I lead him back to my room. I'm tempted to shut the door, out of spite, but I don't.

Plus, Mike is *in my space.* My very soul. Must watch him closely.

"So that wasn't so bad," Mike says as he studies every detail of my room. "Considering the state of your, ah, hinges."

"Caught that, did ya?"

"I did. So what do they do? Like, for jobs."

"Make my life hell."

"Yeah? That come with benefits?"

"Just dental."

Mike cracks a smile, and I get all squishy inside. *Geez,* girlie enough?

"You're cute," he says, but it's like this statement of fact. He's not kidding around or being all jokey.

Some smart-ass response comes to mind, but I forget it as soon as I look into his eyes.

"Thank you," I say, and can feel a damn blush coming on. To chase it away, I say, "Dad's an accountant, and Mom's a . . . mom, I guess. So how the two of them managed to create *moi,* I couldn't say. Mutation, maybe. What about your parents?"

"My mom's a psychiatrist. Dad's in construction now.

Works with his hands." I notice Mike rubbing his thumbs across his palms, but I don't think he knows he's doing it. Still taking in the minutiae of my room, Mike tilts his head back and studies my ceiling faces.

"Those're cool," he says. "So where do you hide the other ones?"

Ouch.

I debate brushing him off. Continuing to hide. No one but Jenn has seen my work, other than when Mom wanders in while I'm working, which isn't often. What if he hates them?

But he already said my ceiling faces were cool, so . . . what the hell. Let's do this.

I slide open my closet door and start pulling out one canvas after another and stacking them on their edges on the floor so that they rest upright against the wall. Before I'm even done, Mike hunkers down and starts going through them, one at a time, while anxiety burns a hole in my guts. Once they're all out, I sit on my bed.

The first several are from what I laughingly call my recent *landscape period*. Lilac saguaro skeletons; Camelback Mountain with an enormous bite taken out of the back; detailed pointillist studies of creosote and Joshua trees. (Think Seurat; *lots o' dots!* Thanks, Mr. Hilmer!)

"You really like the desert," Mike says.

"What? No. I hate it here. I can't wait to leave."

He pauses and turns to me. "Which *here,* exactly?"

"Well, you know. My—" And I stop short. I was about to say *my house.* Which technically is in the desert, but suddenly, the way Mike phrases it, I don't automatically equate the two. I *do* love the desert. I'm one of very few native

Phoenicians. A Desert Rat, born and raised. It's not enough to make me stay, but still: Mike's right.

"Yeah," I say. "I guess I do."

Mike nods and returns to my paintings. The next one shows—correction, attempts, poorly, to show—a naked, eyeless baby doll whose mocha-colored fabric skin has been stripped from one arm and reveals not batting but bare bone.

"Ugh!" I say, and try to cover my eyes, except my fingers are all tangled up in my lap. "Now see, *that* sucks."

"*Does* it?"

"Unless maybe you're nearsighted."

Mike raises one hand and lets it hover over the acrylic impasto. "This texture is wicked," he says. "Can I touch it?"

My heart skips. "No!"

"How come?"

"Because it might get damaged. I mean, sorry, no offense, but no."

"None taken," Mike says, and eases the painting away. "But if it sucks, why care if it gets damaged?"

My eyes narrow as I try to shoot fireballs at his head.

Because he has a point. And he *knows* he has one. Mike's not looking smug or anything, but there's a glimmer in his eyes that tells me in no uncertain terms that he got me. But he also wants an answer.

"Okay, that was mean and totally uncalled for," I tell him.

"Just sayin'."

"Look, you conned me into showing these to you."

Mike moves on to the next canvas. "No, I didn't. You wanted me to."

"*What?*" How in the world could he possibly—

"You wanted me to see these."

"I so did not!" Half-true, anyway.

"Then why be an *artist*?"

Wow, this guy's good. I am getting pissed here. Except not just pissed.

"Listen," Mike says, crossing to my bed and sitting beside me. "I don't want to make you mad or anything. It's just, these are really, really good. Or hell, maybe they're *not*, but I wouldn't know, I'm not an artist. I just know that I like them. And I don't understand why that's such a bad thing here."

I squeeze my teeth together behind a closed mouth for a minute.

"I dunno," I mutter finally. Then I add, "They're not *terrible*." I take a deep breath and manage to pull my hands apart. "Sooo . . . maybe what I should have said is, thank you, I'm glad you like them."

"Did you just admit you might actually be good at this? I can't tell."

"Well, let's not go overboard," I say, but the anxiety in my belly has melted away. "I'm . . . passable."

"Compared to what?"

"People who can sell. Or get fancy scholarships to good schools."

"Ohhhh. Okay." He knocks his knee into mine, and my whole *leg* burns, and proceeds to consume my entire body. Seriously, can't we just kiss again?

"Gotta say," Mike goes, "I'm feeling a little torn about this school thing."

"Hm? How?"

"Well, if it's what you want, you should do it. Find a way,

you know? But on the other hand, I'd hate for you to leave anytime soon."

Mike looks at me, and—remind me again, who am I? Where am I? That's what it feels like to have his eyes locked on mine. I know exactly what he means. I know this is just the beginning for us, and who knows where it'll all go, but for the first time since May, I'm not 100 percent sad that I'm staying here instead of heading to Chicago. It's kinda veering into the fifty-fifty range after those kisses.

My gaze catches the last painting. A jagged, smeared, black acrylic. There's one thing I've got to know now, before anything else happens.

Without turning to him, I ask, "Are you fucking with me?"

Mike rears back. "Sorry?"

"My paintings. You honestly like them?"

"I do."

"Can I tell you something?"

"Sure."

"I really want to sell a painting someday. I mean, I'd do it *anyway*. But I just—I don't think I'll believe I'm any good until someone I don't know hands over a couple bucks for something I did. Is that wrong, do you think?"

He takes my hand. I almost pass out. His hand is warm, rough, soft. Mine fits perfectly into it. "No, I don't. It's fair. As long as you're having fun. And you will sell it, someday."

"So, when you're a rich and famous rock-and-roll star, will you buy one from me?"

Mike grins. "That might be a while. I'll start saving up now."

He flips his bangs back and leans onto his arms, and I'm

suddenly aware of not only how comfortable he is relaxing like that but how happy I am that he feels that way. Glancing around my room, I feel like I'm seeing it for the first time. It's . . . kinda *cool*.

I turn back to Mike.

"So, um. I lack what anyone would refer to as 'moves,' so I'm just going to go ahead and ask. . . . Can I kiss you again?"

"Thought your door was busted."

"I'll chance it if you will."

Mike sits up and leans toward me, eyes closing. Mine close too.

Here's the thing.

The moment our lips touch, time slows. It's unlike our kiss in the carport. This is careful, gentle. Our lips barely move. Our breath mingles between us, still dusted lightly with ice cream sugar. My body stills, internally and externally. And when Mike at last pulls away, I can only sit there with my mouth slightly open, my hands still hovering in place where they had been holding his arms.

The world begins to pick up speed again, and I open my eyes. Mike is looking at me, not smiling but—stunned, maybe. He licks his lips.

"Hi," he says.

"Uh-huh," I say back.

I swallow and widen my eyes to try to get back to the real world.

Mike gets to his feet. "So, listen, I should probably get going. Make sure Dad got home in one piece."

Bummer. Then again, leaving on an up note! I stand. "Okay."

He follows me out of my room and to the kitchen, where my dad is pulling A Cold One from the fridge. He bumps the door with his hip to close it as we walk past.

"Heeeey!" he shouts. "You change your mind about that drink?"

"Uh, no, thanks, I'm good," Mike says, raising a hand.

"Aw," Dad says. He pops the cap off into his hand, then raises it up toward his ear. He snaps his finger and the cap goes flying into the sink. "Haha! Still got it! You sure you don't want—"

"We're *fine*," I say, and open the kitchen door. "Be right back."

"Oooookay!" Dad says, and heads into the living room. There's muttering, then my mom's voice snapping, "*Richard!* Would it kill you to once—"

"Ah, Christ, Miry, relax!"

Mike and I go to my car. I open the door and climb in, slamming the door after me.

"Sorry," I say through my teeth, which have clamped tight.

"No worries," Mike says.

I've gone from totally freaking elated to boiling freaking pissed. I couldn't paint how embarrassed I am. I've gotten used to how Dad acts when he's had some beers, but with Mike there, it was like suddenly seeing Dad from someone else's perspective. What a jackass he looks like.

I drive toward Mike's house and don't say anything, because I can't imagine what to say that could salvage the night after Dad's performance.

Then, a few blocks from his house, Mike puts one hand on my knee, and my rage turns to a simmer.

"Must be rough," he says quietly. "Living with that. Does it happen a lot?"

I nod.

Mike nods back. "We used to rehearse at Hob's dad's house," he says, "till he got so loud fighting with his various and sundry girlfriends we decided to move. Hard to come up with new stuff when it's like that."

I don't say anything, but I pick up his hand from my knee and squeeze it.

The lights are still out at Mike's house when I pull up to the sidewalk in front of his yard. I can see the glow of a cigarette flare near the front door, and make out a huddled shape sitting beside it.

"Well, he made it," Mike says. Without so much as another look at the man on his porch, Mike kisses me on the cheek and climbs out of the car.

"Mike . . . do you need, like . . . help with him or anything?"

"Nah. He's fine. Bad meds, probably. I'll get him inside, he'll sleep it off. Thanks, though."

Meds? I want to ask but don't.

Mike hesitates for a second, studying me under the dome light.

"Take care, okay?" he says finally.

"I will. You too."

"Always. See ya."

"Yeah. Later, skater."

Mike shuts the door and goes to the porch. I watch him shake his father's shoulders. His dad slowly gets to his feet, pitching the cigarette out to the lawn, still smoldering. Mike helps him into the house, stopping briefly to wave at me. By the time I think to wave back, Mike's already gotten his dad inside and closed the door.

As I drive home, I can't help but think about being in my room with him. How easy it all felt. How *good* it all felt. Does that make me shallow or something? To only think about *us* instead of everything else that's going on in the world? His dad, my dad?

Well, then, that's fine. Can I say it now?

Yes. I give myself permission.

I've got a boyfriend.

This little song repeats in my head the entire way back to my house. When I get home, Mom and Dad are engaged in a cage-fighting match in the living room.

Well, screw that. I'm not going to let their bullshit ruin my—

". . . shoulda thoughta that s-seventeen years ago!" my dad shouts.

"Richard, that's not fair!" my mother shouts back.

Oh. That again. They need new material.

I head straight for my room, shut the door, and turn on my stereo. Jane's Addiction pops on. (*Here we go now . . . home.* Thanks, Perry.) I grab a blank canvas, slap it on my easel, and set to work painting tonight's view from Camelback. My assignment for tomorrow is a landscape. Technically, I'm supposed to sketch a painting before jumping in, but frankly, since I'm not a pro, to hell with "technically."

And my walls are made of thinner material than this canvas.

". . . think this's how I wanted things t'turn out?"

"That is not the point. The point is that she deserves . . ."

My hand begins shaking. Can't get the background quite right. The acrylic trembles in the bristles, smearing more than shading. No wonder my portfolio sucked; it's like trying to create in a war zone living here.

Okay, so here's the short version: Dad got Mom "in trouble," as they called it back in the day, and both her parents and his decided the best course was for them to get married, whether they fucking had anything in common or not. Mom was seventeen when she got pregnant, eighteen when they got married and Yours Truly arrived. Here endeth the story.

It's no big. I'm over it.

I *am.*

I mean, the damage is done, right? Dad didn't get to play Irresponsible Teen when most people do, so he's doing it now. Fine, whatever. But Jesus, *if you don't give a shit about each other,* why go through the motions at all? I should perhaps suggest this to them someday. Soon.

Their voices stop, and I hear footsteps in the hall. Mom's. A second later, their bedroom door slams shut.

Good.

Maybe now I can finish my painting.

Except for some reason, the canvas is blurry and my hand is still shaking.

So much for getting my homework done.

ten

Drawing is the honesty of the art.
There is no possibility of cheating.
It is either good or bad.
—Salvador Dalí

Turned out to be no big deal that I didn't finish my landscape, because Doc S didn't even come on Wednesday. She went on to show up late for four classes and skip a fifth entirely. Last Wednesday, after skipping the Monday before, she whisked in ten minutes late and didn't so much apologize as excuse herself: "I was spirited away to spend a perfectly extraordinary afternoon of cocktails and goat cheese with Lindi Taylor!" she said. Lindi Taylor is this American Indian artist who works in the Southwest. Not my favorite style, but she's made a career out of it, which is more than I can say for someone named *Amanda Walsh*.

If Dr. Salinger wasn't so good, I seriously would drop the class. Of course, then I'd have to explain it to Mom and Dad, and honestly, I don't want to bother.

So I played Good Schoolgirl all week, using the times she

wasn't here to work on the techniques she's shown us so far. It's quiet in the classroom, at least. Part of me is sorta happy; I think I might be getting just a bit better. The other part of me wants her to F'ing *show up* and do her job so I can learn more and put together something decent for my portfolio. And I hung out with Mike Thursday and Sunday, not counting a GR show Saturday, so things could be worse.

Today, Friday, Doc S arrives on time and launches into this *glorious* speech about Dada. Normally I'd be all ears, because Dada sort of inspired the surrealists. But her little asides, as she calls them, are filled with heavy sighs and fluttering eyelashes, giving me a headache, so I paint instead, and she doesn't seem to care.

When you're painting, you can see noise. Taste sound. Ten trillion neurons fire in your mind and trigger the fine muscles in your arms to *do*. To create. Your hand moves apart from *You*, this capital-letter thing of fallible flesh. There's technique, sure. You don't just pick up a brush or pencil or stick and breathe life into two dimensions. Still . . . at the time, the rest of the world dissolves away. You know how you sometimes just stare at some fixed point in middle space, unable to blink or avert your gaze? How the peripheral world looks when you do that? Painting and drawing create a similar sensation. You might scratch an itch your consciousness didn't know you had. You might reflexively shake your hand before it cramps. You might stifle a burp (or worse). Your hands, your eyes, your *You* don't care. All that matters is each stroke, each whisper-scratch of the stick, as your creation grows, in stages of shade and depth and color, into something uniquely its own.

And when your gaze breaks, when the moment passes,

whether after a moment or a day, you step back and study what's happened. And the result, for good or for ill, is yours. You are in control of nothing and responsible for everything. Everything you are, everything you may yet become, suddenly gets pulled into crystal-clear focus and rests on this one expanse of once-off-white emptiness. Your mouth dries, and something metaphysical climbs on spider legs up your spine, nesting at last at the base of your skull, where it spreads its long appendages and warms you. It gives you the right to scream.

. . . But anyway. I don't get that at home the same way I do here.

When I check the clock, it's halfway through class and the room is silent except for the whisker-swish of brushes on canvas. Dr. Salinger pirouettes between the easels, offering comments to each student. When she arrives at my elbow, I stop painting so she can get a look at my canvas.

"Good," she says. And for one second, I've attained nirvana.

"But it's . . . *missing* something."

Crap. "What," I say.

"That's for you to know and me to find out," she says, and lightly pats my back. "May I inquire as to the subject?"

I swallow, my throat going arid all of a sudden. She's never asked that before.

"It's, um . . . my teacher."

Dr. Salinger's head twitches toward me, birdlike. "Go on," she coos at me.

"Well," I *go on*, "uh, his name's Mr. Hilmer? And he was my art teacher in junior high? And . . . he was . . . really cool."

"And how exactly did this *Mister Cool* impact your artistic soul?"

I almost elbow her in the gut. Pick your weapon, witch; we will battle and your skull will decorate my bedpost for eternity if you don't watch your tone when talking about Mr. Hilmer.

I clear my throat. "Well, like . . . on the first day of seventh grade, I walked into his classroom and . . ."

Dr. Salinger perches on a stool and props her chin up with one delicate fist.

I don't say this, but the first thing I noticed was Mr. Hilmer himself, an older guy of indeterminate ethnicity, with cloud-white, Cyrillic tufts of hair and an omnipresent turquoise beaded choker. He always showed his teeth when he smiled, which was often.

Second was that his classroom walls were covered floor to ceiling with art posters. Baroque, Italian Renaissance, Romantic—not that I knew any of that at the time. Renoir to Matisse, Warhol to O'Keefe (who, by the way, also briefly attended SAIC); Mr. Hilmer's room was a jumbled gallery of fine art reproductions.

". . . and, um, he had all these art prints," I say. "One of them was Salvador Dalí's *Persistence of Memory*. It was between a Cassatt and a . . . Delacroix, I think."

I shut up for a sec, remembering. I might even smile some.

I went straight to that Dalí poster, which was about eye-level, right near his desk. I barely heard the other kids coming into the room, chattering and teasing. Looking back, I realize now it was the only time and place I didn't hear the obnoxious things people said about me, like they didn't exist in Mr. Hilmer's room.

I touched one of Dalí's famous melting watches with my index finger, as if to feel the intangible impasto I was sure existed on the original—not that I knew what impasto was yet. I didn't learn until later that Dalí didn't use impasto. Turns out he used small brushes and tried to hide his brushstrokes as much as possible. His paintings appear more like photos.

Mr. Hilmer materialized next to me. "What do you think?"

I pulled my finger away, not because he sounded mad that I was touching the poster—he didn't sound mad at all—but because that soft watch repulsed me. And beckoned.

"I don't know," I said. "What is it?"

"Dalí."

I looked for a Barbie or Kewpie doll, and pointed out that there were no such artifacts in this painting.

"Salvador Dalí." Mr. Hilmer smiled patiently. "He was a Spanish artist. Do you like it?"

"I don't know," I said, knowing even then it was a lie. I was *transfixed*.

"Well, let me know when you decide," Mr. Hilmer said. "We have plenty of time. There are some books on the shelf there if you want to see more."

I took all three of his oversized Dalí books to my desk and missed his entire first-day lecture, lost in the books' color plates. Mr. Hilmer never even tried to get my attention.

Dr. Salinger has no such issue. "Miss Walsh? Hello? Are you still with us?"

My body jolts. Dr. Salinger is peering at me.

"Sorry," I say. "Uh . . . he was really nice to me and taught me a lot, and—I dunno, I just wonder about him sometimes. If he's doing okay. He retired after I graduated."

She glances at my painting. It's sort of an homage—or a theft, depending on who you ask—of Dali's *Portrait of Gala*, in which his wife (yes, Gala) is seated, facing out and toward a *second* Gala, seen from behind. I've tried to do something similar with Mr. Hilmer, only more expressionistic, using chunky, thick strokes and lots of matte medium to ghost the image.

"And how do you think your Mr. Hilmer would grade this piece?"

"He wouldn't," I say automatically. "He didn't grade in his art class."

"Ah!" Doc Salinger goes. "So there is no good or bad art."

"Well . . . I don't think that's what he—"

"That is *precisely* what he was implying," she interrupts. She hops to her feet. "Miss Walsh, I take it you fancy yourself an up-and-comer in the world of art, yes?"

My mouth flaps open, closed, open, closed.

"Well? Do you or do you not wish to sell your work? Hm?"

I swallow a couple choice F-bombs, which detonate in my stomach. "Y-yes . . ."

"Well, then, my dear—say something!"

"What do you want me to say?" I'm whining now, acutely aware of how high-pitched my voice is becoming.

"Not with your mouth," Dr. Salinger says, her eyes pleading with heaven. "With your paint. Speak to me, tell me what to *think*. Not what *you thought*. Frankly, Miss Walsh, the world is not terribly concerned with what you think. Do you intend to post signs at the bottom of your frames reading, 'Dear Matthias, This is a picture of my junior high school art teacher, who I think is simply the bee's knees'?"

"Who's Matthias?" This old grandma, Candace, interrupts my mental fit.

"My *lover*," Doc S says airily, fluttering her eyelashes.

Gag.

Dr. Salinger lasers in on me again, dismissing Candace. "Well, Miss Walsh?"

So I go, "I . . . um . . ."

"When I view your picture, I want to think," Dr. Salinger says. "Present tense, Miss Walsh. This," she says, pointing at my canvas, "says *nothing*. I should not have to ask the artist what she has painted, or why. I should feel it in the marrow of my bones."

With that gospel, Dr. Salinger swishes to the front of the class and picks up a thin brush.

"Now, what was I talking about? Ah, yes! Art." She swipes a dab of acrylic from another student and approaches her own easel.

I jab my brush into a crimson blob on my palette and stab repeatedly at the canvas, creating bloody wounds. Think about this, bitch! *Present tense.*

So what if it ruins the picture? Big deal. I stab harder and harder, nearly puncturing the canvas. It's an F anyway, right? Since we're grading now, fine. I'm a failure.

What the hell was I thinking? If I can't even pass an art class at a community F'ing college, then SAIC's going to send me a singing telegram striptease, mocking my audacity in reapplying for a *merit* scholarship. I lack *merit*.

When Dr. Salinger's voice slithers into my ear again, I almost scream; she's approached from behind me. Assassin. Maybe she's taken Mike's ninja class.

"*Now* I'm thinking," Dr. Salinger whispers. "Anger. Passion. That's a good start."

I wonder, if I throw my brush hard enough, will it impale her eyeball?

As soon as Dr. Salinger dismisses us, I pick up my bag and stomp out of the room, feeling a little immature but not caring to hide it. You know what, screw it. I'm dropping.

But the school library is between here and admin, and on an impulse I veer in that direction and slide inside to see if there's anything I can find out about Dr. Salinger. If Doc S is the real deal, there must be articles or reviews on her shows— if she's not lying about where she had her showings. And if she is, then it's an easy case to make for dropping out.

I find a few magazine articles dating so far back they're on microfiche. But it's Dr. Deborah Salinger, all right.

In one small photo, she's wearing a dress that would be dated on my mother. She was thinner then, but not in a good way. The photo is part of a blurb on a show held in San Francisco. These must have been her glory days, as she calls them. Lame.

The entire blurb is a review of her show. I peer closer, hanging on every word:

Deborah Salinger has succeeded in but one way: she has stolen (not to be confused with "imitated") the work of her betters, which, rather than being used for inspiration, has been pirated for works that do not reach the level of mediocrity. Salinger's exhibition is derivative and fraudulently "wistful." The wickedness of such painfully bad art is worth broadcasting. It allows us to study why we praise truly great art. Salinger's work is anything but.

There's a little box at the end of the article with a *D* in it. Looking at the other reviews, I see familiar letters: *A, B, C, D,* and *F.*

Holy *shit!* She got *reamed.* I've come up with some intricately detailed critiques of my paintings, but this guy makes my words sound like they came from a Sunday school teacher. And how about those *grades,* eh, Doc?

"She sucks," I whisper to the microfiche machine. Or she did at one point, anyway.

I go through two other microfiche articles that her name came up in. The reviews are positive but dated *before* that one. As of about five years ago, her name is nowhere to be found.

So wait a sec. One minute she's doing shows, getting reviews; the next she's teaching *community college?* The articles don't mention her education; maybe she got her PhD or whatever after her career fell apart?

Is that what happens if you can't sell? Those who *can't—teach?* I've thought about becoming an art teacher, like for elementary or junior high, following in Mr. Hilmer's footsteps, but I assumed that was a backup plan. Maybe Doc S had the same idea.

Or maybe she had no choice.

I return the films to the circulation desk. The other reviews were written about exhibits at nice galleries in Chicago and Santa Fe. I'd kill to have a canvas in either of their freaking *bathrooms.* So much for dropping, I guess. I can't afford to not find out if she's got more to teach me. Like what I did wrong in my portfolio. She must know, right?

I stop short of the parking lot as I'm heading to my car when I see Dr. Salinger walking all elegantly toward a cherry-red Porsche idling by the curb. This guy gets out, wearing a faux-casual outfit that makes him look like a catalog model. She picks up her pace as he comes around the hood to hug, then kiss her. Man, they're sucking face like the other is their only source of oxygen. Ew.

When they're done slobbering on each other, Doc S gets into the passenger seat and Her Lover Matthias (I assume) gets behind the wheel. He burns rubber peeling out of the lot.

Oooo. I'm *so* turned on. Idiot. I'm glad Mike isn't a "car guy."

I wait till they're out of sight before continuing toward my car. The mystery of Dr. Salinger's career can remain just that, for all I care. All I want now is to pass her stupid class, strip-mine her techniques for anything useful, and move on. Bigger things, better things, or some combination of the two. You want to talk *surreal*? Passing this witch's class would be as surrealistic as it gets—until I see Jenn pacing near a concrete bench just shy of the parking lot.

eleven

Was I really mad? I knew that I certainly was
not. But then, why had I done this?
—Salvador Dalí

I freeze up. Jenn catches me standing here and waves a weak hand.

I could run. Just bolt. And probably should, because what the hell is she doing here? I do *not* need this today.

Four years of friendship become too much for me, though. I walk slowly toward her. At least we're in the open; outdoors, visible. Feels safer somehow. And, ironically, more private.

Jenn is dressed demurely. For Jenn. Blue capris, black cami, and an unbuttoned oxford. Her hair is tied into a cranky ponytail, with wisps of hair sproinging out along her hairline. I don't think I've ever seen her hair pulled back.

"I'm sorry," Jenn says immediately. "I feel like a stalker. But I didn't want to show up at your house. And I didn't think you'd talk to me about this over the phone."

"Gosh, Jenn, talk to you about *what*?"

Jenn looks at the ground. "Do you have a few minutes? Please, Zero."

I sit down and she joins me. I look straight ahead, holding my bag in front of me like a shield. "Fine. Talk."

Jenn wipes her forehead. "It's complicated," she starts.

"*Un*complicate it."

"I didn't mean to do it, Z—"

"*It*," I say. Finally, I face her. "You fucking kissed me, Jennifer. On the *mouth*. For *starters*! And then you . . . do you realize . . . god, I don't even *know*." And, well, there it is.

That morning at her house, I was paralyzed; "shocked" would be a polite way to put it.

I couldn't breathe, couldn't blink. Her hands wandered over my entire body. Not until her touch drifted below my waist did I push myself up. I stumbled around to find my clothes as she sat up, all frowny-face like I'd done something confusing. Jenn said my name, with a question mark, and I just said, "Sorry, I need to get home."

Jenn asked, "Are you okay?"

And I—god, I *smiled*, maybe even convincingly, and said, "Uh-huh! Just gotta get home is all. See ya." Like nothing had happened.

I didn't know what else to say. What else was there?

Jenn lay back down, sighed, and stretched. Her arm snaked out and rested where my head had been on her pillow just a minute earlier. "Okay," she said. "Call me later."

So I found my keys and drove home, took the longest, hottest shower on record, and did *not* call her, did *not* answer the phone for the following week. The next time I saw her was the night I met Mike at The Graveyard. And that was almost a month ago now.

Jenn takes a long, deep breath and lets it out. I don't think she's faking the way it shakes.

"This is a lot harder than I thought it would be," she says.

"Why."

"Well, *because,* Z, I don't—"

"No, I mean, why did you do it? Seriously."

Jenn frowns. "You know, it took me a week to realize why you weren't talking to me. You didn't say anything. I had to figure it out myself."

"Well, I'm saying it now. Why?"

"It never occurred to you? Even a little?"

"What? Hooking up with you? Uh, no."

"No, not—that. I mean, it never occurred to you that I . . ."

I wait. Jenn crosses her stomach with her arms and leans toward me. Something in her expression makes me hurt. Goddammit, I've *missed* her. I'm having a great time with my first boyfriend, and I haven't been able to talk to her about it.

"I wanted to be close to you," Jenn says. "From the first time we hung out. You were *there,* and you seemed to care at least a little. . . ."

"Of course I cared, Jenn! But not like *that.* So, what, you're gay? God, just say so! I mean, in and of itself? Really not a big deal."

She actually *laughs.* "No," she says. "I mean, not exactly. It's only . . . ever been . . . you. In a way."

Wait, what?

"Are you saying you—what, like, had a *crush* on me?"

"That's one word for it," Jenn says. "I guess."

"Okay, so you're bi. You could've just said that, too."

"But I'm not! . . . I don't think . . ."

For the first time, it occurs to me to ask her this: "Have you slept with any girls before?"

". . . Sort of?"

That's news. I shouldn't be surprised. "All right, so there it is. So what?"

"But it wasn't the same thing," Jenn says, her eyebrows bunching together. "It was just—it was sex, okay, yes. But it didn't feel the same. There isn't anyone else I ever felt like this about. I mean, do you know how many guys I've slept with?"

"Um, rounded up? A lot."

"But I didn't love any of them. I know they didn't love me. The next one won't be any different. With you, I could be myself. You're the only person who's ever made me feel that way. Like I was worth something."

Jesus, Jenn. I stare at my boots, taking this in.

"When I'm with *you*, hanging out or coffee or going to those shows . . . it's the only time I feel close to being *me*. If that makes any sense."

I wish it didn't. I wish I couldn't compare that feeling to the one I get when I'm with Mike. I wish.

"But you're *always* with those guys!" I point out. "If you wanted to be around me, why be with them so much?"

"Because sometimes . . . feeling something else is better, I guess. *Anything* else."

Oh.

"I didn't mean to hurt you, Z, and I am so sorry if I did. It wasn't about anything like—you know, like getting together. It was about you."

I hesitate, not sure I want to know the answer to my next question. "So, if I hadn't gotten up, if I hadn't gone home when I did . . . how . . . *far* exactly did you plan on going?"

Jenn angles away. "I really don't know." She pinches the bridge of her nose, eyes squeezing shut. "God, I'm sorry, you must hate me so much right now."

"No," I say cautiously. "I don't. But I mean . . . I never wanted to, like, see you naked, you know?"

"It's okay," she says. "I get it. I wasn't thinking, and I didn't know how to tell you how I felt all these years." Then she adds quietly: "But you didn't stop me."

That pisses me off, but only for a second. Because god-dammit, I knew. I knew it was happening, and I didn't tell her to stop. Maybe it was the way she looked at me, like I was . . . I dunno. Priceless. When Mike looks at me, I feel cool. Badass. Punk-rock. That morning, Jenn looked at me like I mattered more than anything in the world. More than music, more than art.

"I'm a slut," Jenn blurts, and her bitterness is damn near tangible. "It's, like, the only language I speak. I'm good at it. Never been good at anything else. I can't write you a song or paint you a picture. I would have if I could."

"You could have told me. You could have just said it like you did just now."

"And what would you have done, huh, Zero? Given me a nice big hug? Like that wouldn't change everything?"

"And this didn't?"

Twin tears trickle down Jenn's face. I cross my arms, my shoulders bunching up around my ears. Somehow I feel more naked now than I did in her room, and we were *dressed* then. For the most part.

I try to regroup. "Jenn, it's not—look, it's not what you did, it's who you are. You know? It wasn't fair. If you'd just said something, we could've talked about it. But you didn't talk, you acted. Just like always."

Which, even as I'm saying it, I realize is something I've admired about her, despite myself. I could never go around hooking up with people the way she does. Still—there's a confidence to it, no matter how messed up it might be.

I stare at the middle space between us, not meeting her eyes. I don't want to know what I'd see there, whatever that could be. I hate that she's upset, I do. But I mean . . . what now?

"Jenn, I don't know what else to say here."

"Me either. I don't know *how* to talk, that's why I just . . . did what I know how to do. I want to be able to hang out with you again. You know? Like we used to? I don't have anyone else."

Here's the thing.

She's right.

For all the time we've spent at each other's houses the past four years, it's been months since I've seen her parents. And as for all the guys—and girls, apparently—none of them lasted more than a few days. At least when *I'm* by myself, I'm painting or drawing. Maybe it's true I'm not my biggest fan, like Mike said, but at least I get along with me. I don't think that's true for Jenn. I'm alive when I'm alone and working.

What's Jenn got, when she's alone?

"I'm sorry," I say.

"Huh. You didn't do anything to apologize for. Maybe I should've just told you what I was thinking that night about my mom and dad."

"Wait, what about them?"

Jenn sniffs, and rubs at one eye. "They weren't even there, Zero. At graduation. I know you were kinda focused on that scholarship letter, so I get it if you didn't notice. But they didn't even *care.* You did. You were there. I know you were upset, but you still saw me. You hugged me."

God. At least Mom and Dad came to graduation. Dad gave me a gift certificate for Landscapes Art Supply, Mom hugged me, and for just a little while, despite the SAIC letter, everything was good—no arguments or alcohol. Jenn lingered awkwardly nearby. Mom hugged her, too, but now that Jenn's saying all this, I realize it can't be the same as if your own mom or dad was doing it.

"I guess I sorta freaked out," Jenn goes on. "But I didn't want to talk about it. About *them.*"

"It's okay," I say quietly. "I get it."

"I swear to god, I won't ever do anything like that again," Jenn says. "I won't. I mean, unless . . ."

She lets the word hang.

I shake my head. "Look, I don't want to make you mad or

anything, but I'm kinda like looking around inside myself.
right now? And it's just not there. I think I'd know. I'm in love
for the first time in my life, and it's with Mike."

Whoa. Did I really just say that?

Yep. Ohhhh-kay. We'll come back to that.

Jenn jerks her head up. "Mike?" she goes. "The drummer? You're going out now?"

"Pretty much, yeah."

I can see she wants to know more. Until that night, I'd've
told her, too. Told her everything. Now I'm not sure I can.
But I still want to.

"That's cool," Jenn says, clearly disappointed that I don't
give up more information. "So . . . what do we do now? I
mean, can we hang out again? Sometime?"

Part of me wants to say no. But there's this other part . . .
I mean, she is my best friend. And come to think of it, it
must've taken a lot of guts for her to track me down, make me
listen to her apology. I can't just ignore that. If it was me, I
would've just locked myself in my room. Like, *forever.* I
wouldn't have tried to contact her at all. Jenn knows me well
enough to know that, too. But here she is anyway, trying like
hell to make it okay.

Jenn makes no move, no sound. Her shoulders are
slumped, her hands forming tight fists like—

Like her heart is broken.

Maybe for the first time in her life.

"Yes," I say.

She looks up. "You sure?"

I'm not, but I can't say it. "Yeah."

Jenn's expression softens. "Thanks, Z."

We both stand, looking at each other and not.

"Would it be okay if I hugged you?" she asks.

I don't say anything. Just step toward her and wrap her in both arms. She does the same. Gotta say, it's a weird thing; it feels good, like we're going to be okay now, but awkward too, knowing what I know now. And as I hug her, I sort of feel her body relax, like a weight's been lifted.

We split apart, and Jenn smiles a bit. "So, you'll call me?"

"Or you can. Whatever."

"Cool. Thanks for listening to me. And I'm really sorry."

"Tell ya what," I say. "It's done. Everything's out in the open, and . . . we know where we stand, right? So we strike it from the record and go from here."

Jenn, still smiling that little smile, shakes her head. "You're pretty awesome, Z."

"Yeah, I can't help it." I finally smile back at her.

Jenn gives me a short little wave. I watch until she disappears around the library, then sit back down on the bench.

Ever wonder why it's called a crush?

Now I know.

twelve

[I]nstead of stubbornly attempting to use
surrealism for purposes of subversion,
it is necessary to try to make of surrealism
something as solid, complete and classic
as the works of museums.

–Salvador Dalí

"So, you free tonight?" Mike says the following Tuesday night on the phone.

"Nope," I say. "I was planning on hanging with my boyfriend."

Gothic Rainbow played two gigs over the weekend, F'ing killer shows that blew the roof off these tiny dives where there was barely enough room for all their equipment. But they headlined, which on the one hand means they got paid more than the other bands that night, but on the other hand didn't amount to much, since the venues were so small.

"So yes, I'm free," I add, eyeing my next painting for Doc S with disdain. Whether for her or the work, I'm not sure. This one's the skyline of downtown Phoenix, as seen from Camelback, stretching and twisting upward into a sort of black hole in the sky where the moon should be.

"Cool. Can you bring your gear and meet me at Hole in the Wall?"

"My *gear*? Shooting black tar heroin now, are we?"

"Oh, haha. Your art stuff. What do *you* call it? All your charcoals and whatnot?"

"My gear."

I hear Mike chuckle. "You're a mouthy broad sometimes."

"Thanks!"

"So, seven?"

"Sure," I tell him.

We say goodbye and hang up. I pack my bag with a sketchbook and box of charcoals and head out. Rather, I *intend* to, because Mom's busy cooking when I enter the kitchen, and we all know where this is headed.

"Going out," I say automatically.

Mom sighs. And I stop, hand on the door. I turn around.

"I mean, I'm going to Hole in the Wall to meet Mike," I say.

Mom glances at me. "Well," she goes, flipping a steak over. "That must've hurt."

Wow. Low blow, Mom.

Mom turns the steak again. "I'm sorry," she says suddenly. "That was rude of me, Amy. I shouldn't be that way."

My anger cools, almost as fast as it flared. "It's okay," I say. "I'll be home later."

"Oh." Mom goes back to her cooking. "Well, there will be leftovers when you get home. If you want them."

"Thanks." I open the door but hesitate. "Dad gone?"

The steak sizzles as Mom pushes a spatula hard on it. "Yes," she says, shortly.

I stand there for another few seconds, thinking about this. "I'll be home by ten," I decide.

Mom looks at me, maybe surprised. A minuscule grin struggles to make it to her lips, but she doesn't say anything.

I try to smile back and fail just as badly. I go out to my car and head to the Hole, trying to not think too much about Mom or Dad. Too many angles.

I get to the Hole right as Mike is skating down the sidewalk. I watch, tingly, as he effortlessly launches the board into the air and sails over a bus-stop bench, like he's surfing the wind. He lands flawlessly, alternates the nose of his board with the tail, back and forth, several times, and rolls to a stop beside my car.

"Okay, so, *that* was dead sexy," I say.

Mike kisses me. It sears me, no kidding. The time is coming when kissing alone ain't gonna cut it. Not sure yet what that means, exactly.

"Sorry," he says. "I wasn't trying to show off or anything."

"Don't let me stop you," I say, and flick my foot up from the knee to smack his butt.

The Hole is maybe half full when we go inside. I sit across from him at a table and set my bag down.

"Okay, I brought the gear," I say. "What's up?"

Mike grins. "Well, we got a show on the Fourth at Liberty Spike's, you been there?"

"Yeah. Not bad. A little more rough and tumble than I care for, but, yeah. And on the Fourth of July? It'll be explosive! Ha! I should be *pun*ished!"

Mike rolls his eyes but smiles. "Agreed. On all fronts.

Anyway, we usually let Eddie make our flyers because—well, he's Eddie and he figures he has Photoshop, so clearly the job should be his."

"Not reason enough. I've *seen* those flyers. No offense."

"Yeah, no argument there. What do you have to draw with?"

"What do *I* have to draw with?" I grab his hand and shake it. "Hi, I'm Zero, nice to meet you." I pull out my sketch pad and a charcoal. "What would you like?"

"A flyer for the show. Would you make one?" His eyes twinkle at me, and he squeezes my hand.

Wow. Color me flattered. I never would have presumed to ask. Another little splash for my portfolio, even. This is, like . . . being commissioned to do art.

"Yeah, that would be cool!" I tell him. "Is this a paid gig?" I kick his shoe playfully under the table.

"I do wish," he says. "If we could, we would. And if you don't want—"

"Totally kidding," I say. I mean, it'd be cool, but seriously, it doesn't bother me. I'm thrilled to be *asked*.

I give him a quick kiss. "What're you looking for exactly?"

Mike rattles off a list: time, date, all that. Then we get into the design itself. I start with a quick charcoal sketch of Liberty Spike's facade, then add three giant Dalí ants to it. Halfway through my fourth ant, my hand cramps and I lift it off the paper.

"Yeah, that looks—what's wrong?" Mike says.

I stare at the drawing for a second. The style is mine, I recognize it, but there's a *flourish* to it that my charcoals have never had before. And then it hits me: this is exactly the gesture technique Dr. Salinger taught us that first day. The one I couldn't make myself do at the time but that I've been practicing ever since, especially those days when she doesn't show up.

"Um . . . nothing," I say.

Mike gives me a look but lets my nonanswer slide. Thank you, Mike.

I flip to a fresh page and go back to work. Inspired, I gesture-draw a reasonable facsimile of Jackson Pollock's *Greyed Rainbow* as a background, then use an eraser and white pastel stick to create the show information. All right, so it's a stretch; no one is going to look at the swirls of black and white coils and say, "Oh, hey! Jackson Pollock! *Greyed Rainbow*! Hey, that's like Gothic Rainbow but different! What a gifted artist!" But *I'll* know, and right now, that's enough.

We go through an iced coffee and one bathroom visit apiece, and half a sketchbook to get the design just right, and probably spend more time than Eddie would have sitting at his computer.

But it's great. I'm talking to Mike about art, and I'm creating it *for* him. It doesn't get much better.

"Yeah, yeah, that's cool," Mike says, pointing to another Dalí-esque sketch of Spike's.

"Okay. Not a problem. You want it in black and white? Like this?"

"Up to you. You're the artist."

"You're the *client*."

He smirks at me. "Charcoal, then. Sure." He gives me a quick kiss on the cheek, which you wouldn't think would be cause for my body to erupt, volcanolike, into totally useless sexual desire, but it does.

"Could you . . . um . . . do that one more time, please?"

Mike puts his lips to my cheek. My eyes close. He lingers there this time, like he's individually triggering every nerve on my face.

"Okay," I say, a little breathless. "I think I have a *boner*."

"Really."

"Oh, gosh, did I upset your delicate sensibilities?"

"No. My sensibilities aren't that delicate."

I laugh and kiss his cheek in return. Then on my periphery, I catch a glance of copper-colored curly hair and pull away from Mike.

"Jenn?"

Jenn hesitates at the entrance to the room, looking uncertain. "Hi," she says cautiously. She's carrying several catalogs of some kind in her arms. "I didn't know you were going to be here, then I saw your car, and I thought I'd say hi, maybe, but I can go someplace else. . . ."

Man. I've never seen Jenn spin out like this.

"No, no, come here," I say, waving her over.

Jenn gives me a tentative smile, and joins us at the table.

"Jenn, this is Mike," I say, gesturing to him in case she doesn't know which guy I'm referring to. My stomach starts churning my iced coffee into slush. Fact is, I have no idea how this is going to go. It could be weird for her. Under the circumstances.

"How's it going?" Mike says, tucking his bangs behind his ears and reaching across the table for a handshake.

Jenn shakes it, a limp-wristed little girlie thing. "I guess I could ask you the same question," she says, and drops the catalogs on the table. They're from a bunch of different colleges.

"Pretty good," Mike says. "So how do you know each other?"

"Oh, we go way back," Jenn says.

"We met on a field trip to the Phoenix Art Museum freshman year," I say.

"No surprise, right?" Jenn asks Mike, gesturing to my sketch pad. "Her paintings are going to hang there someday, right, Z?"

"Yeah, well . . ."

Mike bails me out of having to flatter myself. "Starting school?" he asks Jenn.

"Hm? Oh yeah. Maybe." She turns to me. "I was thinking maybe culinary school?"

"Totally!" I say. It's the first time she's mentioned anything resembling a future. "That would be perfect. Where at?" I sort through the catalogs.

Jenn shrugs. "Anyplace that'll have me." She assumes Mr. Haight's blustery business voice: "And money is no object, princess!" She rolls her eyes.

"That's really cool," I tell her, meaning it.

Jenn, for the first time ever, looks shy. "Thanks. It's just a thought."

Mike cocks his head at me. "Do you cook, too?"

"I *toast*," I say. "And occasionally reheat. Jenn's really good, though."

Jenn smiles and nudges me with her elbow. "Shut up!"

We all laugh briefly. And then: silence. Awkward, but not quite uncomfortable.

Jenn clears her throat. "So!" she says, and hesitates, like she has no idea what to say next. That makes two of us. Jenn looks at me. "Do I get to—you know. Interrogate?"

I raise an eyebrow, about to stop her. But her gaze is sort of pleading. In all of a heartbeat, she asks me telepathically: *You said we could just move on and be friends again, so we can talk about your boyfriend and my boyfriends and all that and just forget that night ever happened, remember?*

And the truth is . . . I did say that.

So I poke her in the ribs. Jenn screeches and angles out of the way. And just like that, it's cool. Mike watches all this with an amused grin.

"Only if you're nice," I tell her.

Jenn surreptitiously exhales, looking relieved. "Of course," she says. She turns to Mike. "So, Mike. What's it like to kiss the inimitable Amanda Walsh?"

"Jenn!"

She throws me a startled glance. Again I debate steering the conversation somewhere else, but then I understand: if this was a couple of months ago, it's exactly the kind of thing she would have asked. She's defaulting to how we were before graduation.

It's weird, no doubt about it. But maybe she's got the right idea. Forgive *and* forget.

Plus . . . I maybe sort of kinda want to know what Mike'll say.

"You don't have to answer that," I tell Mike, because I gotta pretend like I *don't* want to know.

But Mike nods slowly. "Pretty damn sweet," he says.

"Well, sure," Jenn goes, "but you can do better than that. Is it sexy, luscious, spicy, *caliente* . . . what?"

Mike's eyebrows twitch once, real fast. Still looking at Jenn—but talking to me, I think, I *hope*—he says, "It's, uh . . . a work of art."

Michael? I. Am. Yours. Pinwheels spin my vision kooky. I'm such a dork.

"Wow," Jenn marvels. "You know how to make a girl squirm, don't you?"

"Aaaaand we're done," I say, dropping my arm between them.

"I want to know what his intentions are," Jenn says. "It's my job as best friend to do that."

"That's fair," Mike says. "But as much as I would like to discuss *and* pursue my intentions, I kinda need a break, so, be back in a sec."

He gets up and heads for the bathroom. Jenn and I both watch him go.

Jenn sort of grins. "He really is your first, huh? You know . . . real thing. Like, boyfriend."

"Well! . . . Yeah. So?"

"*So* . . . have you thought about it at all?"

"About what?"

"You know," Jenn says tentatively. "Making love to him."

"Whoa, whoa, whoa, we've only kissed!"

Then I look around, make sure no one's in earshot.

"Okay, maybe a *little*," I whisper. "But not for *real* real. It's only been, like, a month or so." Sure, it's crossed my mind, but in a nebulous sort of way. I mean, I'd *like* to. Someday.

"That's good," Jenn says, touching my arm. "I think it's

great if you don't necessarily want to hook up right away. But—" She stops and presses her lips together.

"Woman, you *really* need to finish that thought!"

Jenn considers for a second. "Look, if he *is* your first love, it might be destined to end the same as most first loves do. That's all. You should see your face when he's in the room. God, Zero, you were *glowing*."

I kick at the floor with the toe of one boot. I know exactly what Jenn means; it's the best description for the feeling I get when I think of Mike.

"I just don't want you to get your heart broken," Jenn adds, and her expression tightens a little, like it hurts her to say it but she means it all the same.

"I see what you're saying," I admit, voice low. "But isn't it a little early to be worried about that?"

"Not if you go off into one of your freaky artistic depressions, it isn't."

I give her my best glare. It doesn't faze her. Jenn's well-versed in my predilection toward locking myself in my room and not emerging for a week, a month, at a time.

"I'm just saying," Jenn says. "You're so—I don't know, sensitive? Sometimes that's good. Sometimes I wish I was more like that. But then other times, it messes with your head. What was that guy's name sophomore year?"

Oh god, here we go. "Joel," I mumble.

"Right, Joel. So Joel asks you out—"

"Jenn, I was there, I remember."

"—and you say yes, and when he shows up at your house—"

"I just *said* I was there, Jenn."

"—you make your dad tell him you have food poisoning and can't go out!"

"It was septicemic plague," I remind her.

"Okay, *gross*. But he was a nice guy, and he was really into you, and you dodged him. Then when he started going out with Kelly Tansy—"

"Who's a bitch!"

"Fact, but irrelevant. When he started going out with her, you spent the rest of sophomore year dressing like . . . like *death*, for god's sake. And Z, that was *without* a broken heart. I mean, like, the real deal, the kind that feels like your heart got ripped out of your body and kicked off a cliff. I just want you to be okay." Jenn scratches her neck. "I hope that doesn't sound weird coming from me. . . ."

"That's what friends do," I mumble, thinking more about Mike than her. Maybe Jenn's right. If anything goes wrong with Mike, how'm I going to handle it?

Wait. No. The one thing I can't do is anticipate that. Because—

Here's the thing.

Jenn *is* right. Mike's my first. Love, I mean. And that's dangerous. I get that. But if I spend every minute we have together worrying about that, isn't it just as likely that I'll screw the whole thing up by *accident*? There's still SAIC to consider, but that's, like, at least a year away, probably two, and what are the chances I'll get into SAIC anyway? I'll probably just end up at Arizona State, like it or not, so we could still be together. . . .

"I don't think I can worry about it right now," I tell Jenn.

"That's cool," Jenn says. "Are you mad at me?"

"For what?"

"Saying all this."

"No, no. I see what you're saying. But I'm not going to think about that, is all. And yes, I'll take it slow. Plus, *if* we ever did it, I'm sure I'd suck, so probably best not to embarrass myself."

"You mean sex?"

"Rebuilding a carburetor. Yes, *sex*, Jenn. I don't know what a carburetor is, either, though, come to think of it."

I lean even closer and drop my voice to a whisper. Kinda crazy to be asking *her, this, now*, but she knows more than I do. "How do you know when? I mean, how do *I* know when? It's not gonna be anytime soon. But."

Jenn takes my hands into hers. I don't stop her. She inches nearer.

"When there comes a point," she says in a conspiratorial tone, "when words aren't enough. When there's absolutely no other way to say what you mean. Like, it's the only way you can make clear how much they mean to you." She squeezes my hands and leans back. "I mean, I kind of loved my first. But that's not why I did it. And I guess I kinda wish I hadn't now. So, yeah, don't rush it."

"But *you* rushed it."

"Which is why I'm telling you not to. Wait awhile. Wait a year. Wait *four*. Whatever. If he's the right guy, he'll wait for you. And in the meantime, I have to say, there's something about just, you know, *touching* and kissing that can get lost afterward, so enjoy it."

Is it in any way ironic that this woman makes so much sense? Discuss.

"Gotta say, it's nice to see you looking not quite so lonely," she adds.

"I used to?"

"Every day, kiddo."

I didn't know that. But I'm not surprised.

"And when I feel that way, I go find someone," Jenn mutters. "It's never enough. It's never real."

"You must feel that way a lot," I go, but grin so she knows I'm kidding with her.

Jenn doesn't grin back. "Yeah," she says softly.

Ouch. God, I *suck*! *And the Bad Timing Award goes to . . . !*

I reach for her shoulder. "Jenn . . ."

But then Mike walks back in, and I drop my hand. Jenn gives me a quick head shake, dismissing my worry, like it's all good. She turns back to him as he sits.

"Miss anything?" Mike asks.

"Girl talk," Jenn says airily. "So are you going to be nice to her?"

"That is my . . . *intention*, was the word, I think."

"Cool," Jenn says. "You can stay." She smiles for him, and I feel relieved somehow.

Jenn gets up. "Well, I don't want to keep you guys. Nice meeting you, Mike." She gives me a hug, which I return. We say goodbye. Jenn gathers her catalogs and dances out of the room. And I feel remarkably good about the whole thing.

"So I can stay?" Mike says.

"What? Oh. Heh. Yeah, as long as you want."

"Whew. So she's your, like, best friend?"

"Yeah. Best-slash-only."

"You never mentioned her before."

Gulp.

"Yeah, well, see, we had a . . . problem. Issue. Movie of the week, or a very special episode. You know?"

Mike nods. "I get it," he says. "It's all good now?"

"Yeah," I say. "It actually is."

"Cool," Mike says, turning back to my sketchbook and studying my drawings. Under his breath, he adds, "Friends are how God apologizes for your family."

Amen to that.

I take Mike home about an hour later—then spend thirty minutes in the car, since, clearly, we have to make out in my front seat before I can even think of going to sleep. Mike knows exactly what to do and not do. He keeps his hands on my neck, or hips, or side. Doesn't try to sneak them to anyplace I'm not ready for. How ready I am is up for debate, but he doesn't rush me. And that makes kissing him so, so good.

Eventually, we peel ourselves off each other, and he gives me a quick smile.

"I'll call ya about the Spike's gig," he says. "See ya later."

"Later, skater!"

I watch him until he goes inside the house, then drive home, all warm and girlie. The night improves even more when I'm able to get into the house without attracting Mom's attention from the living room; Dad's truck, of course, is gone.

But when I open the door to my room, the first thing I think is, *Bitch*.

Mom's been in here without my say-so.

But my second thought is, *What's with all the packages?*

I haven't even crossed the threshold when Mom suddenly appears behind me. "I did a little shopping for you," she says quietly.

I walk to my bed. There are about a dozen flat boxes and fancy sacks. New clothes are in all of them.

"But what—why?"

"Sort of an early birthday, I suppose," Mom says, leaning against my door frame and *not* coming in. "Seemed like a good time. School starting. A new boyfriend . . ." She tries on an uncertain smile.

"Um . . . thanks," I say, and poke through the clothes again. She's, um . . . Well, they're not things I would've picked out, to say the least. But they're not *entirely* lame, either.

Mom clears her throat a little. "So, I've been wondering," she goes, "have you thought at all about looking into any more scholarships?"

"Not especially, no." I'm probably going to fail Doc Salinger's dumb class, based on my last few assignments. While she hasn't told us our grades on anything we've done yet, I'm sure my assignments have been pathetic. I'm not convinced I'm ready to submit myself to the fresh hell of building another asinine portfolio.

"Oh, well, I just thought with your art and all . . ." Mom's gaze lifts to my ceiling, and lingers for a sec on the painting of my mirror-face. "I know you were disappointed about Chicago, but perhaps there are loans or something you might qualify for. You could use your school money for a dorm or something. If you had to."

What is this, a hint? Get the hell out? Listen, lady, the plans are in the works, trust me. "Uh . . . yeah, sure. I'll look into it again." But I don't really mean it. Maybe Arizona State wouldn't be a total loss. . . .

"Good," Mom says. "That's good. You really do need to finish school, Amy."

"That's the plan, Mom." Even if it's not SAIC, CalArts, any good F'ing school? I guess.

"Good. Good. Well, I won't bother you." She gestures toward the clothes. "Let me know if you want to keep any of that. I kept the receipts, I can take it all back if you—"

"No, no, they're nice. They're good. Thanks."

"Well, if you change your mind."

"Okay." I'll change my mind if they make me look like more of a hippopotamus, yes.

Mom sort of nods, and backs out down the hall.

Strange.

I pull out all of the clothes, shut my door, and start trying them on. They're all too tight, I think. Which stands to reason, considering my epic girth. But . . . they're kinda nice. There's even a—wait for it—*skirt* that is actually kinda cute: red-and-white-patterned, tight around my hips, and swooshing out with these sort of ruffles or something. I don't know what you call them. But it looks okay.

I decide to try one of the outfits out the next time I see Mike. Just to see.

thirteen

A painting is such a minor thing
compared with the magic I radiate.

—Salvador Dalí

It's early on the Fourth of July when GR and their now resident artist (me!) show up for the Liberty Spike's gig. GR's opening for a couple of other bands, including Nightrage, which is headlining, so we arrive way before it gets dark, which in July is, like, eight-thirty. I wear a new pair of walking shorts from Mom's trip, red plaid, and two layered tanks, black and white; and when no one's looking, Mike gives my rear a little pat, and I hafta say . . . score one for Mom.

Liberty Spike's is freaking *packed* when Gothic Rainbow takes the stage. I'd like to think it's because of the flyers I designed—I ended up choosing the Dalí ant version over the Pollock—even though that's probably not the case. The crowd starts cheering before they even play a song. Even Hob looks a little surprised at the reception. Spike's isn't known for its welcoming atmosphere. Already there's a group of skins standing in the middle of the dance floor, readying to become bald pillars around which the inevitable pit will form. But they're cheering, too. Not sure if that's a good thing or bad thing.

"What's up?" Hobbit calls into his mic as Brook slaps hands with people at the front of the stage.

The crowd roars back at him. Hob can't hide a decidedly unpunk smile as he plays a test chord on his black guitar.

"Hey, anyone know this song?" he says, and jumps into the introduction of one of their originals.

A *lot* of people know it. There are several screams of recognition, and the people not immediately launching into the pit are trying to sing along.

> *I was standing on the top of the world*
> *Letting the wind blow and shuffle my hair*
> *Into kings and queens and black diamonds*
> *When the earth died and the wind went still!*

They are on fire from the get-go. Mike's beat vibrates my entire body, Hobbit's voice punctures the crowd, Brook's fingers are magic, and even Eddie puts on a bit more of a show than usual. Punks are lifted up by their compatriots and flung about on dozens of upturned hands. Security doesn't even bother trying to stop them. Smart men.

> *Spent my last days with a soda*
> *Glaring out the window at the world*
> *Asked myself just what I'd missed*
> *From the entrance from the outside to in*

The crowd eats up every syllable—everyone except for one guy near the back, who's crossed his arms and seems to be studying the band like Dr. Salinger studies my paintings. Instead of dancing or singing along, he just watches and seems to be taking mental notes. Halfway through the song, he pushes his horn-rim glasses up on his nose and leans over to this Asian girl and says something into her ear. She's maybe in her early twenties but peers over thin oval specs at the band like a grandmother. Weird. Get *into* it, losers!

> *Spent my life living in a hospice*
> *Each day looking forward to death*
> *Eating stale cream cheese and rice cakes...*

I remember this part from the last couple shows. I love it, and so does everyone else in Spike's. The band trails off to silence, but it's like the rest of us have rehearsed this moment.

We all scream at the top of our lungs: *"And smokin' till my very last breath!"*

So I don't smoke, sue me. It just feels right.

Hob's face explodes with joy. Brook rapid-fires a *"One-two-three-four!"* and the band kicks in again. The club screeches approval.

Hob tosses in a few well-placed *pickitup pickitup*s over Brook's solo, and the pit at the edge of the stage obeys him, guys tearing through each other like rabid animals.

I laugh out loud and absolutely burn for Mike. I'm loving the show, there's no doubt, but I have to have him. Sweaty, tired, spent—and that's before I'm done with him, ha!—

whatever condition he's in after the show, I can't let the night end without maybe turning the heat up a little.

Geez. Down, girl.

But I'm ready. I really am.

To distract myself, I check out the two people at the rear of the club again. They're still watching the band and attempting to have a conversation over the glorious noise, shouting into each other's ears. When the song ends and we all cheer, they clap but don't holler.

"Man! Thanks, everyone," Hob says into his mic as Brook's last chord fades. "That was kick-ass. Thank you, sir, may I have another?"

He pounds down on the guitar—a Les Paul, Mike has told me—and the next song starts.

This one is a Misfits cover, which they bring to life wickedly better than the original, in my humble and *entirely unbiased* opinion.

Twenty minutes go by in fast-forward. Spike's fills with sweat and smoke and the shouts of overjoyed punkers as GR creates a canvas for them all to spill their guts onto. My first experience with them at the Graveyard gig was awesome, but this—it's, like, *transcendent.* I see a golden record spinning in my head and flinging itself onto Mike's bare bedroom wall.

Hob glances up at the sound booth in back of the venue. I see the sound guy hold up his index finger.

Hob nods. "Okay, we got one more for ya tonight. This is kinda new for us. This song's by a band outta England called the Levellers . . ."

Three point two people clap. Who the hell are the Levellers? I feel my street cred plummet.

". . . and they play with, like, bagpipes and fiddles and stuff . . . but, uh, we *don't*. This is for a friend of ours out there in the crowd tonight; it's called 'Is This Art.' Here we go."

I'm frozen in place. *Is this art?*

The song consists of heavy bass and just three or four darkened chords, as far as I can tell; not unusual for GR or any other band that plays Spike's. But it punches into me with more ferocity than their other songs. Because—and I *have* to be right about this—it's for me.

The song is basically about how science and technology are worshipped as the ultimate form of art, which the song then questions *(Now isn't nature wonderful/But is this art?)*. So it's not exactly about surrealism or Seurat, but it doesn't have to be.

Halfway through the song, Hob announces, "Ladies and gentlemen . . . drum solo!"

The crowd cheers as Mike's arms blur behind his kit and the other guys play quietly underneath. Somehow, through the whirlwind, Mike looks out at the audience and finds me. He smiles without missing one incredible beat.

Thank you, I mouth to him.

Mike ends with a spectacular drumroll that sounds like there are two kits onstage. They finish the song with a crash, and we their disciples raise our hands and scream.

"Cool, thanksalot, we're Gothic Rainbow, sssssee ya!"

The Vandals begins playing over the speakers while the band tears down their gear. I am parched and sweaty— correction, *glistening*—so I weasel over to the bar for a soda. I end up beside the lanky guy and his Asian chick.

"We could look at November," the girl is saying.

"Eh, we're booked through then," the guy says.

Booked. This term rings a bell.

"Think they can fill it, though?" she goes.

The guy looks around at the crowd. "Dunno," he goes. "But a lot of these guys seemed to know the songs. That's not bad." He picks up one of my flyers from the box office counter and studies it.

I get my soda, but instead of heading backstage to assault my boyfriend, I continue to eavesdrop.

The girl shrugs. "Give them a few months? If BP hits big, we could really kill. What about that last Nightrage show in August?"

I'm pretty sure by BP she means Black Phantom, and to kill generally means a good thing, as in, *make a killing.* These must be promoters. I start to move toward them to ask, but they head out of the building just as the band comes from backstage.

Forgetting the promoters, I launch myself toward Mike. I kiss him hard.

"That was awesome!" I say, *calmly,* not at *all* like a gushing girlfriend-fan.

"Thanks! Felt like it. We're packed up out front . . . you ready to go?"

"Sure, where to?"

Brook squeezes between us. "Pizza!" he announces. "Let's head to Rome's, yeah?"

Mike shrugs. "I could eat. Z?"

"Yeah!" I could keep kissing him all night, too, but that's okay. I'll get my turn.

"Cool!" Hob bellows. "Lemme get our take and we'll head out!"

We follow Hob to the box office. Eddie and Brook walk out of Spike's, trading war stories of the evening's success. Hob waits for a couple of people to pay the cover and come in before stepping up to the counter.

"Hey, Steven," Hob says to this guy running the box office out of a lockbox. "We're outta here, man."

"All right," Steven says.

Hob stands there, waiting. Steven does nothing except dig a finger into one ear and root around.

"So, uh . . . ," Hob goes. "Our cut?"

Steven grunts. He reaches into the lockbox and counts out four ten-dollar bills. "Here," he says, and shoves the stack toward Hobbit.

Hob looks at the money, then back at Steven. "What's this?"

"Ten bucks apiece."

"Whoa," Hob says. "You said ten percent."

"Oh yeah?"

"There's, like, a hundred people here tonight."

"Huh." Steven looks bored.

Mike slides silently between Hob and the counter as Hob lurches toward Steven. "Hell's this?" Hob demands. "How about closer to a hundred bucks, dude?"

"Hob," Mike goes.

Steven scowls in Hobbit's face, and I can *feel* Hobbit's immense frame tensing.

"I got a room fee to cover. Take it or leave it," Steven says.

"How 'bout I take your fuckin' head off!"

"Okay, time to go," Mike says, and prods Hobbit away from the counter.

"This is bullshit!" Hob roars as Mike continues pushing him toward the exit. Other patrons turn to watch. "You know that, man? Real cool!"

"Shut up," Steven says, apparently believing that the counter will keep Hob from tearing his head off.

"I'm gonna fuck you back into your mother, you prick!" Hob screams, and tries to reach past Mike to the counter. Adrenaline dumps into my stomach.

"Get outta here!" Steven yells back, but he's clearly, and rightly, scared pissless.

Thankfully, Hobbit *allows* Mike to pull him to the exit, screaming all the while. The crowd makes a path for him, which I scurry through as well.

We pile out of Spike's. Brook and Eddie are across the parking lot, standing beside Brook's car. They turn toward us as Hob's voice echoes through the night. He's still in full-rant mode when we reach the guys.

"Forty bucks, man!" Hobbit fumes. "What the hell're we supposed to do with this? Huh? How the hell we supposed to live on this?"

"What happened?" Eddie whines.

"Got screwed," Mike says.

I nudge Mike. "What's a room fee?" I whisper.

"Like rent, what the promoters pay the venue," Mike whispers back as Hob continues to rampage. "But Steven's not paying Spike's more than maybe ten percent, and even if he is, he's walking tonight with at least five hundred. Well, five-sixty or more, now."

"Forty bucks!" Hob howls. "What the holy hell are we supposed to do with this?"

"We can order pizza," Brook says, smiling carelessly. Fireworks begin to go off a few miles away. Happy Fourth.

"It ain't about pizza!" Hobbit shouts. "It's about . . ."

He trails off, staring at Brook, whose easy smile has receded but still lingers. Suddenly Hob's rage breaks.

"Huh," he grunts. "Okay. Pizza. Shit."

Brook slaps Hobbit's back. "Place is a dive, man," he goes. "And forty bucks, hey, that's prob'ly more than the other guys got."

"Nightrage'll get paid out full," Hobbit says.

"Everyone knows Steven sucks on Nightrage's tit," Brook says. "We shoulda expected it. No big deal, dude."

"Yeah, and they're dicks, while we're charming and remarkably attractive," Mike says. "We can always fall back on that."

Hobbit laughs at last, and the night is saved.

"You had the whole place going," I tell him, trying to help. "It was an awesome show. People were talking about you." *And* scoping out my awesome flyers, but I don't say it.

Hob pauses at the door to his van, which holds the band's gear. "What people? Sayin' what?"

"This Asian girl and a sorta lanky-looking white guy. They were talking about Black Phantom, I think, and—"

Hob speeds toward me like a bull. "A Chinese chick?" he demands. The other guys all look at each other seriously.

"Um . . . Asian. I don't know if she was Chi—"

"Did you hear their names? What'd they say? They were watchin' us?"

I bunch up my shoulders as if Hob's going to take a swing at me. The other three start edging closer but not to restrain Hobbit; they're all eyeing *me*.

"Yeah, uh . . . they were watching you guys play, but they weren't really getting into it, just sorta watching. The girl said something about booking in August, and that the audience knew your songs, and they should wait and see how BP did because if they hit big . . ."

Halfway through this monologue, Hob turns away and holds his head with both hands, exhaling heavily. Mike, Eddie, and Brook all trade glances.

"Did I miss something?" I venture.

"Holy shit!" Hobbit roars. A firecracker goes off, punctuating his shout.

"It was Four Eyes Entertainment," Mike says. "Most likely." And a skyrocket explodes in the sky, shining white sparkles in his eyes. He looks, like, *mischievous* all of a sudden.

Hob leans over and braces himself on his knees. "Oh, man. Dude. You guys."

"They say anything else?" Brook asks me.

"Not really. I mean, I knew they were talking about *you*, but I didn't know I should be listening for anything in particular. They took one of the flyers with them, if that matters."

"Your kick-ass flyers," Mike says, rubbing my back and still smiling.

"Was that really them?" Eddie gasps, like he's having a coronary. "D'you think?"

"Hell yeah it was!" Hob says. "Think we should call 'em?"

"Nah, bad form," Mike says, sliding his hand off my

back—brushing my rear, which tingles momentarily at his touch—and taking my hand. "They'll call if they want us."

"Which they do!" Hob says.

"All right, then, so let's eat," Mike says, opening my passenger door. "Celebrate the night away."

Hob climbs into his van with a whoop. Eddie, still shaken, takes shotgun. Hob guns the engine. Brook hops into his Bug, and I start up my Peugeot.

"So this is a big deal, right?" I say, turning out of the parking lot.

"Well, Four Eyes typically books a lot of shows at Damage Control," Mike reminds me. "So if they're looking at us to play there someday, then, yeah. Semi-big deal, anyway."

"But DC. That's a huge place."

"It is. It'd mean more exposure, and in this musically backasswards town, that's about the best you can hope for." He starts tapping a rhythm out on his knees.

I take a quick peek at him. "You're pretty excited."

Mike shrugs, but he's grinning when he does it. "We're not talking about opening for a multiplatinum band at a stadium here. It's still just Phoenix. There's not much further to go after Damage Control. We'd have to go someplace like L.A. Or Seattle, I guess, these days. But for where we're at right now, yeah. It would be a start."

I give him a quick elbow. "Just a start, huh? What about that gold record?"

"Oh, that's on the list, but I want to enjoy the ride, too," Mike says, still tapping away.

"So it's not that you don't *want* to be the next big thing someday—"

"Absolutely correct."

"—but you don't want to be successful too fast?"

"I don't want to be rushed into extinction, no. Most bands are only around for a couple years. There's a few who tour constantly because they can and they love doing it. But most of us aren't going to do this the rest of our lives. I want to enjoy the whole trip, you know? Even playing at a dive like Spike's, getting screwed on our take, it's all part of that. It's part of the *fun*. Once we start down that road to being serious, or *more* serious, anyway, then we got to stick with it and play as long and loud as we can before it's over."

I try to absorb this philosophy. Some of it hits a little too close. Maybe instant success isn't the best-case scenario. "Do you think you'll still be playing when you're, like, fifty?"

"Playing? Definitely. Touring, doing it for a living? Hard to say. Easy to say yes when I'm not even twenty." His grin widens. "But I'd be lying if I didn't say that was the plan."

"Sounds like fun."

Mike turns to look at me. His gaze lingers for a sec. oes it?"

"Well . . . yeah?"

e nods absently. "We'd need a good artist. Those flyers esome, you know."

nks, but did they sell tickets? I thought that's what

were a whole lot of people there tonight. I'd say ets, yeah." He gets a strange frown. "Hey, let me mething here real quick. I didn't ask you to do use you're my girlfriend."

little zap when he says that last word.

165

"I asked because you're really good, and whether or not we sold tickets because of them, I know for a fact that bad designs can cost us tickets. So, just saying, you know—it mattered. And we appreciate it."

The back of my neck heats up. "You're welcome."

I pull into Rome's Pizzeria. The other guys have already arrived, and through the restaurant windows, I can see them securing a booth. I park and shut off the engine.

"Well," I say, "I got your back, skater." And I lean over to kiss him quickly before we get out. "Great show again, by the way."

"Thank you." He kisses me back.

So I give him another one. Take that! "What're you doing after pizza, rock star?"

Another kiss from Mike: "I'm free."

"Not anymore," I say, and give him one last kiss.

Well . . . I *meant* it to be a last kiss before going inside to join the fellas. We don't make it inside until most of the pizza is already gone. Fireworks explode in the sky nearby.

No, seriously—*real* fireworks.

fourteen

Painting is only one of the means
of expression of my total genius.
—Salvador Dalí

"**Class, I apologize** for being late," Dr. Salinger says as she floats into the room. We're used to it by now. Half the class has dropped out, while the rest of us just consider it free studio time when she doesn't show. Happily, I've sent out enough Moody Art Chick vibes to keep the old broads from trying to talk to me, so I can paint in peace.

And I've got a good one here. A good canvas. Sketched it out first and everything. *Several* times. I mean, I think it's promising; it's better than the last few, anyway.

"I spent the most incredible evening with Lourdes St. James!" Doc S gushes, and I can't decide whether to choke her with pumice gel or demand a detailed account of the evening. Lourdes St. James paints these fantastic semisurreal portraits based on old high school yearbook photos. They're like caricatures, but more . . . naked.

Dr. Salinger goes on one of her patented bragging tirades. It's like the only reason she's teaching is to have a captive audience to listen to her exploits. If I ever end up teaching, I won't do that. I don't think.

I tune her out and keep working on my canvas. If I can just get the black and white mixture right, I think it'll work. But I'm also trying to apply glossy rainbow colors in a tiny area toward the bottom, and it's proving to be a bit tricky. I lean closer and use a fine brush to dab red, orange, yellow—

"Interesting."

I jerk up and drop my brush. Dr. Salinger leans over my shoulder, eyeing the painting. Gotta put a bell on this woman; she must've stopped talking minutes ago.

"See me after class," she goes, and moves to another student.

Great.

I pick up my brush and spend the rest of the period pretending to be Frida Kahlo. *Soy un mal artista.* Must check exact grammar with my Spanish professor in the fall. Which reminds me; should probably build my schedule soon. One step closer to Chicago. Or not.

Eventually, Dr. Salinger gives us a short "See you next time," and with that, class is over. The room empties quickly. Dr. Salinger watches everyone go, waits an extra couple seconds, then gives me the old hairy eyeball.

"Miss Walsh," she says from behind her desk, "what is art?"

I give her the most theatrical eye roll I can summon. "I don't know."

"Amanda."

I cross my arms and my hip cocks out. I try on a glare for good measure.

"What *is* art?" she repeats.

That's *it*. Had it. "God, what do you want from me?" I say. "It's an asinine question, and it's abundantly clear I don't know! I'll never know it, so can we just forget about it?"

Dr. Salinger *smiles.*

"I'll give you a hint," she says, coming out from behind her desk. "It's somewhere in this room."

I roll my eyes again and look around the studio. It's empty, totally empty. The walls are grimy and paint-splashed, and there are old scuff marks on the linoleum, several skeletal easels, some mismatched stools and chairs, and my—

Hold on a sec.

I point at my canvas.

"What, this?"

Dr. Salinger raises her eyebrows while continuing to slither toward me.

"Are you shitting me?" Man, Mom would punch me in the throat for talking like this to a teacher.

"I should hope not," Doc S goes, and glides closer. "The answer has been in front of you the whole time." She creeps behind my canvas and peeks around it. "This is art. You return again and again to this subject. The rainbow, the mountain. There is meaning here. There is a statement. A story. Whatever that story is, you must search for it, uproot it, tell the truth with it. That is where you'll find your art."

Give me a break. Better yet, a compound fracture. What an enormous steaming pile of excrement. She must be gunning for an Oscar with this performance.

But . . . I kinda want to hear more. I mean, just in case.

Dr. Salinger moves to stand beside me, my painting in front of us. "Do you see a future in this for yourself? Be honest."

Ah. So that's what this is about. She's going to tell me I should pursue something easier. Nuclear physicist. Or garbage woman. Maybe I could learn construction with Mike's dad.

"Sometimes," I say. I don't meet her gaze.

"Sometimes is not enough," Dr. Salinger says. "What might happen if you changed your mind?"

Okay, look. If this is going to be some sort of Disney-fied version of one of those movies where the teacher is a hard-ass and shapes up a class full of social-misfit students by pushing them to excel in calculus or whatever, let me count the ways I do not care. The last thing I need is for this witch to pull some feel-good Fulfill Your Potential speech. Thanks, but no thanks.

"I only took this class because my boyfriend suggested it, and it probably won't even transfer to the School of the Art Institute of Chicago, which, hell, doesn't matter anyway."

"SAIC?" Doc S says, arching an eyebrow. "That's not a school for those who wish to be artists *sometimes*."

I recross my arms and glare at my canvas. She has a point.

"What do you think of this?" She gestures to my painting.

Essentially, it's a jagged still photo in grayscale, as if taken from behind me back in June while I was sitting in the carport with my charcoal pencil and that unreal rainbow hovering over Camelback Mountain. A small girl, no more than a dark lump vaguely the same shape as the mountain, perches at the edge of a Phoenix carport while a black-and-gray rainbow arcs over Camelback. The only thing that's in color is the rainbow the girl is sketching with a pencil. It's the closest thing to a self-portrait I've done, if you don't count the face on my ceiling. "Self-portraits are the artist's best if not only way to reveal themselves to the world," Mr. Hilmer told me once. "They speak volumes the written and spoken word cannot."

But I don't think this piece has accomplished that.

My shoulders bunch up under my ears. "It's okay."

"But you can do better?" It's not a statement.

". . . Sometimes."

Dr. Salinger actually laughs, but not really *at* me. She pulls up a stool.

"You're good, Amanda," she says.

I physically *enter* a Dalí painting. The world around me melts, consumed by ants.

"You're working off passion right now, and that's a great place to start, but I have to tell you, it won't get you any sales, and it *won't* get you into the School. You can shit on a stick if you want, but unless it says something, it's not art, and it won't sell. It's just shit on a stick."

I lift my head.

"If you expect to get into SAIC, of all places, you have to take charge of your art, and that's the one thing I've been hoping to see ever since your first assignment," Dr. Salinger says.

Since my . . . ?

"You're using your tools and your talent, and that is where we begin," she goes on. "But now it's time to *work*. To use your mind *and* heart. Not just your eyes and hands. That canvas you tried to assassinate several weeks ago, with the red acrylic? Passionate! Explosive! But not *intentional.*"

Dr. Salinger takes my hand, with the brush still held in it, and lifts it toward the canvas. She moves my hand until it rests on the miniature rainbow. "Unclutter this," she says softly, and guides my hand and the brush over the rainbow. Chunks of acrylic stick to the bristles, and suddenly, I see it: the image beneath the technique. Like I'd painted over an entirely different—and better—painting.

"See?"

"Yeah," I say, awed that such a little change could make such a difference.

She lets go of my hand. "Now keep going."

I follow her quiet instructions, using the thin brush to stroke away the excess I am so used to applying. The rainbow clarifies, standing out brighter now against the dismal background.

Inspired, I add soft shades of ochre to the shape of the girl sitting on the concrete. The rainbow now lights her from the front, like a discovery. A pinwheel begins to whirl in my belly, blowing tingles through my limbs as I wipe my brush across the canvas, delicate and sharp as a kitten's claws.

"Better," Dr. Salinger says after several minutes of silence. "You're getting it."

I can't stop an amazed smile from crossing my face.

"This is the first step," Dr. Salinger goes. "But only the first. Eventually, you have to put yourself out there. Throw yourself naked upon the brutality of other people's opinions, laughing all the while. That's part of the business. Be a part of the student exhibition this fall, for example. Find a small gallery somewhere that hangs local art. There's a delightful little shop downtown that has a local art program. You should give that a try."

I turn away from the canvas. "Um . . . you don't mean Hole in the Wall?"

Dr. Salinger's eyes widen. "I do! Oh, isn't it just lovely? Eli and I are old friends from a long while back, before he opened the shop. It's a perfect venue to try."

She heaves one of her melodramatic sighs. "Do you know what I'd give to be in your shoes?" Dr. Salinger says, looking all, like, *earnest.* "You can just up and go travel the world if you want, Amanda. This is precisely the time for you to do so."

Her eyes wander to the ceiling. Does she keep her misspent youth up there or something? "I wish I still had that to look forward to," she says. "What I'd give to get back to Chicago myself, or New York, Santa Fe . . ."

Whoa.

Dr. Salinger gives herself a shake. "Well," she goes. "At any rate. I am prepared to make you a small offer. You hang something at Eli's shop, and promise to take my class next semester. If you do, and you continue to take yourself seriously as an artist, we can get together and discuss a portfolio submission—"

"I did that," I say, feeling clouds cover my face. "I mean, I got in. To SAIC. But I couldn't afford it."

"There's a number of merit scholarships offered each—"

"Yeah, well, they shot me down on that."

"For what reason?"

"'Lacking technical excellence.'"

"Technical excellence?" She looks confused, and I'm not sure how to feel about it. Doc S peeks at my canvas. "I'm not sure that's a terribly accurate assessment, based on what you've done this semester. It's really only a fancy term for technique. Easily remedied, if you do the work. I can teach you that. If you wish."

If I *what*?

Doc S frowns, but not at me. "Do you still have the originals?"

"The canvases? Sure."

"I'd like you to photograph them and bring them in for me. If you wouldn't mind."

"No. No, I . . ." I rub my forehead. "But then, why?"

"So I can assess them myself."

"No, I mean—if you're right? And it's not my technique? Then why would they say that, why would they turn me down?"

Doc S taps a finger against her chin. "Well, Amanda, I don't want to leap to any conclusions. Bring me the photos and we'll see what's what."

And for the first time, the possibility of trying again feels like it might be worthwhile. "Yes! God, are you . . . really? You mean it?"

"Well, of course I mean it! Bring me photos of your best work and a draft of your artist statement next week. Something that tells the world what you're all about. Did you really plan on staying at this school for your associate's?"

"Well, sorta. I don't have much choice right now. It's a money thing."

"Then we will build you a new portfolio instead."

"You mean drop out of school?" Mom and Dad would *freak.*

"A change in focus. There's nothing at this school for you, Amanda. There's no school in this entire state that can offer you what you're looking for. But perhaps *I* can."

"But I don't have the money to—"

"Which is why your portfolio is so critical," Dr. Salinger says. "Continue your requirements here if there are financial reasons to do so. That's all well and good. But while you are doing that, your focus must be on getting into SAIC, or one of several other schools that can provide you what you need to move forward. Don't spend the next two years here if you can possibly help it."

". . . Okay. Yeah, um. Yeah, that sounds awesome. Thank you!"

"Thank *you.* Oh, and Amanda," Dr. Salinger says, "I've been meaning to ask you. I've noticed you sign your work with a Z. What is the significance of that?"

"Oh," I say, surprised. "It stands for Zero."

"Zero," Dr. Salinger repeats. "And to what mystery does that allude?"

"It's kind of a nickname?"

"I see. Did you give yourself this name?"

"Um . . . sorta. In junior high."

Dr. Salinger nods. "Well, in my ex-professional opinion, you should consider getting rid of it. This *nickname.*"

"Too unprofessional?"

"Because you're worth more than that."

She arches an eyebrow at me again and leans forward a little, like to make sure this little gem hasn't escaped me.

And it hasn't. But I can't think about it right now. No, I *can't.*

I feel like I should shake her hand or something, but I don't. Instead I drape my painting, pick it up, and head for the door as Dr. Salinger moves back toward her desk.

"Thanks again!" I say. She waves at me, and I walk out into the hall, through the lobby, and into the hot summer sunshine.

What a freaking *epic* day. I've got to tell Mike! But first, I stop and register for fall. Including Painting 205, D. Salinger, Instructor. And Spanish . . . and math and English. Waiting for my receipt, I stare at my school account checkbook. How easy it would be to write myself a big fat check, cash it, and bolt for Chicago *today,* scholarships be damned. Maybe I could get a job or something. . . .

Stupid, I know. Plus, I've got my boyfriend to think about. But it's fun to consider, too.

I cruise home, rerunning our conversation. She did offer to help me with my portfolio, right? I mean, that's what it sounded like. And of course I'm going to take her next class, and as for the Hole . . . well, screw it! Dr. Salinger's right; it's time to just put myself out there.

Wow.

I shouldn't get too excited. Then again, why not? I mean, this could change *everything.*

When I get home, there's a note on the kitchen table from Mom. She's "at appt. till 3." Doesn't say where or for what. Strange, but whatever. Dad's at work.

That means . . . if Mike got here in thirty minutes, we'd have . . . about two hours, at least, to ourselves.

In my room.

Giddy, I call him up and damn near order him to come over.

"Okay," Mike says, easily enough. "You want me to borrow my dad's truck?"

Duh. Mike owns a skateboard, not a Porsche. "Oh, well, yeah, I mean, if you can . . ."

He laughs at me over the phone. "Okay, consider it done. On my way. But not for too long. We got a show tonight at The Graveyard."

I almost literally clap when I hang up, I'm so thrilled. I take a quick shower and even manage to change my sheets.

Wait.

Just so we're clear, I say to myself as I shrug my pillow into a fresh case (Cookie Monster! Shit yeah!), *you're not planning on, like . . . you know.*

No! I respond. *Not that.*

Maybe a little something *like* it . . . God, I don't know, I am *so* making this up as I go. Is there time to call Jenn . . . ?

Knocking at the kitchen door. I give my room one more quick look-over before racing to the door and flinging it open.

"Hey," Mike says, stepping in, "how's it go—"

I cut him off, wrapping him in my arms and mashing my face into his. It takes him a second, but he recovers and returns my assault.

We yank the kitchen door closed and stumble to my room together. "Hi," I whisper between breaths.

"Mm," he grunts back.

A second later, we fall onto my bed.

Here's the thing.

I'm a seventeen-year-old American girl, *eight*een a few weeks from now, *yes!* Sex is all over the place: TV, movies, magazines. I'm told I must weigh or appear to weigh ninety-eight pounds to be considered attractive. On television, I'm shown that sex with lots of douche-bag square-jaw guys is not only desirable but necessary to maintain my worth as a human being. Like, say, *Jenn,* as a sad for-instance. I'm told, indirectly, that anyone asking "Do you have this in a size larger than four?" is a balloon animal, inflated pastel cattle to be mocked.

But today, lying on top of my boyfriend, I am a goddess.

I've never—ever—felt this way in my life.

Which is why, as I'm kissing him, I sit back on my heels and peel my T-shirt off, exposing what little chest I have to him. To do whatever he wants. Everything he wants. Mike's eyes light up . . . but he seems to *recede* somehow.

"Hey . . . ," he says.

I focus on his eyes. "Touch me," I whisper, and in my head I add, *Please.*

He looks at me for a moment, then slowly raises his hands, unclasps my bra, and I shimmy out of it. I let it drop to the floor, and Mike covers my chest with both palms.

His touch is gentle, though his skin is rough, the same way his hands feel in mine when we hold them. His fingers start to move, exploring my body, and I . . . I guess *shudder* is the right word. My eyes close as if I have no control over them, and my head tilts back.

The flip side of this sex-saturated culture we live in is, um, that there's a *reason* it sells.

And while we know, *we know* we shouldn't buy into all the beauty and glamour hype, when all is said and done, we still want to feel sexy. There, I've said it. As Mike is exploring me, so quiet and so perfect, I feel it.

I feel *sexy,* and it feels *good.*

Until his hands drop.

My eyes flip open.

"What?" I say, a single harsh breath.

"We should . . . ," Mike starts, then stops.

My arms automatically move to cover myself. I'm a stupid bitch; that's it. I let him in, so to speak, and it was a mistake, because I *am* fat, and ugly, and—

And he rescues me by pulling my arms back down. It's not me after all.

"It's just . . ."

"Okay, you *really* need to learn to finish your sentences."

He sort of grins. "Sorry. I want to be careful. It's hard to stop, and . . . I'm not ready."

What?

So I say, "What?"

Mike sits up and touches my knee. "Listen. I told you there was a girl. Couple years back. I really felt . . . strongly . . . about her. And things went badly, to say the least, and now I wish I hadn't . . ."

"Had sex with her?"

"Well . . . yeah."

"I don't *care.*" I do, of course. But not enough to have him not touch me again. And as much as I want to know every-thing, I also want to know *nothing*.

"Okay, that's great, but . . . I do." He looks into my eyes. "You are so hot, Zero. You are beautiful—"

Say that again. And *again*.

"—and I do want to be with you. But I . . . I just . . ."

"Do you still love her?"

"Oh god, no! Positive. It's not that. It's not something I'm ready to do, is all. You know?"

"Did you, like, *catch* something?"

He half-grins. "No. No, nothing like that. I checked. *Couple* times, in fact. No."

"It's not me?"

"Absolutely not. I promise."

"Okay, so then—" I debate for a second, then plunge ahead. "What happened?"

Mike takes a deep breath. "Okay," he says. "Well. She came up to me after our first show ever. At Phantasm, you know, before they closed down. She told me she loved the band and all that. So we started hanging out. Then dating. And sleeping together. Pretty quickly."

My stomach flip-flops, but I try not to show it.

"We were on-again, off-again so many times, I think we both lost count. Break up, make up, have sex, break up, make up, so on and so forth. Till eventually she broke it off good and proper. And I didn't respond very well to that." He snorts. "That's one way to put it, anyway."

"What happened?" I repeat.

"Oh, I took a bit of a tumble," Mike says with a grunt.

"Pretty much lost my mind. Major flip-out. Probably woulda ended up in some psych hospital if it wasn't for the guys. They let me bounce around for a while. That lasted till I told them I was never gonna play again."

"Wow."

"Yeah. So one night they showed up to the house and literally dragged me to a show. Black Phantom, in fact. Made me watch the whole gig. Which was awesome, of course. After the show, Hobbit goes, 'That'll be us whenever you get around to being in a rock band again.' Eddie and Brook didn't say anything, just gave me a couple thumps on the back, you know. And we left. Started rehearsing again the next day, and that's when I decided I wanted that gold. Gave me something else to think about."

Mike shakes himself a bit. "Anyway," he says. "Point is, I honestly don't know if *not* sleeping with her would have made a difference, but I do know that I hadn't fallen like that for anyone before. And sleeping with her was totally meaningless. It didn't mean anything with her. *To* her. I don't want to feel like that again. Or let anyone *else* feel that way."

Okay. So that wasn't so bad. I expected worse. And I get it. I do.

But maybe it's because Mom and Dad are both out of the house and we have my room—my bed—to ourselves, or maybe because there's something sort of honorable about his decision . . . suddenly I want him even more than I did when I called him.

I trace a finger down his chest and tug his waistband a little. "So . . . what *can* we do?"

Mike takes a deep breath. "Uh . . ."

"Better hurry," I say, and unpop his button. Mike swallows.

"I—can't have sex with you. Right now."

I shrug. "Okay." I pull his zipper down. No idea what I'm doing here, but I'm pretty sure I can make it up as I go. How tough can it be? Still, I start shaking a little.

"Wait, hold on," he goes, and for a second I'm—well, *disappointed* isn't quite the right word. But then Mike sits up and gently pulls me down to the mattress so I'm on my back and he's beside me.

I wait for him to say something, explain what's going on; then the button on *my* shorts comes undone under his fingers, and *my* zipper goes down.

So, I've been putting on and taking off my own pants for, oh, sixteen-some years now, thanks. But when Mike does it, I can feel my pulse in my ears. Funny how another set of hands makes the mundane so *scintillating*. He tugs a little, and I lift my hips so he can take them off.

With his left hand, Mike explores my entire upper body: hair, face, neck, belly, you name it. He leans over me, kissing every inch of my throat, chest, stomach. My eyes close again, and a shiver starts working its way up my body.

With his *right* hand—

"Oh . . . kay," I whisper.

Several embarrassing vocal sounds and clenched fingers and toes later, I'm half passed-out, I'm breathing hard, and for some reason I feel like crying. It's not a sad or angry crying. It's, like, happy, you know? But I don't know how to explain that. Maybe someday I can paint it for him.

I feel *so good*.

"We can do *that*," Mike says quietly, resting his head on my stomach.

I unstick my tongue from the roof of my mouth. "'Kay," I wheeze.

Breath from his nose tickles my skin as he laughs. "Cool," he says.

We lie there for a while, not talking, our breath slowly becoming synchronized as I run a limp hand through his hair. I have done nothing in my life to deserve this.

After some time, my head finally clears. I think it's that internal clock that warns you that sooner or later, Mom and/or Dad are gonna be coming home. If I want to be able to repeat this afternoon's little escapade, I'll need to get my boyfriend out of the house before they show up. I open my eyes and check the *Three Young Surrealist Women* clock. We have maybe twenty minutes before risking Mom returning.

"So . . . how do you feel?" I ask.

"Good."

"Just good? Not really good?" I lift myself up. "I'm not sure that's good enough."

I scoot over onto my side, and Mike eases down onto his back. His jeans are still open the way I left them, and unless I'm mistaken, he's . . . not quite ready for the day to end, either.

I sit up and hover over him, giving him a long kiss before sliding my fingers between the waistband of his plaid boxers and starting to tug them.

"What're—" he starts.

"Shh," I say, and give him another long, lingering kiss. "My turn."

fifteen

The difference between the Surrealists
and me is that I am a Surrealist.
—Salvador Dalí

Hole in the Wall looks dusty and disused in the afternoon daylight. Nights treat the shop better, when the only real light is one parking lot lamp and the fritzy orange neon sign.

I glance into the backseat. Protectively wrapped in an old tarp, resting flat, is what I consider my best painting so far: the black-and-white one with the colored rainbow Dr. Salinger helped me finish.

It's been a couple days since we talked, and doubt has again built a bell tower from which to snipe away at my pedestrian confidence. She didn't even show up yesterday, which wasn't unusual but irritating.

I go around to the passenger door, open it, and remove my painting, using my hip to close the door. Holding the canvas close to my body, I walk to the entrance of the Hole, and take one last gulp of blistering air before creeping into the café.

Hole in the Wall is cool inside. A delicious aroma of coffee and nutmeg wafts into my nose. One person is behind the cashier's counter. I've seen him before, striding about the shop, behind the register, cleaning tables, serving drinks; whoever he is, he has the run of the place. He'll do.

He offers me a businesslike smile as I approach. "What can I get for you?"

Lifelong acclaim and countless imitators . . . ?

His demeanor relaxes me some, but my hands are shaking.

"Hi," I say, little more than a wheeze. "Um. Actually, I wanted to, um, show you this and, um, see if you wanted to, um, hang it? Or whatever?" I set my future, covered with a paint-stained drape, on the counter.

"Well, let's take a look at it," he says, and carefully unwraps the picture. He lifts it up and stands it on the countertop, holding it at arm's length, his fingers placed gently against the sides of the canvas so as to not touch the paint.

"Hm," he says. "This is nice. Good."

"Yeah?"

"Yes. Yes, I like this. Very nice." He sets the painting down and extends a hand. "Eli. I run the place."

Oh. I shake his hand. "Zer—um, Amanda Walsh."

"Nice to meet you, Amanda," Eli says. "I've seen you here once or twice, right?" He winks at me.

"Yeah . . . once or twice. You're friends with Dr. Salinger?"

Eli's eyes widen. "Deb? We go back quite a ways. Are you a student of hers?"

"Yeah. Yes. Summer school."

"She's a unique personality."

Uh, yeah.

Eli reaches under the counter and produces a tape dispenser and small white tag attached to a thin string. He picks up a pen, scrawls on the tag, and holds it up for me to see.

"Fair?" he asks.

It's the first time I've been here and not wanted something to drink; the thought of coffee curdles my stomach as I stare at the ridiculous numbers he's written. What is that, pi? A hypotenuse? A cosine, maybe? No idea, because no one, on this planet or any other, will fork over that kind of cash. Not for *me*.

"Um . . . you think someone will pay that?"

Eli frowns and looks at his number. "Sure," he goes. "Don't you?"

"I . . ."

"Trust me," Eli says, and tapes the string to the back of the picture so the tag hangs down. He picks up the painting and looks around for a place to hang it. "Ah," he says, and walks a few feet to a blank space on the wall. Right beside the crimson-black tondo I like so much. He hangs it up and brushes his hands together.

"It's a good one," Eli says. "This won't be here long."

Clearly he measures time in ice ages. But I don't argue.

Eli takes my phone number and promises to call when the painting sells, explaining that Hole in the Wall takes 20 percent off the top of the sale. I nod and agree because he can keep it *all* if the thing ever gets picked up, for all I care.

But it's done. I did it. My tiny signature, *Amanda Walsh*, rendered in white gloss, catches the light from an overhead lamp and sparkles.

I say goodbye to Eli, and he gives me an encouraging handshake. I go to my car, get in, and shut my eyes.

"Okay," I say out loud. "Okay."

As I start the car, I catch myself wishing—hoping—that if the painting *does* in fact ever sell, it will be before the start of the fall semester, or at least sometime during it, so I can tell Dr. Salinger.

Still. Whether it does or not . . . I did it.

I head over to Mike's to pick him up. His dad's truck is gone when I arrive.

Mike opens the door. He's in shorts and nothing else. "Howdy," he says with a smile.

"Howdy back," I say, and step in. "Ready to go?"

He glances down at his bare chest. "Sure, why not."

I grin and give his ribs a poke. We go to his room, where he riffles through his dresser.

"You look good," he says casually as he pulls a black T-shirt over his head.

I glance down at myself. Agent Orange T-shirt, cutoffs with my green Dalí belt, and my monkey boots.

"Liar," I say.

Mike winces. *"Really?"*

"I'm sorry, I just meant—"

"Okay, this stops now," he says, and comes over to me. He kicks his door closed, and for the first time I see the cheap full-length mirror nailed to the back.

"What size is that shirt?" he asks, pulling me to stand in front of him so we're both looking in the mirror.

"Large. Obviously."

"Large. *I* wear a large, and I'm not a big guy. You should be wearing a small. Medium, tops."

"You don't like how I dress?"

"I love how you dress. I'm saying it should fit you."

"Well, I don't feel like advertising my fat ass."

"Your . . . ? Okay, take your belt off."

I do, and wonder why. Does he have tantalizing plans for it?

Mike grabs the waistband of my shorts in one hand and a handful of my T-shirt in the back in the other and pulls them both taut. I suck in a breath and stand up straight, shoulders back. My spine offers a tiny *crack!* I should *maybe* consider *possibly* standing like this more often, *sometimes*.

"Now look," he says, nodding at the mirror. *"That's* you. You're swimming in this stuff. You have a kick-ass body." He releases my clothes, and my shorts nearly slip off. I grab them in one hand. "I mean, dress however you want; I still think you're hot no matter what. But it's something to think about. 'Sall I'm sayin'."

Staring at myself, I pull my shorts tight again and study the image. I'm used to seeing a Dalí poster gaze back from behind my reflection; it's weird to just see *me* for once, in an actual mirror.

"You mean it?" I ask him.

"I really do."

I let go of my waistband, and my shorts fall to the floor. Mike takes a step back, his eyes widening. Sweet.

"Something to think about?" I say to his reflection in the mirror.

I watch him run a hand over his hair. He can't keep his

eyes off me. And I like it. I had no idea I could ever feel this . . . oh, the hell with it: *sexy.*

"You want to help me pull those back on, or . . . ?"

"Um . . . not especially."

Just then, I hear the old pickup groan to a halt in the driveway.

"Well, crap," I mutter, and pull my shorts back on. Mike grins and hands me my belt.

"Maybe later," he says.

"Definitely later," I say. I latch my belt just as the kitchen door opens and closes. I look at Mike's door as if I can see through it. "So, time to meet the parent?"

"Eh. I'd rather not. Nothing personal."

"Oh. Okay. No, that's fine."

"You sure?"

"You know better than I do. I'm fine, I swear."

"Okay. Cool. Thanks."

I wait for him to pull on shoes and socks and grab his wallet, and we walk to the front door. We bypass the entry to the living room, which is dark except for flickering blue television light on the ceiling.

Mike pauses and holds up a finger. "Later, Dad!" he calls. Then waits.

About a minute passes, during which I hear nothing other than lame commercials.

Mike nods once, then ushers me out the door and to my car. "There you have it," he says when we climb in.

"I get it," I say. "I'm sorry."

"It's all right. He's just . . . not into people much anymore, is all."

"I get that, too," I say. "You want to get something to eat?"

Mike agrees, and we drive through a Taco Bell for munchies. Lacking another plan, we drive up what I think of now as Our Street on Camelback. Instead of getting out, though, I pull the car around so we're facing the Valley. We eat quickly . . . and then make good on our "later" promise to each other. We focus our kissing on necks, faces, ears; Taco Bell breath is not *conducive* to mouth-to-mouth.

I make myself keep my eyes open, looking out over the valley as Mike touches me.

Oh, man. A girl could get used to this.

About a half hour later, Mike says, "So, I have some news."

"You're pregnant."

He nods soberly. "Twins."

"And we were being so careful." I grab napkins from our discarded bag of Taco Bell and clean off my fingers. Turns out there's a lot you can do without taking off most of your clothes in the front seats of a 1969 Peugeot.

"It's just that my mom called."

I wad up the napkins and shove them back into the sack. "Yeah?"

"Yeah, last night, after the show. She's getting remarried, and I haven't even met the guy. Went on a big thing about me going out there to see her, and I kinda had to say yes."

"For how long?"

Mike snorts. "Week or so."

"Won't you have gigs?"

"Nah, not this coming week."

"Oh. That soon, huh?"

"Yeah. Better to get it over with."

"You don't sound thrilled. Not that *I* would be if it was my mom."

"I'm not." For the first time since I've known him, Mike's expression goes angry. "There's a reason I live here with Dad instead of her."

"Oh . . ."

He rubs his face. "Whatever. It just sucks that it's such a long ride."

I run a quick calculation in my head. "San Francisco can't be more than a two- or three-hour flight."

"Well, if one was in an airplane, that would be true."

"Wait, what're you, *skating* it?"

"Busing."

"Why not fly?" Because if he's taking a stupid bus, that's just gonna add time to how long I *don't* get to see him.

"I don't fly."

A smirk sneaks onto my face. "Really. Why's that? You're afraid of flying?"

"Several tons of steel, several miles in the air, over which I have absolutely no control, separated from certain death by a few inches of metal bolted together by the lowest bidder. Yeah, I'm afraid of flying." He grins at me. "Hob's dad works in aerospace. Told us one too many stories about what goes on in the machine shops or whatever. It's a wonder they aren't falling out of the sky."

"But they're *not* falling out of the sky."

"Not regularly, no."

"Okay, you do know that flying is statistically safer than driving, right?"

"Indeed I do. In fact, I'd rather go out like a rock star. Nice bus wreck."

"Ugh, stop! When do you leave?"

"Day after tomorrow. Monday. I'll get back Saturday."

"Blah. Okay."

Mike stares narrowly at my dashboard. His fingers drum heavily on the passenger door.

"Is she that bad?" I say.

Mike's lips curl. "She never loved him," he says. "She loved the band, the potential. The *record*. Dad was just a . . . means to an end. Sorry if I don't sound fucking delighted."

"Whoa, no, it's cool," I say gently. "I get it."

Mike touches my hand, his hard face softening. "Sorry," he says. "It's not you."

I rest my head on his chest. "No worries."

But I can still feel the tension in his body. I fish for a new topic.

"So if you did fly," I say, trying to keep my eyes open because I'm tired and giddy and absolutely stricken, "where would you go? If you could go anywhere?"

"London, maybe?"

"Ah. So you're a redcoat."

"Right-o. Which makes you a bloody colonial, wot?"

I snicker.

"What about you?" Mike says.

"Not counting Chicago? Florida."

Mike shifts a little in the passenger seat. "Florida?"

"Well, or Spain. But I figure Florida's more likely." My eyes drift shut. "That's where the largest Dalí museum outside of Europe is," I tell him. "St. Petersburg. A lot of his original masterworks are there. Like, the big ones, the famous ones. I want to go to Catalonia too, that's in Spain, but some of my favorite pieces are in Florida."

"Wow," Mike goes. "I knew you liked him, but I didn't know you'd fly across the country for it."

"Time me." I force my eyes open and tilt my head back to look at him. "You doing anything tomorrow?"

"Yeah, we got a band meeting, probably at the Hole, thanks to you. Brook and Eddie love that place now. You want to come along?"

I pull away and look at him. "Seriously?"

"Sure. The guys really liked that Spike's flyer. Hob told me he was going to ask you to do some T-shirts and stickers and stuff. If you wanted."

"Wow! Yeah, count me in!"

I giggle randomly at this news and move back into him. We hang out in my car for a while longer, but I'm halfway to falling asleep, and we decide to call it a night.

I take Mike home and promise him a ride to the bus station Monday. That'll be the last time I see him for a week. A *week*. What am I supposed to do with myself? I crank up the Descendents on my stereo.

I pull into our driveway. The carport light is on as usual, but the kitchen windows are dark. I lock up the car and toss our Taco Bell bag into the trash can around the side of the house before heading into the kitchen.

As soon as I open the door, I get pelted with bright light from the fridge. I cover my eyes and hear Dad laughing.

"Heh heh, gotcha there, huh? Heh!" He slaps the refrigerator door shut.

I rub my eyes and hear him pop open a beer. When the blue spots are gone from my vision, I can make out the outline of his shape drinking from the bottle.

"Ahhhh!" he sighs. He lifts his free hand near his ear and snaps. A second later, a bottle cap whizzes past my head and clicks against the kitchen door. "Still got it!" Dad shouts. "Shit, yeah!"

I swallow something gross. My burrito rumbles uncomfortably behind my waistband.

"Hey, Dad," I say quietly.

"So whatcha up to t'night, huh?" He takes a drink and tilts precariously to one side.

"You're swaying there, Dad."

Dad braces himself against the counter. "I'm not swayin'," he says, and belches.

God.

I start heading for the hallway, but Dad lurches in front of me. "Hey!" he barks, and grabs my arm. I don't think he means to, but it's hard and it hurts. He squints down at me. Beer breath assaults me.

"Hey!" he says again. "You pregnant?"

I pull my arm away. "Dad! God, no! Why the hell . . . you know what, never mind." I shove past him—pretty easy in his condition—but then stop and turn. "Why would you say something like that?"

Dad polishes off the rest of the bottle and lets it tumble into the sink. "I dunno whatcher doin' all night with that kid," he goes. "Prolly same thing I's doin' back then!" He laughs, drunken and stupid. I fight the urge to flying-side-kick his face. (*He's just a pain in the ass/He's a thorn in my side/Why can't he leave me alone?* —Milo Aukerman, lead singer of the Descendents. Thanks, Milo.)

"Jus' remember," he slurs, "ya get preg—*urp!*—pregnant, ya gotta get married. Thass how it works, kiddo."

Oh god. God, god, *goddam* you.

Dad stumbles toward me, putting his hands on my shoulders. "Hey! C'mon. Less go ask yer mom what she did. Hey, Miry!"

He tumbles past me down the hall toward their bedroom, shouting for my mother. I wonder for a second if I should call the cops or something.

Dad pushes the bedroom door open and disappears into the darkness. I hear him crashing around. "Miry! Muh-Miriam! Where-you? Hey!"

There's a soft thud, and his voice becomes muffled. Like against a pillow. I can't make out what he's saying anymore.

That's when I hear it. Off to my right, toward the living room. A quiet, stealthy sound.

A sniff, I think.

I flick on a lamp. Across from me, Mom is sitting at the dining room table, one hand pressed against her mouth, her thin shoulders hunched.

"Mom?"

Mom drops her hand and clears her throat. "You should get to bed, Amy," she says, her voice scratchy.

"Are you okay?" I'm not sure I want to know.

"I'm fine." She stands up and walks over to me. There's nothing unsteady in her gait, but her face is wet. Mom gets to me, gives me a quick kiss on the top of my head.

"You should go to bed."

"Mom, come on."

She hesitates. "What."

"This is bullshit. Sorry, bull*crap,* whatever. Can't you do something?"

Mom touches my cheek. "I'm trying," she whispers. Then she moves down the hall, goes into their bedroom, and shuts the door. I hear Dad groaning something unintelligible, and Mom's voice whispering.

I force myself down the hall, around the corner, and to my bedroom. I go in, shut the door, and turn on the small desk lamp over my easel. My hands shake. I go to my bed and sit down on them.

How can she put up with it? With *him*? Every week the same thing, except usually he's out at a bar or something. Which means . . . Jesus, that means he's probably driving home hammered, now that I think about it. He could kill someone. Or himself. Except it's never the drunks who die, is it?

My eye catches the spine of an old atlas I've had since middle school. I reach over and pull it off the shelf, blowing dust off the top edge. I flip it open to a map of the United States, tracing an imaginary flight to Florida.

Dad lets out a loud groan that penetrates the walls.

I wish Mike wasn't going away. Not even for a week.

sixteen

In the end it will finally be
officially recognized that reality as we
have baptized it is a greater illusion
than the dream world.
—Salvador Dalí

On Sunday afternoon, the band—except for Hobbit, who hasn't shown up yet—commandeers a corner booth that looks like it originally came from a Denny's. It's patched together with a rainbow of electrical tape. I'm between Mike and Brook, while Eddie drags over a couple chairs and takes one for himself.

"Hob's never late," Eddie says, taking a huge slurp of an amaretto coffee concoction that would've put me into a (pleasant, lovely) diabetic coma.

"Anyone talk to him?" Brook asks.

Mike shrugs and Eddie shakes his head.

At which point, the man himself appears around the corner, looking around wildly. I open my mouth to give him a shout, but he spots us first, and before I can make a sound, he leaps into the room and wraps Eddie in a bear hug from behind. He then—this guy must bench-press elephants in his spare time—bodily lifts Eddie up into the air, chair and all.

Eddie releases this high-pitched, girlie yelp, which makes me, Mike, and Brook start laughing at his expense.

"Pumee down!" Eddie shrieks, his masculinity forever compromised.

Hobbit sets him and his chair back on the floor and raises his arms, knuckles almost dragging across the ceiling.

"WE'RE IIIIIIIN!" Hobbit bellows.

The other patrons glance, and look quickly away when they see the size of the monster shouting.

"So what's up?" Brook goes.

Hob wipes his face with one paw and smashes himself down in the chair beside Eddie, who scoots away lest Hob decide to wrestle him again.

"Penny Denton, Penny *fucking* Denton, Four Eyes Entertainment, that's what!" Hob says.

Brook doesn't look laid-back after that. His jaw literally falls open, and Eddie's eyes pop. I feel Mike shift beside me.

Brook leans over the table toward Hob. "Where?"

Hob's smiling so big his face might split in half. "Where you think, brother, exactly where you think."

"Say it. Oh god, say it," Eddie blubbers, like he's having wild monkey sex. And that's an image I do not need, so we can just strike that from the record.

"Damage Control?" Mike says, very softly.

"Hell, yes!" Hobbit roars, and punches Eddie on the shoulder, which almost sends the fat guy end over end. Eddie doesn't seem to notice.

Now I get it. "You're playing there?" I say, and, I'm embarrassed to admit, cover my mouth with both hands, because—

"This is it!" Hob finishes my thought. "We did it, we fu—" He takes a look around; three couples have gathered their things and are leaving the room. "Fricking did it!" Hobbit finishes in a hoarse whisper.

Brook leans back and drapes his fingers across his face. Eddie runs the back of one hand across his mouth.

"Oh, you guys!" I say, and look at Mike.

"Who're we opening for?" Mike asks, drumming his fingers on the table.

"Nightrage," Hob says. "Their last show here before the BP tour. And we go up right before them!"

"That's good, right?" I ask, still looking at Mike.

"Yep," Mike goes. "Means a lot of people will be there."

"Z, we're gonna need flyers," Hob says as his knees piston up and down. "Lots of flyers. Can you handle that? 'Cept, I'm a little strapped right now, but maybe after the show . . . ?"

"No problem, I'm on it," I say. I'll have to dive into my allowance savings, but what the hell. "I can make them up today and take them to make copies. How many do you want?"

"Maybe five hundred? Four to a sheet?"

"Not a problem. Who else is playing?"

Hob digs out what looks like an old receipt. He checks his scrawling on the back in black Sharpie. "Uh . . . Living Room Casket, the Urinal Cakes, and either Just This Once or Peder Parker. Penny didn't know yet."

"In that order?"

"Don't matter, these flyers'll just be for us," Hob says. "Four Eyes'll make up some for the whole lineup."

Brook's eyebrows smash together. "Quick question. What in the wide world of sports is a urinal cake?"

"It's those big breath-mint-looking things janitors put in urinals!" Eddie says, looking pleased to be in the know. Personally, I could have gone the rest of my life without this bit of knowledge, but I'm neither (a) a boy nor (b) Eddie.

I grab a paper napkin and pen. "Doors?"

"Six-thirty."

"Go time?"

"Show starts at seven. We go up at ten, Nightrage at eleven."

"Okay, so when is it?" I ask Hob.

He tells me the date. Next Saturday. Mike's smile drops.

"Ah, shit, dude," he says. "I'm not getting back into town until that morning. That thing with my mom. I'm leaving tomorrow morning, remember?"

Eddie and Brook mumble and look worried; Hobbit chews his lip. "You can't get out of it?" he asks hopefully.

"Love to, can't," Mike states.

"All right, all right, I get it," Hob goes. He blows out a big breath. "Then we need to get the hell over to Eddie's right now and rehearse. And, like, all day Saturday."

"Ehhh . . . I don't know about that," Brook says. "I mean, maybe during the day, but not, like, *right* before the gig. That's bad mojo. Guarantees we'll stink up the show."

"He's right," Mike says. "We've tried that before, back in the day, you know? You want to do like midmorning or something, that's cool, but not right before."

"Okay, okay," Hob says. He turns to me. "Can you help get the flyers out? We only got a week."

"Sure," I promise. "I can ask my friend Jenn, too. She'll help."

"Excellent. We gotta make this a blowout," Hob tells us all. "Biggest show ever. We're gonna need more demo tapes. Eddie?"

"Yeah, yeah, I'm on it." Eddie looks bewildered that his dream is coming true.

"Good, good. Okay. Okay." Hobbit looks around the room, as if the walls have been inscribed with further instructions. He laughs out loud and pounds his fists on the table. "This is *it*, man! I told you! Hey, a set list. We need a killer set list!"

"I say no covers," Brook goes.

"Yeah, me too," Mike says. "If we're gonna do this, let's do it our way."

Hob bangs another fist on the table. "Damn skippy!"

The band breaks up the meeting to get food for their long night ahead in Eddie's basement. Mike walks me to my car. Kinda bummed I won't see him the rest of the day, but Hob's weird about people watching rehearsals. I wouldn't want anyone watching me paint, so I get it.

"Mike, this is so cool," I tell him, feeling a tiny bit jealous. I'm totally happy for him, but passing my painting hanging in the Hole on the way out was a lovely little reminder that I haven't Made It yet myself.

"Yeah, it is!" he says, and brings me close for a kiss. Brook catcalls at us through Hob's open van window.

"So, when you get home Saturday . . . will we have some time?" I ask, flipping Brook a little bird.

"That can be arranged," Mike says with another kiss.

"We'll probably take a break in the afternoon, chill out before we head to DC. I'll call you."

"What do you think this means for you guys?"

He shrugs. "Dunno. Some more fans, hopefully. If we can unload some of those demos, that'll help get the word out. But really, it's just another gig. We don't start making real progress till we tour. And we're probably a ways off from that right now."

The gleam in his eyes says otherwise. I smile to myself and decide not to make him toot his own horn anymore.

"Thanks for doing the flyers on short notice," he adds as Hobbit starts honking. "You sure you can afford it?"

"No problem."

Mike gives me a hug. "Cool, thanks. See ya tomorrow."

"Okay. Later, skater."

He smiles at me and runs to Hob's van, giving me a wave as he gets in. I go home, feeling thrilled and energized to get right to work on the gig flyer. It's gonna be the best night of the summer. I start designing it right away: an acrylic of a giant cymbal with the band's faces reflecting, distorted, off the golden sheen. At least, I think it's a cymbal. Maybe it's a gold record.

Where I'd normally leap in with a palette knife, slathering acrylic like it's a PB&J sandwich, for this, I choose thinner paint and a lighter brush selection. You try to find the right focal point, match the colors on the shadows just so, which isn't the kind of thing I'd normally worry about, but this is like . . . a commissioned piece. It's work for someone else, whether I'm getting paid or not. When you're painting, you should work with the door closed, both literally and figuratively. For me, this flyer painting, which I'll have reduced at the print shop when I'm done, is coming a lot easier since Dad isn't home. Ergo, there is no imminent danger of a nuclear incident with the Nation of Mom.

My focal point ends up off-center, down and left, a wing nut (ha!) securing the cymbal. This will be where the essential lights and darks strike each other. A few hours later, I shake the cramp out of my hand and step back from the easel.

The color temperatures are bold. Striking. You can almost hear the cymbal being crashed by Mike's sticks, which vibrates the reflections of the band members along the rim. When the paint's dry, I'll use a layer of coal-colored lettering to fill in the empty space at the top with the show information.

It's good work, I decide. It's at least not bad.

By the time I've finished the canvas, I already know this one's going into my portfolio. I take a picture of it to add to those I'll be showing Dr. Salinger.

Whenever she decides to show up to class again.

seventeen

The difference between false memories and
true ones is the same as for jewels:
it is always the false ones that look
the most real, the most brilliant.
—Salvador Dalí

"Call me when you get in?" I ask Mike as he pulls his black duffel bag out of my backseat the next morning.

"Promise," Mike says, shutting the door. He walks around the front to come over to my window, which is down. He leans in and kisses me once, then again, for a bit longer. I take his face in my hands, still stained with citrine splashes from my painting last night.

"See you soon," Mike says, and hefts his duffel.

"Later, skater!"

I'm bummed for a moment, watching him walk alone into the bus station. On the way to school, though, my pulse picks up; I've got a stack of photos of my work to show Dr. Salinger.

Class itself is relatively boring, but mentally, I'm turning somersaults. I start grinning like the toolbox that I am when

Dr. Salinger dismisses everyone and motions me to her desk. She sits across from me and begins poring over the photos.

My heart ricochets between my ribs, and I wish for a peppermint cocoa. After screwing up the guts to hang that piece at the Hole, this meeting feels like—I dunno. A step. Large or small, a step in the right direction. And now that Gothic Rainbow's big show is finally coming up, it feels like anything's possible.

"These," Dr. Salinger says as she stacks the last photo on the pile of others, "are remarkable, Amanda."

"Thanks!"

Dr. Salinger smiles. "You do need more work on some specifics, but many of these are impressive." She taps the photos. "I do see what the good folks at SAIC meant, in a roundabout sort of way. How old is the most recent of these?"

I shrug. "Um, I dunno. Three, four months. That one." I point to one of the photos. "Except for the band flyer. Um . . . that one. I did that last night. The others are older."

She examines it closely. "You've improved," she remarks, studying the GR flyer. "But these others . . . you're better than this."

"I am?"

"Given what I've seen in class, yes."

"Well, I mean . . . I've learned a lot since we started . . ."

Doc S shakes her head. "That may be, but this is something different. Where do you do your work?"

"At home."

She nods wisely. "And may I ask how that has been for you?"

I look at the floor. "Not that great."

Dr. Salinger puts a hand on mine. "I'm not surprised," she goes. "An artist needs a space in which she can create. A quiet place."

"But I like to play music when I paint."

"Quiet and silent are not synonymous in this case, Amanda."

I shrug again, but my heart's not in it. I know what she means. At home, with Mom and Dad always bitching, my hand tenses up and it's hard to get my strokes just right. Here in class—after the first few sessions, anyway—my hand is relaxed. Now that she says this, I can feel the difference. Last night was easier because I finished the painting before Dad came home.

Whenever that was.

"I wish I could offer you something more than our three times a week," Dr. Salinger says. "If you have the means, I would encourage you to find a more suitable studio. Because this type of work"—she gestures at the canvas I worked on this morning in class—"should be more than adequate for the scholarship committee next time."

I take a deep breath and exhale slowly. Holy shit.

"Once we've assembled a blue-ribbon portfolio," she goes on, "we'll see about working on your artist statement." She pauses. "SAIC is certainly a bold choice to begin with. What made you choose it?"

"Mr. Hilmer went there."

"Ah! Your former teacher."

"I thought I could maybe teach junior high or something, like he did, if nothing else."

"Those who can't, teach, hm?"

"Oh, no! No, it's not—"

"Quite all right," Dr. Salinger says. "Teaching is an honorable alternative while you work on your career." Her face sort of clouds for a sec. "It's not a solo exhibition, but it suffices." She gives herself a shake. "It's always a good idea in this profession to have something to fall back on, and an undergraduate degree from Chicago will certainly not hurt you."

We sit quietly while I consider the future. I also study Dr. Salinger, and I'm suddenly reminded of Mom. They have the same lines around the eyes, even though Dr. Salinger must be a few years older. Both have this weariness to them, which in Mom's case, after years of dealing with Dad—and maybe me—makes sense. On Dr. Salinger's face, the expression seems misplaced.

"Dr. Salinger? Can I ask you something?"

"Certainly."

"Why did you stop?"

She rests her chin on one hand. "It's simple, really," she says, but doesn't look at me. "I thought I should. I was told as much in print."

I avert my face, in case she can see that I know exactly what she's talking about. It's public record, not a secret or anything, but I don't want her to know I was spying on her.

"Oh, my work sold, and I lived on it for a while," she goes on. "But in the end, I believed what the critics said about me. So I turned to teaching."

God. Now what? Doc S went down the road, tasted success, and still failed. What does that mean for me? Not to be selfish, but—for real?

"You could do it again," I say. "You could try."

"Ah, I've thought about that. From time to time. Every day or so. But no. No. I had my shot, I'm afraid."

"Well, but still."

Dr. Salinger eyes me. Her lips twitch. "Well," she says, "I suppose since you had the guts to put yourself out there, perhaps I'll reconsider. Matthias always says to try again."

"Is he an artist, too?"

"Oh, my, yes. Brilliant. His education is in arts management, but his sculptures are becoming quite in vogue. Goodness, is it so late already? I really must be going. Matthias and I are wining and dining an artist friend from Chelsea."

Yee-ikes! Chelsea's a big-time arts district in New York. Man. Hanging out with *anyone* from there would be a nice gig. I hang my bag over my shoulder after putting my photos carefully inside and draping my canvas.

"Thanks again," I say.

"You're absolutely welcome," Dr. Salinger says, walking me to the classroom door and surprising me with a quick hug. "We'll get together after the summer semester ends and get you started," she adds. "Now, I hope you don't think I've promised you anything. You've much work to do. I will be happy to write you a letter of recommendation, if you wish, provided you do the necessary work to create a truly outstanding portfolio."

Oh god. I forgot the recommendation letter. The one I sent last year was from my high school art teacher, and he may as well have used a rubber stamp reading, "This student is kinda-sorta okay by me." But one from an actual artist, even one whose career hasn't done much lately . . . she'll know how to say the right things.

"Oh, no, no, I understand. Thank you!"

"A number of elements must come together in perfect harmony," she says. "But the first of these is talent, and that you have. So we're off to a good start!"

I feel a blush in my cheeks. "Thanks," I say. "And thank you for meeting with me. See you Wednesday."

"Just a few more classes!" she chuckles. "The time's gone so fast."

No kidding. We say goodbye, and I head out to the parking lot.

Did this really just happen? It was only a couple weeks ago I thought it would be surreal if I even passed the class; now I'll be meeting with Doc S again before fall semester even starts to work on—wait for it—*my career.*

I sing along with the radio all the way home. Mike's supposed to call tonight, and I can't wait to tell him *everything.*

Mom's on the kitchen phone when I walk in. She gives me a quick look and turns away. Smooth, Mom. Not suspicious at all.

"Friday afternoon is fine," she says, lowering her voice. "Thank you, Father," she whispers. "Goodbye."

Um—pretty sure she doesn't mean her dad, who died when I was real little. No, this is one of those collar-and-stole-wearing fathers.

"Who was that?" I ask anyway. Because *this* is news.

Mom straightens her dress. "Oh, Father Larson," she says, trying to sound dismissive.

"Are you going to Mass?" Because she's been home every Sunday morning since I can remember. I've never been to church; Mom had me baptized when I was little, but that's all. Father Larson was the guy who did it, if I remember right.

"Not just yet," Mom says, moving to the sink and searching for dishes in need of cleaning. There aren't any. She turns on the faucet anyway and begins scrubbing her hands.

"I've been speaking with him," Mom says suddenly.

Huh. This sounds deep. "About what?"

Mom continues washing her hands. "Oh, this and that."

"Dad?"

"Sometimes. Yes." Mom turns off the faucet and grips the sink edge. "There's been some trouble at work," she says quietly. "He's been leaving early. Taking very long lunches."

I lean against the wall. My bag, which seemed weightless when I walked out of Dr. Salinger's classroom, is now filled with bricks.

"You mean drinking."

Mom faces me, her expression strained. "We'll work it out," she promises. "I don't want you to worry, Amy. Father Larson has been very helpful. . . ." She looks at me hopefully, like she wants me to agree with her.

But I don't. I can't.

"That's great," I say instead. "If there's something I can do—you know."

Mom wrangles a weak smile. "Thank you, Amy." Her gaze drops to my bag. "How was school?"

"Um. Good. Really good. My teacher's going to help me rework my portfolio."

"Well, that's wonderful. Good for you. I'm proud of you, Amy."

And she is. I can see it. Her voice is weary, her eyes and mouth elongated like a Modigliani portrait, but she really means it. Mom must've been pretty, once. Not that she isn't necessarily now. But she looks a lot older than she should.

Salt leaks into my mouth, draining from the back of my throat. I clamp my jaw shut to keep it from trembling.

"Thanks," I force myself to say, then turn and go to my room.

Inside, I close my door as usual and wipe my nose with the heel of my hand. I drop my bag to the floor, go straight to my easel, and grab my charcoals. I've got a couple hours to kill before meeting up with Jenn to post the GR flyers.

Before heading out to meet Jenn, I discover I've drawn a picture in charcoal of my dad crushing a beer bottle in each hand so hard the glass has shattered. The only problem is, he's starting to melt from the exertion.

I leave the drawing on my easel and go pick Jenn up at her house. I'm surprised to see her dad's BMW in the driveway.

"Hey, you!" Jenn says, springing into my car.

"Hey. Your dad's here?"

"Yeah, just for a couple days. I told him about culinary school."

I pull out of her driveway and head for downtown. "Yeah? What's he think?"

"He likes the idea," Jenn says. She looks happier than I've seen her in a long time. "There's a couple places in Illinois, even. Maybe we could go to Chicago together."

"Sure, that would be cool. My art teacher's helping me with a new portfolio."

"Really? That's great!"

"I know, right?"

Jenn reaches into the sack of flyers I copied this morning and pulls one out. "These are cool," she announces. "Does Mike like them?"

"He hasn't seen them. He's out of town, seeing his mom."

"Do the other guys?"

"Yeah, I met up with Hob real quick before I made the copies. He was pretty excited. That might just be the show talking, though."

"Nah," Jenn says. "It's all you, baby."

We both laugh. "He wants me to do T-shirts and stickers, too," I say.

"Awesome!" Jenn puts the flyer back and rolls down her window to let the breeze ruffle through her hair. "How, um . . . how're things going with Mike, anyway?"

"Great," I say. "Really good. I don't think I've ever been this happy, to tell you the truth."

"Yeah, well, then you didn't see your face when you got accepted to Chicago!" Jenn says, slapping my shoulder. "How does Mike feel about you moving out there?"

"Well, I mean, I don't know for sure that's gonna happen, so."

I wait for a response, but Jenn is quiet. We hit a red light. Jenn's nibbling her lower lip, frowning at the dashboard.

"What?"

She gives a slow-motion shrug. "I just . . . I mean, you wouldn't *stay* here for him, would you?"

"I—I mean, the soonest I could even reapply is in the spring. That's a long time from now."

Jenn tilts her head. "Uh, that's not what I asked you, Z."

I meet her eyes. Jenn's face is tense, eyebrows creasing together. A horn sounds behind me; the light's green. I shake myself and accelerate through the intersection. I don't say anything for several minutes, because the truth is, I don't have an answer.

"Z?"

"I don't know," I say. "I mean . . . no, I guess I wouldn't."

"You've been talking about that art school since we were, like, fourteen."

"I know. . . ."

"Honestly, I'm not liking this," she says quietly.

"*What?*"

"I'm glad things are going well with you two, I really am," Jenn says, watching the world cruise past us through her window. "But suddenly you're okay with even considering *not* going to Chicago if you got a scholarship? That's not like you. I never figured you for a groupie."

I hit the brakes hard at the next red light. Jenn jerks forward and gives me a surprised glare.

"I'm not a groupie!"

"Okay, okay, sorry, I didn't mean it like that. I just mean that you've always known who you were, what you wanted to do. And I'm, like, feeling that for the first time myself, and it's awesome, and—you know, I originally had a date planned tonight."

My anger subsides; talk about not being yourself! "You did?"

"Yeah, but I broke it off. It was kinda nice. I figured me and you could go out somewhere, or if we didn't, then I could stay home or see a movie, or *whatever*. Maybe even have dinner with my dad . . ." She snorts a bit, like she's shocked to hear herself say it.

"That's cool," I say cautiously, and pull into a parking garage near Damage Control.

"It is," Jenn says. "And what I'm saying is, now that I'm sort of finding my way here, I'd hate for us to trade places."

I find a space and park. I shut off the engine and face her. "Trade places how?"

"Settling," Jenn says, putting a hand on my knee. "Settling for anything less than what you really want. I'd hate it if someone decided *for* you what you were gonna do. That's all."

"It's not like that! This is all hypothetical. I already bombed the scholarship once, so I might do it again, in which case I'll be stuck here anyway. . . . And if I *do* get it, well then . . . I'll figure that out when I get there."

I twist my fingers in my lap for a moment.

"But I wouldn't turn it down," I say, surprised that I'm surprising myself with the decision. I've gone to great lengths to not think about it, and it was easy, because there wasn't anything really to think *about*. Not until I resubmitted my portfolio. Now that Jenn's showing me the possibility in cold, hard reality, the truth is, I couldn't ignore the opportunity.

If it happened.

"Well, then, cool," Jenn says. "I mean, you know I'm behind you, whatever you do. But don't give up on what matters most to you. 'Cause that would suck."

The concern in her voice is partly aggravating, like I'm

being a total idiot for even thinking about staying in town for Mike. But I also suddenly feel *way* grateful that she's here and cares enough to say something.

"I won't do anything stupid," I tell her. "Promise."

"I know," she says. "That's *my* job."

We both giggle, then head out to paper the area around DC with Gothic Rainbow flyers. With Jenn batting her eyes at all the right guys—she hasn't ditched *that* skill—we get stacks of flyers in businesses all over the place.

Whatever happens, this is going to be a *huge* show. I put worries about school out of my mind even as I let myself admire the flyers a little. Just a bit.

eighteen

Well, I have a few minor inner conflicts.

—Salvador Dalí

"Too tight," I tell my reflection in the *Young Virgin* poster while Social Distortion plays on my stereo.

The black and gray pinstripe shorts Mom bought hug my hips more tightly than *I've* ever hugged *her.* And my red Minor Threat shirt from junior high is too clingy, making my boobs pop out and emphasizing my belly pudge. My thighs are dead tree trunks.

Except . . .

Here's the thing.

I turn around for myself, checking all the angles. Do a little *sexy dancin'* just to see how it feels. Hunker down and stand back up to see how much room I still have in the fabric.

I *know* I'm wrong, but . . .

I think maybe I look kinda good.

"Wow," I whisper. When the hell did this happen? When did my hair fall just right, my legs look this sharp, my whole short body fill these clothes so well?

I'm not talking supermodel quality, here. No one will ever take covert glances at my chest (except maybe my *boyfriend*! giggle!), and I don't lack for ass.

But it isn't *bad.*

(*In the nightclubs, baby, when the lights shine down, she's a knockout.* —Mike Ness, lead singer of Social Distortion. Thanks, Mike!)

Maybe I should wait and wear this outfit tomorrow when Mike gets home.

Nah! I look too *good,* and who knows if it'll all fit the same tomorrow? I might gain eighty pounds by then.

"Weird," I say out loud. I grab my bag and head out for class.

So I feel pretty good on the drive to school. And when I sit down at my usual place in Dr. Salinger's room and she's not there, it's a bummer but no big. She's missed probably one-fourth of our classes entirely. She didn't show up Wednesday, either, which truly sucked, because I wanted to show her my flyer design as it looked on paper.

But when some old dweeb in tweed skitters into my classroom, my first thought is that I've accidentally gone into the wrong room.

Even as this gray-haired dork is slapping down a briefcase on Dr. Salinger's desk, I look around at my classmates. No, this is the right classroom, right time, right date.

"Uh, hello," the dork says. He's dressed like a turd, all

greens and browns. "This is painting, right? Intro to Art? Is today your final, or is that next week?"

"A week from today," old grandma Candace says helpfully.

I raise my hand. "Um, excuse me?"

Mr. Turd squints at me through his glasses. "Yes?"

"I'm sorry, where's Dr. Salinger?"

He shakes his head and pulls some papers from his brief-case. "Dr. Salinger has decided to try her hand elsewhere," he says.

He keeps talking. What I hear is: "It appears *mutter mumble mutter* no grade book *blah blah blah* passing credit *whistle snort vomit* final project next week *mumble mutter mumble . . .*"

In the distance, someone with *my* voice asks, "Where the fuck is she?"

Someone gasps a bit, and I couldn't care less. Mr. Turd puts his hands on his hips the way only a dork knows how to do. "Miss, I need to ask you to refrain from using that language."

"Yeah yeah fine, where is Dr. Salinger?"

He lowers his head, trying to look all severe over the top of his glasses. "Dr. Salinger. Has moved. Out of state." He cocks an eyebrow as if to say, *Is that clear?*

Which, um, *no,* it's not.

"Are you kidding me? Did she leave a number or an address or anything?"

"I couldn't say, miss."

"But this is *important*!"

He offers me a bland turd smile. "I understand if some of

you are upset by the school's decision to not give letter grades, but it was the best they could do under the circumstances. If she'd done even *some* of the work an instructor—"

"Oh my god," I say, and grab my bag.

"Miss, you'll need to fill out this—"

"*Shut up!*" I scream, and shoulder through the classroom door, into the hall, and outside.

There has to be a mistake. I just *saw* her, for god's sake. How could she suddenly decide now to take off? That can't be right. I could ask at administration. Mr. Turd got his facts mixed up, is all.

No, they won't tell me anything. Wait! Maybe . . .

I race for my car and speed to the Hole, praying Eli will be there. Luck—such as it is—is with me; he's handing someone a tall iced coffee when I rush in.

I practically body-slam the patron to the ground to get to Eli.

"Excuse me," I say to Eli, "but have you heard from Dr. Salinger?"

Eli blinks. "Not personally, but she left for New York on Wednesday evening, I heard."

Something invisible socks me in the abdomen. I clutch my (thick, gelatinous) gut.

"But when is she getting back?"

"She's not. Her current love interest got a job as a curator at a gallery in the city." He smirks, like this doesn't surprise him.

My intestines twist, snakes in a dry burlap sack. "You mean Matthias?"

"Right, that's him. He's probably why she tagged along.

She's a bit of a hanger-on these days, I'm afraid. Kind of a groupie. But he is quite the up-and-comer, so I can't say that I blame her."

I struggle to breathe. "D-do you know which one? Which gallery?"

"Mm, no, sorry, not a clue."

"Well—is there—did she leave a number or anything?" My heart beats as if attacked by Mike's double-bass pedals.

"I've got her old home number, but I can't really give that out. Sorry. And she's not there, at any rate."

"But she might've left a forwarding number or—"

"Oh, I kinda doubt that. You know how she is."

I thought I did.

"This is about par for the course for Deb," Eli goes on, shredding my heart with razor teeth. "Comes and goes as she pleases, and the heck with anyone else." Eli squints at me. "Is there something I can maybe do for you?"

My eyes drift over to my painting, collecting dust on the wall. The little colored rainbow on the driveway has lost several shades of luster.

"No," I whisper. "There really isn't."

I turn and walk out of the Hole.

I need Mike, need to tell him everything, let him hold me, because it's coming, boy, the tears are already massing in my stomach and waiting to come up, and I need his arms around me to let them loose, but of course—"*Shit!*"—he's in California.

Today. When I need him more than ever, *today* he's out of town.

I can't go home. Even if I thought I could talk to Mom,

she's got that stupid appointment with the good reverend or whatever you call him. Shit *shit SHIT!* And Dad, well, good old Dad is either (a) at work or (b) completely shitfaced or (c) *both*, right?

I make a left. Camelback looms ahead of me. My mountain, my navigator.

I know where else I can go. But I have to make it fast, because my vision's already going blurry and the last thing I need is to wreck my car to top it all off.

On the other hand, why the hell not? Just toss my entire fucking life in the glove box and take us both off a cliff.

I hold my breath almost the entire way to Jenn's house, because if I don't, I'm going to have a meltdown that cannot be measured with existing technology.

She'd better be home.

I pound on her front door and open it without waiting for a response. Another advantage to having a best friend.

"Jenn!"

Jennifer appears from the doorway to her kitchen. I can taste but not smell garlic, rosemary, basil floating into the room, and hear the stove-top exhaust fan going. She's cooking, of course. She looks startled for a second, then races toward me.

"Zero? What's going—"

I grab her, and I swear to god, I *bawl*. My eyes slam shut and squirt tears from every corner, my forehead aches, my chest constricts.

I mean, holy *shit*, do I fucking cry.

"Zero, what is it? Is it Mike? What happened?"

I shake my head into her shoulder. Goddam you, *Doc*.

Goddam you. Jesus, I practically told her to leave myself: *You could try.* And I guess she did. . . .

"Come here, sit down," Jenn says softly.

I follow wordlessly, sobbing like a big tub of crap, as Jenn leads me into her gorgeous living room, something out of a lifestyle magazine. I perch on the couch as Jenn runs back into the kitchen. I hear her twisting dials and moving pots around.

"*What* is the matter?" Jenn says when she comes back, kneeling in front of me, her hands warm and damp on my knees and (ridiculous, clownlike) new shorts.

I take a couple of breaths. My sinuses are all clogged up.

"It's my art teacher, that bitch. . . ."

I unwrap the whole sordid tale. How she was going to help me, *change my entire life,* and then bailed. Jenn nods and shakes her head at the appropriate times. How am I supposed to know if I'm good enough now? How am I supposed to build my new portfolio? Or get her recommendation letter, *shit!*

"That is royally messed up," Jenn says when I'm done and not crying anymore. "What can I do? Can I get you something? Water? Or we have some soda. Or I could fix you a—"

Jenn stops. "Or maybe not that. Sorry."

"No," I tell her, dragging an arm under my nose. "Go ahead. Fix me whatever." Maybe Dad knows something I don't. Maybe this is how it all goes away. Because feeling something, anything, has to be better than this. *You fucking witch.*

"Well . . . maybe later," Jenn says. She sits down beside me on the couch. "Sounds like a rough day, kid."

"Huh. Yeah. A bit." Oh, and one more thing: *"How could she do this to me?"* I scream, and Jenn doesn't even blink. "You don't just up and take off on people like this. It's not fair!"

Jenn puts a hand on my back, frowning sadly for me, and says nothing.

It is not, not, *not* fair. I feel another sob coming up but I choke it down. Jenn puts her other hand on top of mine.

"I'm so sorry," she says. "But it's not the end of the world, Z. You could—I don't know, come up with some other way . . . ?"

"Whatever," I mutter.

"You gonna be okay?" she whispers.

And those words, so simple and stupid, just make me come unglued. I cry into her shoulder, quietly this time, and after a moment, Jenn surrounds my shoulders with her arm. This is the first time I've been inside her house since graduation.

When the worst has passed, I look up into her face. "Thanks," I say sickly.

"Anytime. I'm glad you came here instead of being alone."

"Yeah," I say. "Me too. I'm glad you were home."

And I really am. We came so close to never speaking again. God, where the hell would I be now? With Mike gone, and no Mom, no Dad, and now no fucking future . . . what the hell is left?

Still looking up at her, I lift my right hand and touch her chin with one finger. Jenn's eyes slide down, trying to watch me.

"Z, what . . ."

"Does it work?"

"Does *what* work?"

"With those guys. You know. Does it really make it all go away?"

Jenn slowly reaches up toward me.

And moves my hand away from her face.

"No," she says.

I don't believe her. I don't believe anyone. Why should I? I lean toward her.

And Jenn leans back. "Zero, stop. You don't—"

"How do you *know*?"

"Because you *told* me."

I pull back and jump to my feet. "Are you—seriously? Two months ago you like make a *pass* at me, and now . . ."

Jenn stands, lifting a warning hand. "Hey, hang on, that's not—"

"Jesus, what is it with me? What do I have to do to get something right? Why does everyone *go*?"

"Z, come on, don't say that."

"God . . . *Fuck* this!" I bolt for the door.

Jenn runs after me. I fling open the front door and race for my car.

"Zero, *please!* Wait!"

I get to my car with her voice echoing after me.

I drive. Drive till the needle hovers over Empty. Might as well gauge my, you know, *soul.* I cover the entire metro area. I don't know how; the city passes in mosaic, fragmented. I avoid Camelback Mountain.

It's dark by the time I get home. I can see my mother and father through the kitchen windows as I pull into the driveway behind Mom's car. As soon as I step onto the pavement, I can hear their voices. Screaming.

I clutch my belly, which has been lurching up and down since Jenn's. God, *now* what? Not tonight, please, please not tonight . . .

I creep toward the kitchen door, trying to avoid detection. Neither of them sees me. Mom's got a handful of papers in her hand and gestures angrily with them; Dad's hands are on his hips, his shirt unbuttoned and sleeves rolled up. His face is one shade removed from violet. Vermilion, perhaps; must do a color study . . .

I make it to the carport and lean against the cool brick wall beside the kitchen door. I can hear each word perfectly.

"Richard, how could you let this happen?" Mom is shouting.

"I didn't set out to, if that's what you mean!" Dad shouts back.

"You wouldn't know it, the way you've been carrying on!"

Something heavy shatters against the interior wall near the door, and I jerk. Another few inches, it sounded like, and whatever had been thrown would have careened through the door's window. Which, had I been standing *there* instead of against the wall . . .

"*I try!*" my father screeches.

I have never heard such rage except in my own head.

"*I do my best, goddammit, and all you can do is criticize me!*"

My mother says something too low to catch. Whatever it is, Dad must have missed it, too. "What?" he demands.

Mom doesn't scream this time. "I said get out."

Silence.

I move my hand from my stomach up to my throat as my heart beats madly beneath my skin. I'm gonna throw up. Right here and right now, please don't let me throw up. There is nothing, absolutely nothing, worse than puking.

Well. Maybe one or two things.

The door opens so swiftly that I rear back, shoulders raised defensively, forearms pressed against my chest. Dad bolts through the doorway and turns toward me as if heading for his car. But my presence catches him off guard, and he skips backward a step.

"*Jesus!*" he bellows, then glares at me.

For one second, I truly and absurdly think he is going to hit me, and I sorta want him to. I could hate him then. Like, legit. Dad's lips are pulled back from his teeth, eyes bloodshot, crisscrossed with red tendrils, arms shaking with wrath, both hands balled into fists. Beer breath shoots into my nose, careens down to my stomach, and gives it a good shake.

But he doesn't move. I can only stare back, frozen, terrified at the sight of his darkened face. He's not drunk, either. He's had a beer, maybe two, but isn't drunk.

As he looks at me, some of the anger seems to leave him. He walks past me to his truck, his hand fishing for keys in his pocket. He finds them, gets into the truck, and squeals out of the driveway. The scent of burnt rubber wafts into the carport, sliding into my nose, down my throat, settling on top of all the snot I swallowed from crying. Yum.

The carport light comes on, blinding me. Hands touch my shoulders.

"Amy?"

Weak and shaking, I let Mom guide me into the house. I glance over my shoulder at the wall as Mom ushers me through the kitchen. A large stain dribbles beer from an impact against the wallpaper, and brown shards of glass litter the floor. Great job, Pop. I wonder—did he throw it at her? Did she use her secret ninja abilities to dodge?

Mom guides me to my bedroom, where she sits me down on the edge of my bed. "Are you all right? I expected you home hours ago. You had a phone call—"

"What happened?" I interrupt, trying to keep myself upright. I am so tired.

Mom covers her mouth with one hand. "He's, ah . . . Your father lost his job."

". . . Oh."

I ought to be upset by this news, but I'm not. I think too much has already happened today. I stare blankly at my feet, try to curl my toes. See if I have any sensation in them. "Are we gonna have to move?" Wouldn't *that* be ironic.

"No. It's not quite as bad as all that, not yet. You should still have your college account. That's something. . . ."

I swallow hard and say nothing. I should be hungry, starved, but I'm not.

"Where were you all afternoon? Jennifer called a little while ago and asked if you'd made it home."

All afternoon? Let's see . . . I was going stark raving fucking loony tunes, that was fun. Oh, also, I tried to—

"Am I okay?"

"Okay?" Mom repeats, putting a cool hand against my forehead. It feels good.

"I mean, am I even halfway normal? Am I weird? What's wrong with me?"

"Of course you're not weird. You're very creative. . . ." She pointedly looks up at my ceiling paintings. "And perhaps a little sensitive. Amy, what happened to you? You don't look well."

I lower myself to my bed and curl into a fetal ball, wrapping my shins with both arms. "I don't know."

"Do you want to change? Put on some pajamas?"

"No."

"Should you call Jennifer back? She sounded worried."

"I can't." Ain't that the truth. Boy howdy, I tell ya, when I decide to make a shit situation shittier, I commit.

"All right," Mom says. "I'll go ahead and phone her, if you don't mind. Just to tell her you're safe."

"'Kay."

Mom retreats to the doorway. "Can I get you anything?"

"No."

"Well, I'll come check on you in a little while."

"'Kay," I whisper again.

I don't know if she ever does check in on me or not, because I go *out* straightaway, and stay out till after eleven the next morning, when my phone ringing wakes me up. I answer it without thinking. What if it's Jenn? I can't talk to her now, no way, not after what I pulled, but I've already picked up the phone and it's too late.

"Hello?"

"Hey," Mike says, and his voice is dark. "I'm home. So how was *your* week?"

nineteen

More and more I am preoccupied by
the idea of chastity. For me, it is an
essential condition of the spiritual life.
—Salvador Dalí

I'm grateful he's home. Sincerely. I'm grateful he agreed to go out this evening, after having spent all day rehearsing at Eddie's, so we could *talk*, so I could tell him about Dr. Salinger, and my dad, maybe even Jenn. Tell him *what* about her, I don't know. Better not to think about it.

But now that we're together in my car, I have nothing to say. Even the words I rehearsed all day are dim and distant. Maybe it's because we're on the clock. We've sorta got plans tonight, after all . . . kind of a big show coming up.

And I feel worse, because all I can think about is me.

"So," Mike says. "What's on your mind?"

Everything.

"Nothing," I say.

We've already been driving twenty minutes. I have no destination in mind. I'm afraid if the car stops, I'll tell him everything, and I just don't want to. What if I totally freak him out? And shouldn't I? I mean, after everything that's happened, what I tried to do . . .

"I just need one happy thing, you know?" I say.

"Actually, I don't."

"What?"

"Sorry, but I don't know what you're talking about."

"Yeah. Whatever."

"Whatever, huh? Cool. Swell."

"Mike, it's not you, it's me. I just . . . I really need to be distracted."

"Yeah, well, take a number."

I glance at him, sitting tense in the passenger seat. He's rubbing his thumbs across his palms, hard, fast.

Through his window, I realize we're nearing Hole in the Wall. It'll do. I pull into the dirt lot and park far away from the flickering orange neon sign. It's giving me a headache.

"Is this okay?"

Mike shrugs. "Sure."

"And can we just . . . talk? I mean, can you just talk to me?"

"About what?"

"Anything. I don't care. I just need you to talk."

"Okay," Mike says with this little frown. It hurts me to see his face like that. "But we'll have to head out in an hour or so. Brook's picking me up at my place for the show tonight."

Damage Control. Mike's biggest night. I'm such a useless, selfish bitch.

"Sure. No problem."

I shut off the engine, and we walk inside.

The café is maybe half-full, if that. Weekend nights don't treat the Hole well; most people don't hang at coffee shops on weekends. We go up to the counter to place our orders.

My gaze goes directly to my painting, hanging nearby. God, why don't they just take it down?

Eli is running the register. "So it's still here, huh?" I ask as he hands me my drink.

"What's that?" he goes.

I point. How can he miss it? It's that shit-on-a-stick painting. "My painting is still here. No one bought it."

Eli looks at the painting, then at me. It takes him a second to make the connection. "Oh, right!" he goes. "Sure. Well, it takes time. You need to be patient. Someone'll pick it up." He gives me what he must consider an encouraging smile.

Which I disregard. "Sure," I mumble.

"Any luck tracking down a number for Deb—"

"Thanks," I say, anything to interrupt him.

Mike watches this all unfold without a word. He follows me into the purple room and sits down across from me.

"What was all that?" he asks.

"Hm? Oh. Nothing. That one's mine."

Mike glances over his shoulder. "You put a piece up here?"

"Sorta."

"You put a piece up here and didn't think I'd want to know? How come?"

"Um, specifically to avoid talking about it."

Mike reacts like someone jabbed a needle into his belly. "Oh," he says.

"I'm sorry," I say. "I didn't mean to sound like such a bitch."

"Okay. No problem."

I strain to focus my attention on him. A unique sensation; usually it comes pretty easily. "How was the trip?"

Bad call. Mike squeezes his mug so hard I'm afraid it will shatter.

"Shitty," he says.

Since there's an opportunity to make things worse, naturally, I go for it. "How come?"

"Because my mom's an idiot and the guy she married is a tool. Next item?"

I slouch in my chair. "Anything."

"Okay . . ." Mike drums his fingers on the tabletop. "So, Nightrage almost broke up," he says after a moment.

"You don't say."

"Yeah, Brook told us this morning. Guess they're really stressing about this tour with Black Phantom."

"Mm. Too bad."

"I guess," Mike says. "I mean, they *are* a good band. But their guitarist got pissed off about something their drummer wanted. . . ."

Mike continues speaking, but I don't hear him, because this couple, maybe twenty-somethings, have approached my painting and are studying it. *Intently.*

I sit up in my chair and watch as they talk to each other, tracing my whirls and lines with their fingers an inch or so away from the paint.

". . . but I don't think Brook would do it, since . . ."

The couple step back, move to one side, step closer again. My heart races.

Oh god, please. Pick it up, take it to the register. I need this right now.

". . . regardless of what Four Eyes thinks, because they're so . . ."

The guy picks up the small white price tag Eli attached to my painting. He turns to his girl. I fight the urge to get up and feign getting a fresh cup of coffee so I can hear what they are saying. The woman frowns slightly and seems to be weighing the price in her mind.

Come on, come on!

". . . not that Mom or her stupid dick even asked about the band . . ."

The couple glance around the room at the other paintings. The woman points at my piece and nods enthusiastically, and I suck in a deep breath; the guy also nods as he looks around at the other pieces once more. Then he points to the painting . . . *next* to mine.

The crimson tondo.

No, I order them. *Take mine; just pick it up and make me the happiest fucking person in the world for just a little while!*

They study my painting one last time—then the guy gestures toward the tondo again. Eli cheerfully takes it down off the wall, wraps it up, and puts it into a sack. The guy hands over some cash, and he and his skank walk out of Hole in the Wall. The empty space beside my painting is outlined in dust.

Sonofa*bitch*!

Son of a bitch, why did I come here? Of all the places to go. Why am I so stupid? Am I, like, biologically incapable of making a good choice or what? I didn't need this, not tonight—not ever, okay, I admit that, but goddammit, definitely *not tonight.* Salvador Dalí himself is laughing at me, doubled up with hysteria over the fact that I would dare to be so dumb.

". . . so clearly what's going on in my life is of no possible interest to you, so maybe we should just head out, okay?"

"Uh-huh," I say, then snap to attention. "Wait, what?"

"Jesus, Zero. My mom's . . . No, forget it. I got a show to think about."

I slouch further into my chair and shut my eyes. "Sorry."

"'Sokay." Mike scoots his chair back. "We should get going, huh?"

"Oh. Sure."

Leaving our coffee untouched, Mike guides us out of the café. I refuse to look at my stupid painting or stupid Eli or the stupid dust ring where the painting I loved so much has disappeared forever. Just like everything else.

We climb into my car. Mike's pissed. Maybe not pissed, but shut down. My fault.

It's all my fault, isn't it.

Dr. Salinger, Jenn, my dad, my ridiculous painting in that lame-ass café. Just once could I get something right?

I glance over at Mike, my hand on the key to twist the ignition.

"You're mad," I tell him.

"Yeah. Sorry, it's just . . . fucking . . . family, you know?"

"Kinda."

He looks at me, and the way the car is parked under the single parking lot lamp, the only light that creeps in happens to fall across his eyes like Morticia Addams. Even though the light is yellow, his eyes shine white.

"I really thought I'd be excited about tonight," he says.

"And instead, I can't get my mom out of my head, and I don't know what the hell's wrong with *you,* and I just want it to stop for a second so I can have a good time playing this gig. You know?"

"Yeah," I say.

We both stare at the dashboard. Just wanting it to stop for a second. And then, without my permission, I ask:

"Do you love me?"

Oh, *there* ya go! Yes, great choice, Amanda, you are a *gem.*

Mike shuts his eyes. "Zero . . . I'm not having this conversation tonight."

I'll take that as a no.

Problem is, my answer is yes. Why, because I have nothing else? No, it's not that.

Maybe—

Maybe I don't have to even say it. Maybe I can—

I lunge across the seat and pin him against the passenger door. Mike yelps as his shoulder crashes into the window.

"Zero!"

"Shut up."

I force my mouth onto his and make some attempt at sucking his lungs out. I bite, chew, slurp, anything I can make my mouth do to make his obey.

"Z . . . Zero . . ." He tries talking around my tongue.

I move down to his neck, kissing and nibbling. I hit a sweet spot; Mike's breath catches in my ear.

"You . . . trying to . . . cheer us up?" he gasps.

"Uh-huh."

I shove my hands under his shirt, feel the outline of his stomach and chest under my fingers. Mike makes another gasping sound. I keep attacking his neck, and soon his hands move to my hips.

Here's the thing.

Fuck it.

I somehow manage to lean back on my shins and tear my shirt up over my head. Mike's eyes blossom, but he doesn't say anything. It's okay. Other than the one strip of yellow light, we're in total darkness, and the lot's almost empty anyway.

Even as he says the hesitant nonword *um* to me, his hands find my ribs. Mine find his zipper.

"Zero—"

I shake my head. His fly button pops open beneath my fingers like it's done so many times before tonight.

Like an old pro at this, I grab the waistband of his jeans and pull backward until my back is against the steering wheel. His jeans come off with an audible denim plop.

There's no going back. No, there isn't.

I scoot down and bring my legs up to my chest, shoving my old cutoffs up toward my knees, then down again past my ankles and feet. Our pants kiss quietly, dejected, in the backseat.

I see in his eyes a moment of hesitation. I hear and ignore his past reasons for not going this far.

I guess he does, too, because with his help, an awkward few seconds later, I'm in nothing but my bra. I loom over him again, kneeling, reaching, grabbing, hoping I'm not hurting him. And not caring all that much after all.

I balance, precarious. I use my other hand to touch myself the way Mike does. A second later, his hand joins mine.

Mike's eyes are now squeezed shut, he's breathing hard, and I wonder if he'll accidentally open the door and topple out, which would be funny as hell if you think about it, which I'm not, and who cares, his body is responding.

"Careful," he whispers, voice jagged at the edges.

I shuffle my knees up a little so I won't slip off the edge of the seat, then force myself into the passenger seat in reverse, facing him.

I take hold of him, and lower my body onto his. Mike's eyes fly open.

Turns out there's a lot you can do without taking off (most of) your clothes in the front seats of a 1969 Peugeot.

And me . . . well, I hurt.

"Ow, fuck!"

"You okay?"

"I'm fine—I'm fine—I'm fine," I say. "Ow. Shit. Ow . . ."

And then I freeze solid. Complete and total motionlessness as I realize that this is happening. He is inside of me, really inside me, and it hurts in so many ways and feels good in so many others.

Mike takes in a deep breath through his nose, his hands helping to support my weight by clinging onto my hips.

"Oh," I whisper. Then add, " 'Kay." I spend thirty seconds trying to swallow something dry in my throat.

My motionlessness breaks, and my entire body starts shaking. Quivering. It's not sexy; it's not because I feel good. Partly it's because I'm having trouble balancing on the seat, but that's not all. My heart pounds, threatening to pump right out of my chest.

"You okay?" Mike whispers again.

I grab the headrest of the passenger seat with one hand and use the other to brace myself against the dashboard.

I pull myself up just a bit, then down again. God, ow.

I do it again. Everything goes black, and I wonder if I'm passing out, but no, it's just that my eyes have closed without my permission.

I find what I think approximates a rhythm of some kind for all of what I assume to be a minute. No idea, really. When Mike takes in a sharp breath and squeezes me between his hands, I stop.

Here's the thing.

Just once, have I gotten something right?

Mike lifts his left hand off my skin and forms a fist, which he throws into my radio. Hard.

"God . . . *dammit.*"

"It's fine," I say, my breath escaping in rags. "It's okay."

He opens his eyes and stares—*glares*—at me.

I stare back at him. *What?*

And instantly I discover just how exposed I am. In every possible way. I kneel there, motionless, an *écorché*, naked and skinless against him.

I slowly lift myself off of him, slide into the driver's seat, reach for my clothes, pull them on fast, feel wetness sliding thick out of me. At least I get my clothes on in the right order.

I'm fully dressed again before I realize my fingers are sticky and colored crimson. I stare at my hand in the darkness. It's me. My blood. My blood and—

In the seat beside me, Mike is getting dressed, too, extending his body awkwardly to try to shimmy his jeans back on. He zips up and sits back down, and his hands fall into his lap, shaking.

I find a fast food napkin under the seat and wipe my fingers clean. I suddenly have no idea what to do with the napkin when I'm done. So I just hold it.

Just sit there.

Looking at the neon Hole in the Wall Café sign buzzing orange a few yards away.

Where my painting hangs unsold. Where my best friend and I spent so many hours.

The wind picks up, tossing an empty beer can *rumple-crinkle* across the dirt.

So this is where it happened. The parking lot of a coffee shop.

No music, no satin sheets, no rose petals. Not even the traditional backseat.

"Oh god," I whisper.

Mike says nothing.

I slowly turn toward him. He's grabbed hold of his pant legs and twisted the denim into his fists as he sits unblinking, looking at nothing. There's a thin trickle of blood running down his hand.

"Mike?"

Mike doesn't move.

"I didn't mean—" I start, and can't say anything else, because *yes,* I did.

Mike sniffs. "I need to get home," he goes, his voice nearly inaudible. "The show."

"Okay," I whisper back, and twist the key in the ignition.

I'm in pain the entire drive to his house. It's not exactly crippling, but it ain't no fun, either. This is awful compared to how I usually feel after being with Mike.

But then we were never together like this.

And may never be again. More of that intuition stuff, maybe. It tells me that this—what should have been so good and so wasn't—was absolutely the worst thing I could have done.

When I pull up to his house and park, Mike opens the door right away.

"Are you mad?" I ask as he climbs out.

Mike hesitates with one foot on the sidewalk. "I don't know," he says. "You still coming to the show?"

"I—I don't—"

"Well, I'd like you to. Think about it. See ya."

Then he's out, shutting the door and walking up the path to his front porch. I watch him go inside.

I shift into drive and cruise home in silence. Mom and Dad's room is black when I get there. I make it all the way into my room before realizing I still have the bloody paper napkin clenched in my hand.

I throw it into my garbage basket and climb into bed alone.

I make sure to bury my face against my pillow so Mom won't hear how hard I'm crying.

Here's the thing.

I don't remember when I started.

But I do stop soon enough to shower, change, and still make it to Damage Control on time.

And the Bad Timing Award goes to . . .

twenty

I have this daydream. It's gonna sound contradictory, but it's not, not really. I'm at an opening at some big gallery. My biggest show ever. I'm selling for thousands of dollars. Then some hotshot comes in. Maybe a Hollywood producer or something. He sees this one painting, and he's all, "I have to have it. Price is no object." Or something like that. Except when he whips out a checkbook, I tell him, "Sorry. This one's not for sale." And he gets all mad, right? Tells me he'll pay me one million dollars, right here, right now. And I just say, "Nope. Sorry." So he goes up to two million, then three million, but each time, I tell him no. Finally, he gives up and storms out of the gallery. But see, he doesn't get it. He doesn't understand that I can't sell this particular painting because it is absolutely the best painting I've ever done. I can't sell it, not for any price. I'm too proud of this one piece to ever let it go.

Now, the reality is that the chances of this happening are less than zero percent. No pun intended.

But that's not the point. The point is, someday I will paint this masterpiece. I don't know what it is yet, or when it'll happen. But it is out there. I have to know what that painting is. A piece so beautiful or disturbing or both that I could never let it go.

Like I said, it's a daydream. But it's my daydream.

Tonight, it comes back to me in the greenroom downstairs at Damage Control, where Mike and the band are gathered, waiting for the show to start. I didn't even know there *was* a downstairs, and a distant part of me now feels extremely badass. Every wall of the greenroom is a study in collage, band posters pasted up over other posters of bands who've long since broken up, died, or gotten real jobs. Brook has taped my flyer dead center on each of the walls, where I'm afraid it will blend in, get lost, but it doesn't. It stands out from the others like one of Mike's beautiful blue-green eyes— the color I used as a backdrop behind the cymbal (or record) reflecting the guys' faces.

I just wish I could enjoy it.

Three of the guys are amped up, pacing nervously, making jokes, slapping fives.

The other one sits quietly on a folding chair, not making eye contact with me.

"Don't we get, like, lobster or something?" Brook says, showing his teeth.

"Next time, next time," Hob says, and (almost) everyone laughs.

The energy is bright, electric, but I can't share in it. Upstairs, Just This Once is doing the last sound check of the night before the doors open.

"C'mon, Michael!" Hob says, shaking both of Mike's shoulders in his massive hands. "Aren't you jazzed, man?"

"Yeah," Mike says. "Just getting in the zone."

"Oh, hey, no problem," Hob says, releasing him. "Do what you gotta do, man."

Mike nods and finally gives me a quick glance. I can only stare back. Of all nights . . .

Right then, Penny Denton of Four Eyes Entertainment barrels down the stairs and into the greenroom. She looks around at everyone, and she's *pissed.*

"Who's Jonathan?" she demands.

Hob turns around. "That's me. How's it going? We've only met on the pho—"

"We need to talk," Penny barks, and stomps back up the stairs.

The rest of us turn to Hobbit, who's watching the door slowly swing shut. He pulls on a scowl and follows after her.

"What the hell was that?" Eddie says to Brook, then immediately repeats it to Mike.

"Probably nothing," Brook says. He gives Eddie a smile, but it's not quite as big as it was when we got here. Mike glances at them, at me, then back at the floor.

We sit in silence for about five minutes, during which I try to figure out how many ways there are to say "I'm sorry." Around number 362, there are heavy footsteps on the stairs.

We all stand. Hob comes in and shuts the door quietly behind him.

"There's been a change," he says, staring at the ash-stained carpet. "In the lineup."

"What?" Eddie cries.

Brook kicks one of Mike's empty drum cases. "What'd they do, move us to first now?"

Hob shakes his head. Brook storms up to him.

"What, did they boot us? Is that it? 'Cause that would be bullshit!"

"We're last," Hob says.

The guys turn into statues, staring at their leader.

"Say again?" Brook goes.

"We're last," Hob repeats, and slowly begins to smile. "We're *headlining*."

Brook sits down fast on a folding chair. Eddie covers his face. Mike only gives a little shrug of his eyebrows—but the eyes beneath show more. Life. Distraction. Something other than whatever he's feeling after what happened—

"I just shit my pants!" Eddie gasps.

"Is that, like, a metaphor, or do we need to go find some size forties real fast?" Brook asks.

Eddie nervously shakes his head. It almost makes me laugh.

"What happened to Nightrage?" Mike asks Hob, like he's still trying to comprehend what Hob has said.

"They broke up," Hob says, rubbing his hands together. He looks a little *too* pleased at the thought. "Like, literally an hour ago. Imploded. They're done, they're history!"

So their blowups onstage weren't an act after all. And who

cares—now the way is clear for Gothic Rainbow to *arrive,* so to speak.

Just wish it was under different circumstances, personally speaking.

Mike finally moves from the chair. He goes into the center of their circle. "Okay, you guys? This doesn't change anything. We got moved up. That's cool. But most of the people up there came to see them."

"Yeah, but they're gonna leave sayin' they saw *us*!" Hobbit says. He turns to me. "Zero, listen. We got a merch table set up at the back. Can you run up there and man it for us?"

"Um—sure," I say.

Hob frowns at me and sneaks a look at Mike. "What's up with you two?"

Brook and Eddie likewise check us both out. I swallow something dry. How to answer *that* little question? *Well, Hob, it's like this: earlier this fine evening, in a fit of mutual pissy moods, Mike and I . . .*

"We're fine," Mike says. "No worries."

Huh. Sure.

I clear my throat. "Okay, so, yeah, I'll head up. Break a leg or whatever it is you're supposed to break."

Mike comes over and opens the door to the stairs. The other guys say thanks, and Mike takes me up to the top.

"Listen—" he starts.

"No, I know," I say. "Just have a really great show, okay?"

Mike looks into my eyes, and it hurts how much I care about him, about this, about us. I touch his arm, briefly, before heading into the venue to find the merchandise table.

I get there as Just This Once begins playing. I find GR's merch table and take a seat behind it. There's not much to show off; just copies of the band's demo tapes with hand-written labels. But I sell two almost right away. The people at the box office counter are busy explaining to everyone who comes in that Nightrage is off the bill. I don't see anyone choose to leave.

After Just This Once wraps up, I feel a tug on my sleeve.

"Hey, you."

For a moment, I almost don't even turn, convinced I must still be suffering from a Stupid Fucking Mistake hangover. But when I do, it's Jenn all right, wearing a worried smile.

And before I know it, I move into her and hug her tight. She hugs me back.

"Thought you'd be here," she says, while Bad Religion plays over the sound system.

"I'm so sorry," I say.

"Forget it," Jenn says, squeezing me. "I just wanted to make sure you were okay."

We're still embracing when some tool walks by us, leering. "Hey, all right, girl-on-girl action!" he says. Do guys find this approach *normally* works? Discuss.

Jenn, without breaking her hold on me, barks, "Hey, piss off, jerk!"

The dude blinks and hurriedly goes to the bar. I start laughing; can't help it. Jenn giggles back, and we separate.

"You want some help?" she asks, gesturing to the table.

"Yeah," I say. "That would be great." Oh, you mean selling tapes? Yeah, that too.

She finds a folding chair and brings it over to the table to join me. We both take seats as the capacity crowd shouts for drinks and music while another band preps for the next set.

"So how you doing?" Jenn asks me.

I shake my head. "Jenn . . . I'm the stupidest person on the face of god's green earth."

"Nah. *I'm* gunning for top spot. Did something happen?"

I look around, biting my lip. Not a conversation I want to have, period, never mind at Damage Control on the night of GR's big show. But it's so loud and crowded that it permits an ironic sort of privacy.

"Okay," I say, and scoot my chair closer. Then I vomit. Not, like, puke, but everything that happened tonight. Jenn listens carefully, eyebrows furrowed. I can't tell if she's angry, disappointed, or sad, or at *who*.

"God, Z," she says when I'm done. "I don't know what to say."

"Tell me I'm not a jerk."

"You're not a jerk," Jenn goes. "You were really upset and confused. Trust me, I get it."

The next band, Living Room Casket, starts up, and it's way too loud to talk without shouting. So we wait thirty minutes till they're done, and Jenn turns right back to me.

"It was a mistake," she says firmly, like she's taken the time during the music to formulate her opinion. I didn't hear their set at all.

"I know."

"No, you don't," Jenn says. "It really was. The one thing he specifically asked you not to do, and you did it."

"This is not helping," I mutter.

"Yes, it is. You need to understand that if you're going to make it work. Sex changes everything, Z. *Everything.* Even under the best circumstances, which this wasn't."

I nod and cover my face. I know. I *do.*

I feel her hand on my shoulder. "What does Mike think?"

"No idea. We haven't had any time to talk about it. God, *tonight,* why'd it have to be tonight?"

"Well, it didn't have to be. That's all on you."

"Jenn!"

"Do you want me to be your friend or not?"

"Well, yeah, but—"

"Then I'm going to tell you the truth," Jenn says. "And if that hurts, I'm sorry, I really am, but if I didn't say it, I wouldn't *be* your friend. Okay?"

". . . Okay."

"So obviously, you have to talk to Mike," she goes on. "But maybe not tonight. I know you want to, and he probably does, too, but give it till tomorrow. You have your own things to worry about first."

"Like what?"

"How about getting pregnant?"

Oh, holy hell. I almost throw up for real, right then and there.

"And diseases," Jenn goes on, like it's a list that she's well versed in, and I suppose that she probably is. "You'll have to get checked out. See your doctor, all that."

"Yeah," I say. "Okay. I mean, I'm not worried about it. He said he'd been tested before."

"It doesn't matter what he said. Ever. You have to. When's your period?"

Ladies and gentlemen—mostly ladies—this is the single best night of my life, yessiree.

"Dunno," I say into my hands. "Couple days, maybe."

"That's good. If you get it, chances are good you're not pregnant. But even if you do, you should wait a week or so and then go make sure."

I nod wearily.

"Good. Now as for you and Mike, I think you should both just chill. Let him get his head together, too, you know? It has to sink in."

She's right, I realize. It's been *hours*. I still hurt a little, for god's sake. It is too soon to go having a big discussion. Not right after the show.

"The show," I say.

"Huh?"

I stand up. I'm, like, angry, but not in a bad way. Maybe *defiant* is a better word.

"This show," I say. "We should have a good time. I should try, anyway. I don't want to miss this." Especially if it's going to be the last show I'm ever allowed to go to . . .

Jenn stands beside me. "There you go," she says, and looks at me as if proud.

The houselights lower, and the third band, an acoustic punk duo called Peder Parker, starts up. And suddenly, I start to hope. Maybe everything will be okay.

At a quarter after eleven, Gothic Rainbow takes the stage of Damage Control.

The cheers from the audience are deafening. The club is packed now, wall to wall. There must be two hundred people, standing on the dance floor and draped over the railings upstairs. They rub against each other, as if their friction will get the show started sooner. A row of punks press against the edge of the stage until they are practically bent into Ls, their faces fierce and ready. Their girls squeeze behind them, screaming as the band walks to their places.

That's when it hits me: these people *are* here to see this band. Maybe they came to see Nightrage, too, like Mike said . . . but they know exactly who has walked onstage.

If the band is disturbed by the sheer number of bodies or the ruckus they're causing, they don't show it much. Brook slaps hands with nearby punks. Hobbit stands center stage, arms crossed over his chest, surveying the audience, beaming. Eddie's *blushing*, and even from my spot near the rear wall, I can see he's shaking. Mike, as usual, is partially camouflaged behind his kit and shadow, his face a ghostly disc hovering in darkness.

I wonder what he's thinking.

Hobbit strides to his microphone. "How's everybody doin' tonight?"

Thrilled screams welcome him. Fists puncture the air. I try to add my voice above them all, and succeed only in tearing my vocal cords. Jenn howls alongside me, face alight.

"All right. We're Gothic Rainbow," he says, after playing an experimental chord. "This song's called 'Let's Pretend.' I hope—"

But even with his microphone, he can barely overpower the shouts of the crowd. Hob smiles wickedly, and waits for us to quiet down.

"I hope you like it!" he finishes, his voice pleased and perhaps surprised. Then he pounds down on the guitar strings.

A mosh pit starts even before Hob begins singing. The air, congested with sweat and smoke, surges vigorously. The crowd slams through the pit or bops along on the outskirts.

Gothic Rainbow is *ferocious.* The stage lights, high-tech compared to the other venues they've played, swirl and dance multicolored beams across the band and audience alike. Crimson, cadmium, chrome, a Monet palette highlighting the audience's wild hair.

The first song ends, and we all cheer ourselves hoarse.

"All right, this next one's *not* about a girl," Hob says. Somehow we cheer even harder. I try not to think too hard about whether there's a hidden meaning in his words.

Mike taps out a four count and the song begins. A guy with a violet Mohawk jumps onstage before security can stop him, and launches himself at the crowd while Brook laughs and Eddie shits himself (again). Security uses flashlights to spotlight the kid, who's nearly crying with joy as the crowd passes him overhead. Eventually, he is set down, unharmed and forever young. He escapes punishment from security by leaping headlong into the pit.

Forty minutes pass in a rush of adrenaline. Damage Control is a living canvas, painted with impossible impasto, thick and complex. My fingers twitch for a charcoal pencil, something, anything. There's no paper, no canvas, no surface large enough to contain what I want to paint.

Which is probably a good sign, all things considered. Who knows what my hands would reveal.

It's almost midnight when Mike unleashes a *livid* assault on his drums that extends well past the normal four-count opening the band favors. The crowd screams, recognizing the introduction of one of their favorites. Instinctively, we know this will be the big finale.

The audience bounces on their feet, anxious for the song to begin in earnest. The rest of the band kicks in simultaneously over Mike's percussion, creating an explosion of power, rage, and ecstasy in four simple chords.

Hot white lights swing across the stage and the audience. Hell-red washes flare on the wall behind Mike's kit. Hobbit approaches the mic, cranking down on his guitar, and screams as if fire will belch from his mouth. Brook dances around, bobbing his head and smiling wildly; still in the song's introductory chords, his head falls back on his neck, and he laughs out loud. It's inaudible over the noise, but his face gleams with sheer delight. Even Eddie, normally still and focused, is grinning broadly and bouncing on his toes. Now he's *looking* for someone else to dive off the stage. Jenn grabs my arm and shrieks, and I join her.

The band is having the time of their lives, taking us all with them.

"All right!" Hobbit shouts into the mic as the opening chords ring out. "Let's wrap this sucker up! This song's called 'Last Breath.'"

We cheer until the concrete beneath us trembles.

"Ready? All right." Hob spaces his next words out to match the melody. "One. Two. *One, two, three, four!*"

Hob's voice is raw, unharnessed. *Unleashed* to assault us.

The horde sings along. The song punches into my chest and pounds on my heart and lungs. Excitement, pure stimulation bursts out of me; I scream incoherently into the air, the only release possible *sans* paintbrushes. The music from these Fauves, these wild beasts, would've made Matisse envious; the song is an audio masterpiece of violent distortion and strident, invisible color.

> *I was standing on the top of the world*
> *Letting the wind blow and shuffle my hair*
> *Into kings and queens and black diamonds*
> *When the earth died and the wind went still!*

The rhythms continue as Brook conjures magic on his guitar. The strings squeal and sing beneath the crunching melodies issuing from Hob's and Eddie's instruments. Brook is laughing again as he bends and twists the neck of his guitar for greater distortion.

> *Spent my last days with a soda*
> *Glaring out the window at the world*
> *Asked myself just what I'd missed*
> *From the entrance from the outside to in*

We all sing along:

> *God, what is this hell?*
> *You never knew, you never will!*
> *Oh god, what is this hell?*
> *You never knew, you never will!*

I try not to let the chorus be about me. Mostly succeed.

Hobbit slowly lets his guitar fade. He closes his eyes and mouths the mic, as if to kiss it.

"All right, bring it down," he says. Sweat floods his face, pools at his boots. Girls *reach* for it. Guys shake their own heads, showering punk sweat on the rest of the crowd.

The band follows Hob's directions while the audience shrieks for more. The music goes on for another few beats. Hobbit's eyes stay closed. Brook slows down, then stops, so all we can hear is Mike tapping lightly on his drums and Eddie playing quietly on bass.

Hob's eyes open, and he surveys the crowd. He has us all right where he wants us. He is *king,* master of this domain. Hob stands straight, shaking back his mane of dripping hair, savoring every moment. Mike looks . . . like Mike. Unperturbed but intense.

Hobbit comes back to the mic. "All right, I'm gonna need some help here; you know the words," he says. "Let's hear it."

Hobbit moves his mouth, but he's barely projecting into the mic anymore. He whispers the verse. Two hundred zealous fans scream the song back to him, word for word. Magic.

> *Spent my life living in a hospice*
> *Each day looking forward to death*
> *Eating stale cream cheese and rice cakes . . .*

Hob pauses, letting his hands float downward to cue us all. Near silence fills the club, underscored only by the hum of amplifier static and random screams. Hob lets this near silence hang for a blissful moment. The audience stills at last, slack-jawed at the anticipation of what's to come. The lights dim.

At last, as if neither he nor his audience can stand the delay any longer, Hobbit puts his mouth up to the mic and inhales, his barrel chest expanding to Herculean proportions.

And smokin' till my very last breath!

We cry the line into the air with him, united.

"One-two-three-four!" Brook shouts.

The song explodes again into the final chorus, and the crowd roils. The lights blare to life again, bathing the stage in smooth greens, blues, and violets, and washing the audience with rainbow strobes and rotating spotlights.

I catch sight of Penny Denton near the box office, her arms folded over her chest, standing next to the lanky guy I saw her with at Liberty Spike's. Her eyes blaze behind her thin glasses, and one corner of her mouth turns up in a confident smile. Her expression reminds me of the way Mr. Hilmer used to look at my drawings.

They made it.

Four Eyes has to book them now, here at DC for a while, but soon in bigger venues. Opening for national bands. After that . . .

The band plays the song to a crescendo conclusion with one final simultaneous crash.

"Thank you!" Hob calls into the mic. "We're Gothic Rainbow, ssssssee ya!"

We applaud and shout our praise as the houselights rise.

Mike gets up from his kit and vanishes backstage. The rest of the band slaps hands with fans at the foot of the stage as recorded music is piped in over the speakers.

"That was awesome!" Jenn says, giving me a hug.

I hug her back. "Thank you!" I say, and laugh because what did I do, really?

But as people slowly begin shuffling out of the club and I see them grabbing up GR flyers from tonight's show as souvenirs, leaving behind the full-lineup flyers Four Eyes made, it occurs to me that maybe I had something to do with it after all.

"I'm meeting up with these guys from ASU," Jenn says, primping her hair in an invisible mirror. "You want to grab Mike and the band and come with?"

"Nah," I say. "I'm out." After everything that's happened tonight, I could use a good decade of sleep. "But thanks for asking. Maybe some other time?"

Jenn smiles. "That would be cool. We should do coffee soon. If you want."

"Totally," I say.

Jenn's face brightens even more. "Cool," she says. "Call me later! Let me know how—you know. Everything goes? I'll be there."

With that, she squeezes out from behind the table and heads out.

Half the club is surrounding Hobbit, Eddie, and Brook, who have conquered the world. Inhalers appear in the hands of several kids who are gasping for breath. Girls engulf their boys, lipstick sharks. Bodies are fondled, gripped. The air is humid and glorious.

Finally, the band gives one final wave and exits backstage. Mike hasn't returned.

Backstage.

He must still be back there, avoiding the attention. I start to move from the merch table but get swamped by people clamoring for tapes. I have to spend about twenty minutes selling them, taking in cash and shoving it into my pocket, making change with this improvised cash drawer. When the crowd thins out, I shove the remaining few tapes into a pile and am about to rush downstairs when one last straggler ambles up to me. He's got spiked, bright-red hair and wears all black, head to foot. Two wide black leather bracelets decorate his skinny arms.

"How much're these?" he asks.

He looks familiar, but even with the houselights on, DC isn't terribly bright. Also: don't much care. Must get downstairs.

"Three bucks," I tell him.

He pulls a wallet out and removes a ten, handing it to me. "I'll take three."

"Really? Um—yeah, okay!" I hand him the tapes and a dollar. He gives me a backward nod and swaggers toward the box office, stopping to talk with Penny Denton and the lanky guy.

There are only five tapes left, which means we sold more than twenty. *Awesome!*

When I get to the greenroom, three-quarters of the band is almost literally bouncing off the walls, while one-quarter sits casually on a folding chair drinking a bottle of water.

Three guesses, right?

As soon as Hob sees me, he howls and tackles me, swinging me up in the air and nearly braining me against the ceiling. I don't mind.

"Zero, you are totally *killer*!" he shouts, setting me down.

"We did it, we did it!" Eddie's chanting over and over, while Brook slaps him on the back and laughs his head off.

Mike is quiet. Smiling, though. That's good.

I pull the cash from my pocket and hand it to Hobbit, who gives a great hyena giggle and starts counting right away. Brook and Eddie watch him, eyes wide and hungry.

I scoot over to Mike and give him a hug. "You did it," I whisper.

He says nothing, just squeezes me.

And right then, I'm sure we're going to be okay. "I'm gonna go home," I whisper to him. "Can we talk tomorrow?"

Mike looks a little surprised. "Yeah," he says. "You sure?"

"Unless you want to—you know. Talk about it now."

Mike glances at the guys and grins a bit. "Tomorrow's good."

"Okay. Cool. And Mike, I'm so—"

"Nah, don't," he says. "We'll hang out tomorrow. I'll call you."

I kiss his cheek and stand to leave.

"Hey, you're not takin' off, are ya?" Hobbit demands.

"Yeah, I'm out," I say. "You kids go have fun."

"Well . . . all right, then. Catch ya later. Hey, wait, Z." Hob counts out some cash from the wad of bills and shoves it into my hand. "Couldn't'a done it without ya," he says, giving one of the flyers on the wall a quick rub.

"Hob, I can't—"

"Too late," he says, grinning.

I give him a hug. Then I wave at Mike, and he smiles for me.

It's okay, I say to myself the entire drive home, over and over.

It's okay.

twenty—one

Mistakes are almost always of a sacred
nature. Never try to correct them.
On the contrary: rationalize them,
understand them thoroughly. After that, it
will be possible for you to sublimate them.
–Salvador Dalí

I'm still a little sore in the morning. Correction—midmorning.
Quite the reminder, thanks.

God, what did I *do?*

The entire night's memory crashes into me. Holy shit,
how bad is it? What if Jenn was right, what if I'm—

The smell of coffee creeps under my door and into my
room. Mom's up, of course. Dad's . . . wherever unemployed
drunks go. To Mass, perhaps? Ha.

I get up, use the bathroom, and take a shower. Long and
hot. Insert clever, poorly timed joke here. Even though technically last night ended up more or less okay, now that I've
had the night to sleep off the pain, guilt, exhilaration, and
whatever else, it's like today is set for my execution.

Despite the summer heat, I get dressed in jeans and a
long-sleeved T-shirt, and don't know why. I sulk barefoot into

the kitchen, where Mom *and* Dad, I'm surprised to see, are both sitting at the kitchen table.

It's not a fight; not yet. But they're laying the groundwork. I can hear it in their voices as I shuffle in.

"Then you explain it to her," Mom is saying.

Great. This sounds promising. . . .

"It was a mistake, okay?" Dad says fiercely over a steaming cup of coffee. "I made a mistake, and I'm sorry. What more do you want?"

"I want Amy to have a fair chance, Richard!"

Okay. Enough's enough. After this weekend, I'm pretty much gassed; this has to stop.

"Fair chance at what?" I say.

They both whip around.

"Hey!" Dad says quickly with a big grin. His eyes are bloodshot. "Mornin', kiddo!"

I raise a hand. "Dad, don't," I say, feeling exhausted all over again. "I really can't today."

Dad's face freezes. He turns back to his coffee and stares into the mug.

"So?" I ask, moving closer and leaning against the fridge. "Fair chance at what? Huh?"

Mom leans back in her chair. Dad spins his mug.

"I really don't think Amy needs to hear this," he mumbles. He never calls me that.

"We are a family, Richard," Mom says, and her voice has this confidence in it I've never heard before. "She needs to be involved."

"This isn't about her!" Dad explodes. Mom doesn't even

flinch. "She's got her own thing going on, and I'll *handle* it, okay, Miriam? I'll handle it!"

"Can we not talk about me like I'm not here?" I suggest.

Dad spins. "Oh, that's great. Yeah, that's what I need this morning, more of your attitude."

"Look who's talking."

Mom looks nervously at me, then at Dad. Dad looks— well, *shocked* would be a kind word for it. He stands up and races toward me, but like Mom, I just don't care anymore, and don't even wince.

"Just what in the hell is that supposed to mean?" he growls.

"It means I can't do this!" I shout up at him. "You two screaming at each other, wondering if you're going to get home safe after drinking all night . . . *all of it*!"

"Now wait just a damn minute!"

"No! I won't wait. I'm tired of it, Dad, I'm tired of this whole mess you got yourself into, and it's killing me inside! I can't do my work like this!" Because at the end of the day, Mike and Doc S were both right; being here is killing my art.

"Oh, I see!" Dad bellows, pacing in a tight circle. "It's *my* fault you didn't get into some damn art school? That's how it is?"

"I *did* get in. I lost a scholarship because my work wasn't good enough yet, and it wasn't good enough because dealing with you made it impossible to do it well."

I suck in a breath. I've never said anything like that out loud. But the reality, the truth of it, I think, hits me harder than it does him.

I got in. I really did. And that *means* something.

"How can you talk to me like this?" Dad says, sounding like a five-year-old. "After everything I've done for you!"

My hands crunch into fists. "You've given me a place to live, and clothes, and a car, and food, and you know what? Thank you. Thank you for doing that. I appreciate it, I really do. And you've never tried to stop me from going after what I wanted, and that's great. But you've never really been behind it, either."

"Oh, Christ!"

"Well, have you?"

Dad lurches toward me, sticking a finger in my face. "I've given you . . . !" he starts, but can't seem to figure out how to follow up.

I am so tired. And I still have to talk to Mike. And make some phone calls, but crap, it's Sunday—those'll have to wait till tomorrow morning.

"Whatever," I say, shutting my eyes. "I can't put up with it anymore, Dad. So just—either get a divorce and call it a day, or get your shit together and get *better*." And although my stomach is twisted, gotta say, it feels good to just get it out.

Silence.

I open my eyes. Dad's still angry, sort of, but there's something else in his face now. Fear, maybe.

Mom clears her throat. "Actually, Amy," she says softly, "that's what we were talking about."

Dad runs his hands through his graying hair and stands by the sink, gripping its edge. I move to stand between them.

"About what, exactly?"

Dad shakes his head and looks out the kitchen window. Mom eyes me carefully.

"I've asked your father to get help," she says, her voice steady. "If he doesn't, then I will have to leave. And you would be welcome to come with me, though with your birthday coming up, I suppose it would really be up to you."

I wait for a ton of bricks to crush me. It doesn't come. I must be too tired. Or just not surprised. It was only a matter of time.

"Dad?"

"We don't have the money even if—" he says, but cuts himself off.

Money for what? Getting sober somewhere? Money well spent, I'd think.

"We could take a loan out on the house," Mom says.

"That's horseshit," Dad spits.

"Getting *hammered* every night is horseshit," I shoot back.

Dad's shoulders slump. Just a bit. No one says anything for a long, long time.

"I'm done talking about this," he says finally, and heads for the door, jangling the keys in his pocket.

"Off to Scotty's, then?" I call after him.

His hand freezes on the doorknob. Mom and I watch and wait.

After another uncertain length of time, Dad mumbles, "Fuck this." He walks out to the carport, slamming the door shut behind him like a cranky adolescent not getting his way. Mom and I don't even flinch as he squeals his tires on the driveway and takes off down the street.

Slowly, I sit down across from Mom. She looks about as wiped out as I feel, rubbing her index fingers against her temples. After a sec or two, she opens her eyes and says, "So how was your night?"

I actually laugh. It's a sick, sad sound, but Mom does the same.

For the first time I think *ever,* I want to tell her everything. Jenn, Mike, the band, Dr. Salinger—all of it. I don't know why; maybe I'm just too drained to fight it. Or maybe it's the way she just talked to Dad, like she meant business, that she wasn't going to roll over anymore. I wonder if her talking to that priest guy helped or what.

"Mom," I say, toying with Dad's cooling coffee, "last night. I—"

My phone starts ringing. My head automatically turns in the direction of my room.

"Is that Mike?" Mom asks.

"Oh yeah. Um . . . almost certainly."

"Amy? Are you all right?"

I stand up. "I will be," I say. "Look, can we . . . talk? Sometime? Later? I have to tell you some stuff and I might . . . need some help."

Mom blinks. How long has it been since I asked to talk to her? Since I needed help? Long enough that it registers on her face that it's been some time.

"Of course," she says right away. "Anytime. About anything. Are you sure you're all right?"

"At the moment. Thanks," I say, and walk quickly down the hall to my room. Even before I reach the phone, I've decided; I will talk to her, and I will tell her everything.

"Hello?"

"Hey. What's up."

"Mike, hi." My stomach instantly turns in on itself as I try to anticipate where our conversation is going to go, exactly. I need to apologize, I know that much, but—

"So, um, we need to have a chat," Mike says.

"Yeah, I know, I really—"

"Noooo . . . ," Mike interrupts, "I don't think you do. We really need to talk."

"Um—all right. You want me to come over?"

"How soon?"

What the hell? Why the sudden rush? I don't like this.

"I need to grab something to eat . . . about an hour? Maybe less?"

"Sounds good. I'll be here. See ya."

He hangs up.

I put the phone down. Eat? Right. After that little introduction? I pick up my keys and wallet and leave my room without shutting my door.

Mom's washing out Dad's mug in the sink. "Going to see Mike?"

"Yeah," I say. "Might be awhile."

"That's fine. I'll be here when you get back." She shuts off the faucet. "That is, if you still want to talk. Or anything."

"Probably," I say. "See you soon." I hesitate by the door. "Where do you think he went?"

"Daddy? Who knows? But, Amy, you have to understand . . . I was serious. I meant what I said. If he doesn't get help . . ."

"I get it," I say. "I'm with you."

Mom smiles sadly, eyes shining. "Thank you."

And I go to my car. I debate stopping for food somewhere, but by now, there's no way I'm forcing anything down my throat. I do get an iced coffee. Not at the Hole, though. Not yet. Maybe not ever again.

I race to Mike's house, my coffee gone by the time I get there. I go to the front door and knock. Mike answers almost right away.

"Hey," he says. He's wearing those black shorts I like, and a plain white T-shirt. "Come on in."

I come on in. Mike shuts the door and leads the way to his room. No hug? No kiss? This can't end well.

Mike goes to his bed and sits on the edge, heaving a sigh as he does it. I stand near the doorway, like I shouldn't even come in here anymore.

"Can I start?" I ask.

Mike gestures toward me.

I take a big breath. "Okay," I say.

"So . . . it was a mistake. Last night, it was a mistake, and I'm really, really sorry. The one thing that obviously meant a lot to you, and I just destroyed it, and I'm so sorry. I didn't mean to, exactly. I mean, well, I did, sorta, but not like that, and not so soon. This weekend's been like the best and worst of my life, and I don't even know where to start, there's so much to tell you about. . . ."

Relieved I'm getting it all out, I step into his room and pace, hardly noticing that all the papers usually scattered around are gone now. The hardwood floor squeaks beneath me. I watch my feet, afraid to look him in the eye, what I might see there.

". . . but the main thing is, Friday, I had this *terminally* bad day, because my art teacher was supposed to help me with my portfolio and write me a recommendation letter and all this, and I was really super excited, and then she left, didn't tell me she was leaving or anything. . . . And you weren't home, and I went to Jenn's, and . . . god, that's a whole other thing I never told you about her, but that can wait, it's just . . . And then my dad had this major blowout when I got home, and Mom kicked him out, at least for the night, but he came home, and—oh my god, he *lost* his job, and Mom said if he didn't stop drinking she was going to leave him. . . . But I'm really talking around this whole thing, I know, it's just . . . when I saw you, last night, I just wanted—you know, it's funny but not like a joke funny, Jenn said this to me once and I thought I understood, but I didn't, and now I really do, but anyway—I just wanted to feel something other than what I was feeling, and so I, like, *attacked* you last night to try and make it go away, but it didn't, I just made everything worse, and . . . and god, I am so sorry, Mike, and I really don't want us to be over."

I stop. Take another breath. Force myself to look up.

And notice his black duffel bag on his bed, stuffed full and zipped shut.

"Um—what's that?" I ask dumbly.

Mike sort of nods to himself for a second, and puts one hand on top of the bag.

"I'm going to L.A. with the band tomorrow. We're hitting the road."

twenty—two

I believe the moment is at hand when by
a paranoic and active thought process
it will be possible . . . to systematize
confusion and contribute to the
total discredit of the real world.
—Salvador Dalí

"Wh-what?"

Mike takes a breath and looks into my eyes. *God,* his eyes. Then he says:

"Here's the thing."

I can't wait a second longer. "*What?* What is it, what happened?"

He swallows hard; I don't think I've ever seen him do that before. Nervous-like.

"It's Black Phantom," he says. "They were at the show last night."

That's it—the guy who bought the GR demo tapes. It was Jason Alfaro, lead guitarist of Black Phantom.

"They'd made plans to come see Nightrage, but, uh . . .

well, of course, that's not what happened, so they saw us instead, and, um . . ."

He runs his hands over his hair and licks his lips.

"Mike . . . ?"

"And they're starting that tour next Monday," Mike goes on. "Which was supposed to be a double bill sorta thing with Nightrage. They got the whole thing mapped out. The label's even got them into a couple cheap motels, which is pretty impressive. And since Nightrage fell apart . . . well, they talked to Hob last night and offered us the gig. We had to decide right away, because there were other bands in L.A. they could ask, so. We had to take it."

"You're going on tour?" I repeat. "Mike, that's awesome! God, I thought something was wrong. That's great!"

"Okay, well, yeah, it is, but let me finish."

Oh.

"The tour is about three, three-and-a-half months," he says. "All over the country. Couple dates in Canada, too, up near New York? We circle around and end it in L.A. around Halloween. We'll swing through Phoenix, too, it sounds like. But just for the one night."

Three months. I don't know how I can live without him for that long. I fall butt-first straight to the floor. Melodramatic enough? Just in case it's not, I cover my mouth with my hands.

"Oh," I say through my fingers.

"Yeah."

I look up at him. His face is being torn in half, one side thrilled, the other terrified.

"And, um . . . if things go well on the tour, there's a decent chance the label might pick us up, too. Which means we'd have to get started on an album. And we'd have to stick around there."

"There? You mean Los Angeles?"

". . . Yeah."

My stomach tightens as if a corkscrew is slowly spinning my organs inside out.

I feel my mouth evaporate inside. Sonoran desert sand replaces spit.

"So you're moving away."

"No, not—actually . . . yes. Probably something exactly like that."

He peeks at me through his bangs. "Which is why I called you." He swallows hard again, and stares at me.

"Interested?"

Dalí has a painting called *The Three Glorious Enigmas of Gala*. When I first saw it in one of Mr. Hilmer's books all those years ago, I thought the painting was of clouds, or maybe vanilla pudding. Just three progressively larger soft blobs of yellow-white. Then I realized it was Gala's profile, facing down. I could never look at the painting again without seeing her faces, unable to recapture that first impression.

The feeling in my body right now is a combination of both sensations: soft, fluid whiteness and a certainty that nothing will ever be the same.

"What?" I whisper.

"Do you want to come with?"

No way did he just say that. No. Fucking. *Way*.

"Z, listen, last night—you're right, it was a mistake, but I didn't exactly stop you. And that's not why I'm asking you this now. What d'you say?"

What do I say?

How about something along the lines of *freakin' time me!* Except I don't verbally say that. I think it. I think it *hard*. This is fantastic, ridiculously incredible; it makes up for all the shit that's been happening, it's a big old finger to Doc Salinger, it's a kiss-my-ass to my dad—

And Mom. And Jenn. Things are back to something resembling normal with her, and god knows she came through for me last night. . . .

And what *about* Mom, and Dad?

Shit. Wait.

"It seems . . . fast," I say slowly.

"Yeah. It does."

"That doesn't scare you?"

"Hell, yeah, I'm scared! You scare me to death, Z. I don't know what this is, but . . . there's nobody else I'd want to come with me more than you."

Go for the joke: "That's awfully romantic comedy of you."

"It is. But we're only going around once, you know? I mean, we're not going to be able to do this when we're twenty-five, thirty. *Forty*. If we're gonna screw up, let's do it now while we still can."

Suddenly, it's not Mike sitting on that bed; it's Dr. Salinger. Waxing poetic about how now is the time to try things, to just go and travel the world.

It made sense at the time. It even makes sense now. Just up and go and to hell with everyone else. Be young, have fun, seize the day.

Which she turned right around and did to me.

Is that what artists do? Act flaky and dumb and chalk it up to "Oh, well, I'm an artist"? But Doc S, like, ditched me; Mike's not doing that. He's here. Inviting me to go along.

"And you leave *when*?" I heard him the first time, but maybe I was wrong.

Mike looks at the carpet. "Well, see, that's sorta the catch. The guys left this morning."

"This *morning*?"

"Tour starts next week. They were planning on Nightrage, so. Everything was already set up. We have to rehearse, go over stuff with the label. . . ."

"Wait—so then why are you still here?"

Mike looks at me again. Straight in the eye, straight to my guts. His eyes dazzle me into submission.

"To ask you face to face," he says. "I got a bus ticket for tomorrow, at noon. Thought you'd need a little time to think about it."

"So, twenty-four hours to think about moving out of *state*?"

"Zero, I gotta go. I can't . . ." He stops, pressing his lips together.

"Mike, I'm *seventeen*. And there's so much going on right now. . . . What about school?"

"What about it?"

I start to get pissed at the carelessness with which he asks that, but the anger turns to something else. Doubt, I guess. Because, yeah—what *about* it? After Doc S's little dodge, how am I supposed to come up with better work, or the recommendation letter, to get that scholarship? Plus, it occurs to me: I haven't told Mike the entire story. Not just that she left me in the lurch, but that we were going to be working on it at all, that it might be as early as spring when I resubmitted.

Why hadn't I mentioned that?

"What happened to if I want something I should go get it?" I ask.

"I still think that. Clearly. If I didn't, I wouldn't be going on tour."

"Okay, so? What do *you* want me to do?"

"I *want* . . ." He pauses, sighs. "I want you to do whatever is going to make you happy," he says, dropping his voice. "I mean it. But I also want you to think about this chance. It might not come around again. C'mon, we could see the whole country. We're playing a show outside of Chicago, you could go visit that school even, if you wanted. Maybe you'd get there and see it and change your mind."

Something inside me bristles. "You want me to change my mind?"

"I didn't say *that*."

"No? What'd you say?"

He forces in a deep breath. "What I'm saying is that art schools are always going to be there. Touring with the band might not be. Listen, I'm not trying to be melodramatic here, Z. The absolute truth is this is much more likely to be our last tour than our first. Know what I mean? There's no guarantees. And it's only three months. You could still work on your portfolio, fill out applications, whatever it is you have to do, but you could do it with . . . me."

The bristling part of me softens. Because he's right. On the other hand:

"But you said you'd be staying in L.A. afterward."

"Well, it's possible, yeah. But c'mon, there's got to be some great schools in L.A., of all places. I mean, I dunno, what about, like, UCLA, or one of the Cal universities or something?"

There are, of course. Plenty of great schools with great programs. I gave them only a brief glance when I was prepping my application for SAIC, though, because that was my dream. For all I know, SAIC is the absolute *wrong* school for me. I know that's possible. But it's been at the top of my wish list for so long now, I can't imagine going anywhere else.

But Mike sure as hell isn't going to be moving to Chicago.

Right then I get this black-hole suction sensation in my gut. Like I'm being twisted inside out. The absurdity of the whole thing suddenly hits me right there, right in the belly, where for all I know, a little Baby Mike or Baby Amanda is growing even as we speak. What are we going to do if I have a baby, move in together? People twice our age wait longer than we've *known* each other to do that. Well, most of them, anyway, I assume. We shouldn't even be talking about this.

Except . . . we are.

And I *like* it. I'm scared to death, and the one thing that's taking my mind off my fear is that maybe I'm one of those lucky ones who find the right guy the first time out. I mean, it's possible. Isn't it? There *are* other schools; they *aren't* going anywhere. I have money. Instead of going to school, I could use it for an apartment. Food. Baby food. Child care . . .

I push my palms into my eyes. "What if I'm pregnant?"

Mike freezes. His face goes blank; then he nods.

"Okay. Well, if that happens, obviously I'll come back."

"Mike, that's a huge, big thing."

"So was last night."

And frankly, that all but settles it in my mind. It *was* a big thing. He knows. And despite the whole moving away part, in one sense, he's not going anywhere. And where he *is* going next, I could tag along.

I squeeze my eyes tight, try to think.

"How long'll it take to find out?" he asks gently.

"Jenn says maybe tomorrow, a few days. If I get my—you know. Then probably I'm not."

"If you are," he says, "then I'm all in, whatever you want to do."

"But the tour."

"No, uh-uh, forget the tour. Zero, come on. Just because I didn't want to doesn't mean I didn't *want to.* I was there, too, remember?"

Yeah. Pretty clearly.

We sit in quiet for a long time. My thoughts spin so quickly that the only thing I can think to do is pick one thing to focus on for right now. What's in front of me.

"You're right," I say at last. "You can't not go."

"I know. And I'm glad that you do, too."

I look behind me at the framed album on his wall. It could be his someday.

Mike catches me looking at it. "A record would be cool and everything," he says, "but I also want . . . I'd like to see where it is *we're* going. You know?"

I shut my eyes again and lean over my crossed legs, trying to make myself breathe normally. Not happening.

"Mike," I say, "I can't move to Los Angeles. Or go on a three-month tour. I can't."

"Actually, you can. If you want to. Z, I don't know where this is all headed, but I want you there for it. And I mean, it's not just me, the guys want you to come, too. We'll need flyers, posters, T-shirts, buttons, stickers . . . whatever. All that stuff. And hell, in a few months, we might even need to start talking about cover art for an album, you know? We all want that to come from you."

I can't tell if I'm suffocating or merely having a cardiac arrest.

Mike gets down next to me and puts his hands on my shoulders. "Think about it," he says quietly. "Just think about it. I've gotta get to L.A. with the guys and work out some details and stuff, but I mean, you could even take the whole week, if you need it. And if—you know, *everything's okay*, you could meet us there."

I hear a loud pop and look down at my hands. I've tied my fingers into sailor knots, so hard one of the knuckles cracked. The feeling of my fingers tightly woven together like this is familiar but displaced, like trying to suck your thumb a year after you stopped.

I realize I haven't made this gesture in some time, this finger-lacing thing. It's been a while.

And it kind of hurts.

I pull my hands apart and stare at my fingers, which are still cramped into talons.

These are my tools, and I was destroying them.

"Mike, I can't."

"Yes, you can. You don't have to, and I'll understand if you don't. But don't say you can't. About anything."

I want to.

Of course I want to go.

It's a rock band tour. I'd be making art. Probably sleeping in a van or strangers' houses, sharing space with four guys I've known only a few months, one of whom happens to be my boyfriend, who I would probably curl up to every night. And if it turned out I was—what'd they call it?—*In Trouble*, well, we'd be back way before it would become an issue.

How many people get a chance to do something like this, *ever*?

There are other advantages, too, I think as I stare past Mike at his empty bookshelf. I'd be away from Mom and Dad, the residue of Dr. Salinger, everything. In other words, *not here*. Like I've always wanted. Like I always planned.

Of course I want to go.

"Mike . . ."

"Think about it," he says again. "Dad's giving me a ride to the station, but we could . . ."

Move to California. With my boyfriend. It sounds so . . . stupid. Like, *trite*. Typical. I'd be living up to my self-imposed reputation—moody art girl meets musician and they run away to Cali. Love, sex, and rock and roll. Take off and to hell with everyone else.

"After everything you told me when you got here," Mike says, "your parents and all . . . well, hell, why *not*? I mean, what have you got here?"

What do I have here?

What *do* I have here.

So I tell him, "Okay. I'll think about it."

For the first time since I first saw him, I don't have an urge to kiss him. I'm too confused, too muddled, too—everything. I get up, go down the hall, out to my car, and drive home without looking back.

When I get home, Mom asks if "now's a good time." I say no, I have work to do. I go to my room, and for the first time, I not only look into my *Metamorphosis of Narcissus* poster at my reflection, I sit down in front of it and stare. My eyes glaze back and forth between the painting and my face, like a cheap version of a stereogram, those posters made up of all dots that when you cross your eyes create a 3-D picture. Mine is only two dimensions, but I get equally lost.

Run away to California. That's what I'd be doing, essentially. Running away from home.

I leave my room only long enough to go to the bathroom or grab food from the fridge. I play music. The Adolescents, Agent Orange, Bad Religion. (*I tried to make things make sense but I can't.* —Greg Graffin, lead singer of Bad Religion. Thanks . . .)

I almost call Jenn but don't. I have to do this for me. I'm a big girl now, right? I can make my own shitty, fucked-up, stupid decisions just fine. The only question is, stay or go: which one is the shitty, fucked-up, stupid decision?

A shaft of moonlight bounces off my floor and lights up the faces on my ceiling. When did the sun go down? I stare at those faces even as my eyes try to close from exhaustion.

No. Not yet. Plenty of time to sleep later.

I go through my stack of blank canvases and pick the

biggest one I've got. I throw it onto my easel and reach for my acrylics and gels. Then I remember: sketch first, paint second. Kinda like measure twice, cut once. So I grab my sketchbook and a pencil and spend a few hours preparing this painting, the one I've been wanting to do for about two months now. When the sketch is done, I attack the canvas.

I lose track of the night entirely, working on this piece. By the time I can barely lift my hand anymore, it's nearly complete. I think. Hard to say. I clean up my brushes, change into flannel pants and my D.I. shirt, and take one last look at it before hitting the light.

But my fingers freeze over the light switch.

Did I really just paint that?

It's a pair of eyes. Mike's, of course. I've gotten the emerald-sapphire mixture just right, and the high gloss shines almost as well as the real thing.

I've got them. I did it. Captured the right color, the right feeling, the—

There's something else there, too, I realize. Something I didn't see before.

In both pupils, there's a reflection. Slightly rounded and distorted, like an Escher drawing, like you'd see if you were looking into a spherical mirror, but clearly recognizable.

It's me, reaching toward the eye, out of the canvas, as if *I* am a painting, right now, and the artist in the pupil is the real thing. This reflection is reaching out with a paintbrush; it's me, painting my own image in Mike's eyes.

I don't want to get all melodramatic here . . . but *holy shit.*

I hear Mr. Hilmer's voice, distant but distinct. *Self-*

portraits are the artist's best if not only way to reveal them-
selves to the world. They speak volumes that the written and
spoken word cannot.

It's not my first self-portrait, if you count the shattered
reflection on my ceiling or the Camelback Mountain picture
hanging at Hole in the Wall. But it's my first intentional one.
I *know*—I know how angsty and ridiculous it is—but I think I
know what I've been seeing in Mike's eyes this whole time.

Stop, no. I can't go there. Not now. It's too much. I have
way too many things to think about, and I am dead tired, and
I might be pregnant, for all I know, and I have to get some
sleep if I'm going to make any kind of decision here.

What should I do? I ask my faces, my hand still hovering
over the light switch.

What should I do?

My faces are stoic, judging, asking me my own question
back. I remember now that it was just a few weeks ago I came
so close to painting over my rendering of Jenn, and how glad
I am now that I didn't.

But I also realize there's something I need to do instead.

I climb onto my bed with a jar of white acrylic and my
biggest brush. It takes only a few minutes for my mirror-face
to disappear, buried beneath blank whiteness.

What should I do? The only thing I *can* do.

"Is this really happening?" I whisper-ask *The
Hallucinogenic Toreador.*

Thunder rumbles in the distance.

A storm is coming.

twenty—three

The next thing I know, it's Monday morning, and rain is playing snares on my awnings. I lie in bed, trying to organize my thoughts. A minute later, I cover my face with both arms and cry with relief as I realize: I won't be having a baby.

Okay. So that most likely solves that. But I have to be sure. I roll out of bed and go to the bathroom to shower and clean up. After that, I pull on my baggy jeans, then drop them and kick them into a corner. I choose a new pair of pants that Mom bought instead. These actually fit me. I'm surprised when I double-check the size.

Then I call our family doctor and make an appointment for the earliest I can get in. I try hard to ignore the nurse's tone when I tell her, why I need to come in. But I feel better, for the most part; safer.

My phone rings.

Mike! It's already eleven.

"Hello!"

"Hi, is this Amanda Walsh?"

Un. Real. What is this, a salesman? I do not have time for this.

"Yeah," I say, *not* nicely.

"This is Eli at Hole in the Wall Café. I hope I didn't wake you up."

Actually, you didn't, but I have somewhere I have to—

Wait, *who*?

I go, "Uh-huh?"

"Listen, your painting sold last night, so I owe you some money. Minus the twenty percent, of course."

My what whatted when?

"So if you want me to send it to you, I'll need a mailing address, or I could hold it here for you to pick up, since you're one of our regulars. . . . Are you still there?"

Thunder rumbles the roof; rain patters against my window. I want to open my mouth to the sky, drink the rain, because my mouth and throat are as dry as a Phoenix summer.

"I'm sorry," I say. "Did you say my painting sold?"

"Yep. To an older couple moving to California. Said they wanted a piece of Phoenix to take with them, and your painting of Camelback Mountain was perfect."

California.

I check my Dalí clock. Less than an hour.

"I . . ." I have nothing to add after that.

"You want me to just hold on to it for now?"

The money. Someone is paying me for my painting.

I did it.

I'm an *artist*.

"That would be great," I say, and open my top drawer, riffling for a clean shirt to pull on. "I can come by. . . ."

"Sounds great, I'll be here. Hey, congratulations, huh?"

"Thank you," I whisper, and hang up.

What was I talking about? Ah, yes. Art.

(But is this art?)

I yank on the T-shirt and my boots. My blue cabbie hat hangs on my desk lamp, so I grab that and pull it over my uncombed hair just as Mom knocks on my door.

"Everything okay, Amy?"

"Yeah—no—"

She cracks the door open and peeks inside. "Say again?"

"I sold a painting," I say. "My first sale, and I have to—I've gotta . . ."

"Amy, that's wonderful. Good for you!" She comes in, hugs me tight, and kisses my forehead. "I knew you would."

"Thanks. . . ."

"Listen, your father's home," Mom says, releasing me. "You might want to talk to him. Before he goes."

Before he—

"He would appreciate it," Mom says gently, and leaves my room.

I follow her and catch Dad in the hallway. He's pulling a wheeled suitcase behind him.

"You're really leaving?" I say. Guess it runs in the family.

Dad stops, blinks. "Oh. Hey, kiddo."

"Got yourself a nice apartment somewhere?"

Dad looks confused, then closes his eyes. "No."

I fold my arms.

"It's, um . . . this *facility.*" He sneers at the word and opens his eyes. "Some place a friend of your mom's recommended, I guess. Some priest or something." He shakes his head like he can't believe it.

He also looks scared.

I drop my arms. "You mean you're not moving out?"

"Just for a few weeks," Dad says, not meeting my eyes. "Get, um . . . you know. Dried out."

Oh my god.

"For real?"

"Yeah." He squints at me. "Thought you'd be a little happier than this."

I look at him, around him, through him. He's really going? Really going to try?

"I am," I whisper. "I really am. That's great, Dad. Thank you."

He lets go of the suitcase handle and comes over to me. Lifts my hat, ruffles my hair. "I should thank you," he says. "You called me out good and proper, kid. That took guts. I appreciate it, Z."

"Amanda."

Dad blinks. "What's that?"

"Could you start calling me Amanda?"

Dad half-smiles. "If you want."

"I kinda do."

"You got it. Amanda." He puts my hat back on my head. I adjust it so it falls right. "Think I could get a hug from you?"

I don't say anything, just wrap my arms around his

middle. Dad hugs me tight, his cheek pressing against the top of my head.

"I'm sorry," he whispers, his voice hoarse. "For—yeah."

I squeeze him tighter.

We let go of each other. Dad grabs the handle of the suitcase and wheels it behind him to the kitchen. I follow silently.

Mom is pulling her purse over her shoulder. "Ready?" she says softly.

Dad nods. He goes to the kitchen door, pauses, and looks back at me. "See you in a few weeks," he says. "Unless you, you know. Come visit."

He trundles into the carport, headed for Mom's car. Mom and I watch him go.

"Is he serious?" I ask her.

"I think so, Amy. It's a start, anyway. There might be some rough spots, but . . ." She lets out a tired little yelp and flaps her arms up, then down. "Well, what the hell."

I stay silent again.

Mom watches Dad load the suitcase into the backseat of her car. "Any ideas about what you want for your birthday?" she asks absently.

". . . What?"

"Your birthday? It's just around the corner. It is a big one. And I'd like to get you something nice." Mom turns to me. "Or perhaps do something together . . ."

God. I'll be eighteen in about a week. So soon?

What do I *want*?

"Tickets," I say.

"Tickets?" Mom repeats. "To a show of some kind?"

"Plane tickets."

"Oh. To where?"

I rub my face. "I gotta go out for a bit," I say. "We can talk about it later. You should get going."

"Where are you headed?"

"Nowhere—special. And, um . . . I still need to talk to you about some things. Okay?"

Thunder erupts again, and the kitchen rattles. Mom glances out the window, and I know from experience she doesn't want me to drive in the rain.

I wait for her to tell me not to leave. To stay home.

"Okay," she says after five decades have passed. "Please be careful."

I look into her eyes. "I will."

Mom comes over and gives me a quick hug. "See you soon."

I don't move as Mom follows Dad out to her car. They climb in, and she drives carefully out into the road, then on down the street.

See you soon.

I don't know how long I stand in the kitchen, but when I finally look up at the clock, I see I've got maybe twenty minutes to make it to the bus station.

I run to the Peugeot, climb in, and drive fast, switching lanes and zipping through yellow lights as if my life depends on it. Maybe it does.

I careen into the bus station parking lot and park in the first available space. I race toward the station, shielding my eyes from the rain. My boots get soaked running through oily puddles, disrupting iridescent rainbows.

I burst into the building and follow signs to the boarding area, where the buses sit awaiting their passengers. I fling open the doors and nearly trip down the iron steps to the sidewalk. Wiping raindrops from my eyes, anxious, I search for Mike among the throng of passengers climbing on board the nearest bus.

There.

"Mike!"

Mike turns. His board dangles from one hand, while the other is passing an attendant his duffel bag to be stowed in a storage compartment. He's wearing his Ghost of Banquo shirt, which is starting to stick to his body from the rain. Mike quickly surrenders the board to the attendant, then steps toward me, his face breaking into a smile. Like he's so happy to see me.

I'm already on my way. We meet near the rear of the bus, and I grab him with both arms, pulling him close. His arms encircle me, holding me tightly.

My eyes close as I grip Mike. "I had to tell you," I breathe against his chest. "I had to tell you in person. . . ."

But I don't, can't, finish my thought. I lean back, away from the warmth of Mike's body, and take his head in both hands, like I did that night on Camelback Mountain. Mike meets my lips halfway, kissing me hard, his hands clenching fistfuls of my shirt and drawing me near until we're pressed together even more closely than we were that night in the parking lot of Hole in the Wall.

We kiss; frantic, agonizing, relentless. Mike's hands seek all of my body. I feel every touch along my back, my neck, and my face, while my fingers run through his hair, his bangs beginning to drip from the cascade above us. The rest of the world fades into background noise, then away completely, until we're alone, and together.

At last I pause and rest my head against his cheek, exhausted, my face warm and flushed. "I love you," I say, eyes tightly closed. "I really think I love you, and I just had to tell you that." I lean back again and look up at him. "I'm not pregnant. I mean, I'll find out for sure later this week, but— probably not."

His relief is so immediate and plain that I'd laugh at him if I wasn't standing in the rain at a bus station.

"All right," he says. "That's good. Good. Wow. Okay." Then his relief fades, and he studies me. "So, does that mean you've deci—"

"And I sold that painting." I have to interrupt. "The one from Hole in the Wall. It sold."

"That's *awesome*, Z. That's great." Mike's eyes shine beneath the ashen sky. "I knew you would."

"Yeah." I touch his face, studying his features with my fingers, memorizing the texture. "I know."

A baby begins crying somewhere, followed by the soothing murmurings of a mother. A baritone voice calls, "All passengers boarding!" and suddenly the world is back, all noise and color, a kinetic painting.

Mike tugs on my sleeve. "So what do you think?"

It's not too late. Like he said, I could meet up later in the week and—

"I can't," I say. "I want to, so much, but I can't."

Not today, and not later this week.

I want to. Oh god, fucking A, I want to.

But the thing is, I have to see what's next for me. I don't

want him to go, either; I want him to stay and go with *me* wherever *I* end up. And I know he can't.

We can't. Not like this. Not now.

Mike looks down at the wheels of the bus, which will soon go *round and round.* He nods a bit, like to himself, before facing me again.

"Well. That's okay. You do what's right for you. You can change your mind. . . ."

"I know. But there's so much going on. . . . My dad's getting help, he just told me. And my art—I have to try again. I have to do this."

Mike nods again. "Okay," he says. "I get that. I understand. Sucks. But I get it."

"I'm so sorry."

"No, don't be," Mike says, and sniffs. "Don't be. You got stuff to do. That's all right. And I mean, anything can happen, right?"

"You never know. . . ."

"We'll be passing through in October."

"I remember."

"So I mean, we'll know more about where we're headed by then, I'd think."

"Tell me all about it after the show."

"I will." He brushes rainwater from my forehead. "Well—I have to go."

He embraces me again. I hug him back, then release my hold and take a backward step.

Mike looks once more into my eyes and, quite unexpectedly, smiles. It lights his face and eyes and makes my knees weak.

Mike reaches for my head and snatches my cabbie hat. He flips it so the brim goes backward and yanks it over his head. "If you want this back . . ."

I brush my hair out of my eyes. "I know where to find it."

"Exactly." Mike takes a deep breath and nods once at me. "See ya," he says.

"Yeah," I say. "Later, skater."

Mike's emerald-sapphire eyes sparkle at me one last time. Then he turns, walks to the bus, and leaps on board. I wait, expecting him to pop his head out a window and wave, but he doesn't. There's a hiss of air, and the bus starts rolling out of the lot. Still I wait.

A flash of red brake lights reflects on the wet pavement, and I think, *Yes.* He's told the driver to stop, there's been a mistake, he has to get off the bus right now and go back to—

The bus turns the corner and is gone.

Dreamer.

But then, I'm an artist. That's what we do. Isn't it?

I turn and head back through the station and out to my car. Halfway home, the storm breaks, and sun shines down on the valley. It looks like it's going to be a beautiful day. Glancing out my window, I wish for a rainbow arching over Camelback Mountain.

Aren't rainbows supposed to be a promise or something?

I veer toward home and think of my painting, resting in some couple's car, maybe draped and upright in the backseat, on the way to California right this second. Talk about surreal. I think of Mr. Hilmer and Dr. Salinger. Of Salvador Dalí.

And of Florida.

That's where I want my birthday tickets for. Florida, round

trip, so I can visit the Salvador Dalí museum. Always wanted to go there. Spain might be a bit too expensive, *ha!* I'll bring Mom and Dad, because they need to get out of that house for a while. I need to show them, explain him to them, *teach* them. Maybe they won't get it, won't get who and what Dalí is all about, but that's okay.

They'll get *me*. That's enough. And if Dad gets his shit together—or at least collected in buckets around his feet, and I think he might—then we're all going to need some kind of common ground. What better way to do that than art?

I don't know what'll happen now. The School of the Art Institute of Chicago seems further away than ever. But I'm going to make it. Somehow, I know I'm going to make it.

And maybe someday, when even *I* least expect it—maybe I'll get a ticket to L.A., too. Lot of art going on in L.A.

And a lot of music.

Might be cool to feel it out firsthand. Check out the scene. Maybe see some bands. See who's playing. Just for fun. I mean, I'd hate to wake up in the middle of the night thinking, *What if?* You know?

But not today.

Half the city is bathed in morning light, the other blanketed by clouds sketched in charcoal. But there's still no rainbow over Camelback. No new promise today, I guess. Or . . .

Here's the thing.

Maybe it's in the backseat of a car headed to California.

I am about to begin . . . I begin . . . We have begun!

–Salvador Dalí

acknowledgments

First and always, thank you to my beautiful wife, Joy, without whom I would be utterly lost. And probably not know what day it is. This one's for Tobias. We love you!

For Joel and Teena; Tim and Erin; Matt and Abriel; Bishop and Erin; Michael and Rachel; and Jeff and Anna. Thanks for calling it like it is. And thanks to Greg, Jay, and Tony, who stick around. I love all y'all.

Super ultra deluxe thanks to Jennifer Mattson and Michelle Andelman, my agents, who whipped the story into shape; and to my editor, Suzy Capozzi, who still gets me. Thank you so much! And thank you to Heather, Casey, Ellice, and everyone at Random House who gave me the chance and make it look good.

Here's to Mr. Breazeale, whose name I probably misspelled; to Fran, Julie, and everyone who read the first drafts back in '93. I miss you, and thanks. Here's also to Dana-Lynn, Amanda, and Vivian, my faithful friends and first readers, who tell me the truth.

Many blessings and undying gratitude to the Book Babe/ Card Night gang. No one told me you were part of the deal, and I can't imagine life without you in it now. And thank you so much to the Arizona YA author crew who make the trip all the more enjoyable. You guys all rock, and it's so awesome to be—well, Joy's Husband. (Love and ponies!)

Special, crucial thanks to all the bands and fans at Chyro. Talk about a crash course in the music business. On that note, thanks especially to Living Room Casket, Peder Parker, and Just This Once, for letting me play.

For Mom and Dad, and for Tully and Goldie.

For Blueberry, who we miss.

Matthew Sixteen-sixteen.

An unsolicited endorsement: check out kidsneedtoread.org. There's a reason it's not called "Kids should maybe read sometimes dot org."

And thank *you*. Hope you enjoyed it. Ssssssee ya!

TOM LEVEEN is a native of Arizona and has lived within sight of Camelback Mountain his entire life. He has been involved with live theater as an actor and director since 1988, and has been the artistic director and cofounder of two theater companies. *Zero* is his second novel. You can visit him at tomleveen.com.